SIENA SUMMER

The year is 1918 and the Great War is drawing to its grim close. Kit Enever, is recuperating from a leg wound and the innocent friendship of a small girl, Poppy Brookes, is a gift to lighten his heart. It is, however, Poppy's older sister, Isobel, who captivates and—against his better judgement—ensnares him. A decade later Poppy, twenty now, receives a letter from her sister entreating her to come to Siena, where she and Kit have settled. When Poppy arrives to nurse her pregnant sister it is to find a disturbing undercurrent in Isobel and Kit's relationship, and an equally disturbing third party on the scene; a Frenchwoman as cool and calculating as she is beautiful. Poppy's own venture into love is overshadowed by the insanity of a war long ended, and a bitterness and desire for revenge that, with tragic consequences, inevitably, damages most the totally innocent.

SIENA SUMMER

Teresa Crane

CHIVERS PRESS
BATH

First published 1999
by
Little, Brown and Company
This Large Print edition published by
Chivers Press
by arrangement with
Little, Brown and Company (UK)
1999

ISBN 0 7540 1311 1

British Library Cataloguing in Publication Data available

Printed and bound in Great Britain by
REDWOOD BOOKS, Trowbridge, Wiltshire

PART ONE

Kent, England,
autumn 1918

CHAPTER ONE

So immersed was the child in her own affairs, and so efficiently did the swirling river water mask sound, that she was quite unaware of the young man's halting but soft-footed approach along the footpath. He stood above her on the grassy bank, leaning heavily on his supporting stick, watching her, smiling a little, contemplating the remembered self-absorption of childhood. Dressed in a brown corduroy smock, heavy woollen stockings—despite the warmth of the day—and small brown boots, she looked, he thought, like nothing so much as a little mouse. Even her straight, untidy hair, into which had been tied an improbably bright scarlet ribbon, was brown. She was sitting cross-legged by the water, beside her a carelessly discarded straw hat and a small fishing-net sheathed in slimy river weed, and before her a string-handled jam-jar full of murky water into which she was staring intently. Beyond the river the rolling, sun-dappled hop gardens and apple orchards of one of the most fertile counties in the land basked in a mellow sunshine that was as benign as it was surprising in this year of almost unremitting cold and rain.

The peace of the unremarkable little scene suddenly and unexpectedly twisted in his guts like a stab of physical pain. He had almost forgotten there was a world such as this. A world apparently untouched by the barbarous, the inexplicable brutalities of war. A world of innocence.

Innocence. Who could put tongue to such a word after the past four years? Who but a child?

He shifted a little, easing his leg. The movement caught the girl's attention. She looked up. As he had expected—as he had known—her eyes, too were brown—brown and bright and solemn. A mouse, he thought again, touched and amused. A little brown mouse.

There was a moment's silence. Then, 'Hello,' she said.

'Hello.'

'Are you lost?'

The unexpected question brought the barest shadow of a grim smile. God Almighty—out of the mouths of babes! 'No,' he said. 'At least, I don't think so.'

She was studying him, frankly and interestedly. So far she had not smiled. 'Not many people use this path. Well, not many people until the hop-pickers come. Then they use it all the time. To get to the pub, I think.'

This time he grinned in quick amusement. 'Sounds like a good enough reason to me.'

She nodded matter-of-factly, and transferred her attention to the jam-jar.

'What have you got there?'

4

'Sticklebacks,' she said, not looking up, her small face intent, 'and some other little things. I don't know what they are.'

'May I see?'

She nodded.

With great care he manoeuvred his way down the gentle slope to the riverside. She held up the jar for his inspection. Straggling strands of her soft brown hair were plastered to her flushed cheeks. Her clothes were of solid good quality, and her accent was clear and precise, holding nothing of the soft Kentish burr. He studied the jar. She studied him. 'I don't know what they are, either,' he said after a moment and with perfect honesty.

She laughed, suddenly and with an edge of delight. 'Perhaps I've invented a new fish.'

He smiled. 'Discovered,' he said gently. 'I think you may have discovered a new fish.'

She was unabashed. 'That's what I meant.' She cocked her head, looking openly into his face, her brown eyes narrowed against the setting sun. 'What have you done to your leg?'

His smile was wry. 'I didn't do anything to it. Someone else did.'

'Was it the war?' The question was matter-of-fact.

'Yes,' he said after a moment. 'It was the war.'

The child's attention was back on the jar. 'Hugh and William went to the war,' she said. 'They were my brothers. But they were killed.'

Again he was taken aback by the frank calmness of the words. 'I don't remember them much. I was only six then. I'm ten now. Nearly eleven.'

What have we done? What have we done to our children? Will this little one grow up thinking it natural for young men to die or be maimed in war?

He turned his head, looking back the way he had come. On the ridge behind him that lifted above the river, the path had passed a memorial, shaded by oaks and well tended. 'Do you live in the house up there on the ridge?'

She glanced at him. 'Yes. Tellington Place. O—oh!' A light voice had called in the distance. The child screwed up her face in a fierce and rueful grimace.

The voice called again. 'Poppy! Po-ppy! Poppy, where are you? *Poppy!*'

'That's Isobel. I've stayed out too long again.' She scrambled to her feet, shook out the enveloping brown corduroy; for the first time she seemed to take note of the mud and river weed that stained it. The scarlet ribbon was sliding down a lock of fine brown hair. Distractedly she tried to push it back up.

'Poppy? Where are you?'

'I'm coming! *I'm coming!*' She cast a glance at her companion, shrugged with a beguiling roll of her eyes. 'I'm sorry. I have to go. I'm late. Isobel's mad. I can tell from her voice.'

'*Poppy!*'

The child took the jam-jar, went to the river's edge and, with infinite care, emptied the contents into the deep, shadowed water below the overhanging bank. Then she stooped to pick up the dripping net and set off up the slope to the path that led through the grove of ancient oaks towards the house.

'Hey—' adroitly the young man scooped the straw hat from the ground with the end of his walking-stick. 'Haven't you forgotten something?'

Poppy accepted the hat with a quick grin. 'Thanks. I'm always forgetting things. It gets me into trouble.' She pulled a comical little face. 'I sometimes think that everything gets me into trouble.'

He watched her up to the path. She turned and lifted a hand. He smiled, and she was gone.

He turned, stood for a long time, watching over the river, listening to the silence. The blessed silence. Birds sang. The water gurgled sweetly beneath its banks. The hop gardens were green and shadowed, glinting gold. There was no war here. No incessant, pounding thunder of artillery, no unnerving and constant threat of death, no demand beyond human endurance. No sniper lurked in the woodlands beyond the river, the sky was innocent of danger. The smell of death did not haunt the air, nor taint the muddy ground. This was

7

normality.

Was it? Or had that other, anguished world somehow become the norm? What was normality?

He hunched his narrow shoulders a little, leaning on his stick, favouring his damaged leg. The little girl whose brothers were dead had begun to sing as she walked up the path towards the distant house. He could hear her high, clear voice above the sound of the river.

With some difficulty he hauled himself back up the bank and set off in the opposite direction, towards the village and the pub.

*   *   *

When their paths next crossed a couple of days later, Poppy saw him before he saw her. She watched the tall, slim figure limp down the path towards the tree in which she sat. He was wearing the same blazer, flannels and open-necked shirt as before, but this time he carried a small satchel on his shoulder. He was hatless, and the dappling sun glinted on his thick, soft, light brown hair, gilding it to gold. She sat quite still in the fork of the tree; not until he was almost directly beneath her did she move. Then, 'Boo!' she said, and jumped down on the path beside him.

The young man gasped, stumbled, dropped the satchel, and all but fell. Alarmed, Poppy put out a small hand to steady him. 'I'm sorry.

I didn't mean to startle you.'

The man's quick grin was rueful. To her surprise she saw that a faint sheen of sweat stood suddenly on his forehead. 'What do you do when you do want to startle someone?' he asked. 'Fire a pistol?'

She giggled. 'Don't be silly. I haven't got a pistol.'

'Thank the Lord for that!'

She laughed again, bent to pick up the canvas satchel, and handed it to him. He swung it back on to his shoulder. His hand was trembling. She fell into step beside him, her head cocked to look at him. 'Where are you going?'

'To the river. I thought I might make a few sketches.'

'Sketches?' She skipped a little, swinging her arms. 'Can you draw?'

'It's what I do for a living.'

'Oh?' She stopped in surprise, then ran to catch up with him. 'I thought you were a soldier?'

He shook his head, smiling. 'Not a proper one. I think they gave me a uniform just so that I didn't feel left out.' He seemed to have recovered himself; the jumpy edge had left his voice. 'I draw the war rather than actually fight in it.'

'But—' She glanced at his stiffened right leg.

He smiled again, gently. 'To carry a pencil

9

rather than a gun doesn't stop people shooting at you,' he said. Nor does it ease the terror of a barrage, or the nightmare sights and sounds of death and dismemberment. He glanced back down at the child skipping beside him, was struck again by the innocence of the small, solemn face. How many men had died in the mud and agony of Flanders with a picture of just such a young face tucked in their pocket? Hundreds of thousands. Perhaps millions. How many children like this had lost fathers and brothers to this war to end all wars? How many of the survivors would come home unchanged to the children who waited? His heart suddenly ached for this youngster, who barely remembered a world not at war. He knew too well—few knew better—the brutalising effect that prolonged exposure to the terrible inhumanities of total conflict could have upon the sanest and most sensitive of men. A nation of innocents like this one would find themselves dealing with more than the loss or the physical maiming of their loved ones when the ghastly business was at last over. Which surely it must be soon? He wondered, not for the first time, how long it would be before he had to go back. If the newspapers could be believed, the Germans were being pushed back at last, disheartened by their demoralising defeat on the Somme the month before. Surely now they would sue for peace? Surely, soon, the killing must stop?

They had come to the edge of the woods. The river glittered beneath them, and beyond the water the fields and orchards and hop gardens lay still and warm beneath the sun. In the distance a cluster of tiled roofs, the typical circular roofs of the oast-houses that were used to dry the hops, stood in contrast to the rich verdancy of the countryside. An ancient tree had fallen. The young man perched himself on the log, his game leg stretched out in front of him. The child dropped unselfconsciously into the grass, reached for daisies to make a chain. She was wearing a pinafore today over the brown corduroy—a pinafore already woefully stained from her tree-climbing activities. Her brown head was bent, her face intent. He reached for his sketch-book.

Moments later, she lifted her head. 'What are you drawing?'

'Wait and see.' His pencil flew, his hand sure. He was smiling a little. 'There!'

She scrambled to her feet, came to his shoulder. 'Oh! It's a little mouse—' She stopped, put her hand to her mouth, her eyes huge with delight. 'No, it isn't! It's me! It's *me!*'

'It's what you remind me of. A little brown mouse.'

She was staring, speechless at the drawing. 'It's *lovely*! May I have it?'

'Of course.' He tore the page free and handed it to her. 'Here you are, little Mouse.'

11

She giggled. 'My name's not Mouse. It's Poppy. Poppy Brookes.'

'And I'm Kit. Kit Enever. How do you do?'

She gurgled with laughter again, her serious little face suddenly alight. 'I like you,' she said. And with the words an unlikely but lasting friendship was born.

*   *   *

Poppy told no one about her new friend; not that there were many to tell if she had wanted. She was, by nature and by circumstance, a self-sufficient child used to keeping her own counsel and to making her own amusements. Her mornings were spent with her governess, Miss Simpson, a demanding and unimaginative custodian who thought more of clean fingernails, polished shoes and the tedium of tables by rote than of the wonders of Lewis Carroll's *Alice*, the delightfully gruesome workings of the Inquisition, or the romance and terror of the French Revolution, that were the kind of subject more to her charge's taste. So Poppy plodded obediently through her mornings and in the afternoon lived in a world entirely her own.

Her mother and elder sister seemed always absorbed in things womanly and grown up that were to Poppy as arcane as Popery and as boring as the declension of verbs. Her father was often away in London; and, anyway, as long as she could remember he had never taken any notice of her except to give her expensive presents on her birthday or, on the odd occasion, to make vexatious—and invariably unflattering—comparisons between the pleasing virtues of her elder sister and her own graceless shortcomings.

Since Hugh and William had died, Poppy frankly preferred her father's absence to his presence; there had been little warmth and no laughter in him these past three years. Images of the two young men—killed in the same action within hours of one another in the spring of 1915—filled the house. Their pictures were everywhere: in the hall on the table beneath the sweeping oak staircase, in the drawing-room on the mantelpiece, the silver frames draped in black, in the dining-room, in her father's study, on the landing— even two portraits, commissioned after their deaths, in the conservatory that her mother rather grandly referred to as 'the Orangery'. Poppy remembered them only vaguely as large, noisy, genial people, often on horseback and always with a dog in tow, who had treated her with the kind of off-hand, sometimes even rough affection that they might have afforded a favourite puppy or colt. She had liked them, and sometimes the portraits made her sad. But then she did not like the Orangery anyway— the heat, and the perfume of the rare tropical plants that were her mother's passion made her nauseous the moment she set foot in the place—so she did not often have to look at them, and that was the way she preferred it.

In this as in anything that she feared or disliked, as, for instance, the threat—the certainty—of being sent away to school, Poppy reacted with a practical, live-for-today approach: don't think about it. Think of something else. There was always something to think about, something to escape to; a book, a secret adventure, a conversation with the imaginary companion with whom she spent the best part of her time, the closest she had to a friend. The house, whilst not vast, was quite big enough for a small girl to lose herself in, to evade the supervision of those who, in truth, were often none too concerned about her whereabouts in any case.

When the lost sons and Isobel had been young, there had been what her mother always called 'staff' to watch them; nannies, and maids and gardeners. Now things had changed. There Was A War On—Poppy always thought of these words with capital letters—and 'staff' was otherwise occupied, in the forces, in the factories, on the buses and trams. Now the Brookes family had Miss Simpson, who lodged in the village and came to the house each day on her bicycle, a cook whose name was Mrs Butler, though Poppy had never fathomed if there had ever been a Mr Butler, or what had become of him if there had been, and two girls who came in from the village each day to help in the house, and whose concerns were more for their absent sweethearts than for a pragmatically subversive child with an independent mind and a talent for disappearing. Mrs Butler was the only one who 'lived in' and she rarely left her kitchen or her rooms in the old servants' quarters in the attic.

Kit Enever remained Poppy's secret for a whole month.

It was not a kindly month from the point of view of weather; the same wind and rain that made such a misery of the trenches of Flanders and Verdun afflicted the whole of England. As elsewhere, the harvest in Kent, hop and fruit, was an interrupted and dismal affair. But rain or shine Kit walked the footpath to the village, exercising his damaged leg, and more often than not stopped along the way to sketch; and more often than not found himself with a small, interested companion.

'Where are you living?' she asked. She was sitting on an abandoned apple box, watching him as he sketched.

'At the old rectory. The Reverend Harold Matthews is my uncle. I don't have any other family.' He was absorbed in the intricacies of a hop-bine. A field or two away the hop-pickers were working, calling and shouting in good-natured ribaldry, but here it was quiet. Quiet and vaulted and shadowed, like the aisle of a church. The wet, furrowed ground smelled

15

pungently of life, of the cycle of growth and harvest. The sun struck suddenly through cloud, glinted and gleamed like blades of gold through the canopy of leaves.

She stared at him, fascinated. The idea of not having a family was a new one to her, and not totally unattractive. 'What—no one at all?'

He shook his head, still absorbed. 'No one at all.'

'No brothers or sisters? No mother or father?'

'No.'

She sat still for a moment, her chin on her small fists, contemplating the strange thought. 'I've got a sister,' she said. 'And a mother and father.'

And two dead brothers. He turned to look down at her. 'Your brothers must have been a good deal older than you.'

She nodded. 'Mmm.' Her attention had been caught by a bird that flittered amongst the bines. There had been a sudden shower a few minutes earlier and glittering drops of water caught the light. 'So's Isobel. I was the last. There were two others in between but they died of the fever before I was born. Mama was poorly after that. Do you like reading?'

'Yes.' He grinned. This ability to change the subject without drawing breath was, he had discovered, as characteristic of her as her frank and unselfconscious curiosity. If Poppy wanted

16

to know something, she asked.

'So do I. It's one of my favourite things. Have you read *The Wind in the Willows*?'

'I have.'

'That's what I'm reading now. It's funny, isn't it?'

'It certainly is.'

'Mama says I'm always off in a corner with a book. She thinks it's bad for me.' Something in her tone made him glance down at her. Her attention had been distracted; she was looking past him to where, in the shadows of the far side of the hopfield, there was movement. Cheerful voices called. Women, skirts kilted about their knees, trudged two by two into the rows of bines, hauling with them the simple wood and sacking bins into which they picked the hops. Muddy-legged wild-haired children whooped and called. Reluctantly, Poppy stood up. 'Oh, bother. I suppose I'd better go.'

'Why?'

'I'm not supposed to play with the hopping children. Papa doesn't even like me to talk to them.'

'Oh?'

She was watching the influx with a certain wistfulness. 'They are a bit rough,' she said, 'but they seem to have a lot of fun.'

He ruffled her hair.

She sat down again, her small mouth set in a sudden, obstinate line that Kit was coming to recognise. 'I don't see why I shouldn't stay for

17

a little while. I'm with you, after all, aren't I?'

Kit nodded, amused. From the things she had told him over the past couple of weeks and from what he had gleaned from his usually benignly tolerant uncle, he did not somehow get the impression that 'Papa' would be any happier to know that than he would be to discover his daughter pelting round the hopfields with the pickers' children, but he did not say so. Harold Matthews had come as close to being caustic as his charitable nature allowed when questioned about Poppy's parents. 'One would have thought,' he had said gently, 'that losing the boys so tragically would have taught them that there is more in life than the pursuit of wealth and the niceties—or otherwise—of social climbing. The father, I'm afraid, is an old-fashioned martinet of Victorian inclinations, and the mother, whilst charming, is an unmitigated snob.' Not for the first time Kit found himself wondering how such a pairing had produced his friendly, open, inquisitive little Mouse.

Two children, a small boy and a girl of about Poppy's age, barefoot, dark of skin and eye and thin as rails were approaching them. They stopped a few yards away, faces wary. Poppy watched in fascination as the mud oozed between their bare toes. The girl smeared at her nose with a filthy hand. Poppy was enthralled. Kit had turned a leaf of his sketch-book, and his pencil was flying.

18

The older child looked at him suspiciously. 'What yer doin', Mister?'

Kit for a second did not reply. Poppy had climbed on to the box to watch. 'He's drawing you,' she said.

The girl, unsmiling, grabbed the boy's hand and stepped back a little. 'Wha' for?'

'Because it's what he does.' Poppy was patient. She glanced back at the other girl. 'He's ever so good at it,' she added reassuringly.

Kit's lips twitched.

The dark eyes narrowed. 'What d'yer pay?' she asked.

Kit's pencil stilled for a second. He tilted his head, looking at her. 'I'm sorry?'

'What d'yer pay? Fer drawin' someone?'

Poppy answered for him. 'He doesn't pay. People pay him.'

The tousled head shook emphatically. 'Oh, no. No fear! You wanna draw me, you pay me.' She tapped her narrow chest with her thumb, then stuck out a thin, dirty, well-shaped hand, flat out.

Poppy stared at her.

Kit laughed outright, parked the pencil behind his ear and fished in his pocket. 'Here,' he said.

Long, dark-skinned fingers with nibbled nails curled about the penny. A brief, wicked, smile flashed. 'Ta, Mister.' And with one fleet movement she turned and was gone, hair tossing, bare legs flashing as she ran.

Kit looked at the little boy, who had shoved a filthy thumb in his mouth and was watching them with huge black eyes. 'Would you like a penny too?' Kit asked gently.

The child nodded. Kit put his hand in his pocket again, handed a coin to the boy. The boy snatched it, turned and scampered after his sister.

Poppy fidgeted a little uneasily on her box. 'Papa says you shouldn't do that,' she said. 'He says they're here to work, not to beg, and that if you give them things they'll only come back for more. He says it encourages them to steal. And anyway—' she added, suddenly stern '—he didn't say "please" or "thank you".' She jumped from the box, brushed industriously at her skirt.

Kit tucked his book away into his satchel. 'Well, neither did he,' he said peaceably. 'Perhaps no one's ever told him that he should?'

That startling thought silenced her for a while. That there could possibly be a world not dominated by 'pleases' and 'thank-yous' and 'may I?s' and such like was a notion of such novelty it took some considerable stretch of the imagination to get to grips with it. It went, she supposed, with bare feet and uncombed hair and wiping your nose with the back of your hand. And—wonderful thought!—no times tables, no samplers to embroider or, in

20

Poppy's case to spend hours unpicking and re-embroidering, no lists of dates of the birth and death of kings. But no books either. None of Mrs Butler's delicious apple pies. No comfortable bed each night, in your own pretty room with fresh sheets and a nightlight and Mama's sweet perfume as she bent to kiss you goodnight. Poppy had seen the huts being disinfected and readied for the pickers; she knew the families slept together on a single plank bed and a mattress stuffed with straw, that they cooked on open fires and ate off tin plates. She thought of the gypsy girl, of that sudden, wicked, flashing smile, of the bare legs and the tossing hair. That one didn't lie awake at night fretting at the thought of being sent away to school, that was for sure. But then—what of comfort, and the fire in the drawing-room on a winter's evening, when Mama or Isobel would give in, laughing, and read you a story? The other girl hadn't given the impression that she even knew of such things. Poppy frowned ferociously. It was all such a puzzle.

'Do you want one too?'

She looked up at her companion. Kit had taken another penny from his pocket and held it out. She liked his hands. They were long, and competent, and the nails were square and very short and clean. 'Pardon?'

'A penny—' his eyes were laughing '—for your thoughts.'

She giggled. 'I was just wondering—' Her voice faded. It was difficult to put into words exactly what she had been wondering '—what it would be like to be that girl,' she finished, lamely.

Kit regarded her for what seemed like a long time, his eyes suddenly sober. Then he sat down on the box, bringing his face down to the level of hers, and took her hands in his. 'Don't be fooled, Poppy. There's precious little romance in destitution. Precious little dignity, either.'

She kicked at the box with the toe of her boot and gloomily voiced the thought at the forefront of her mind. 'I'll bet she's not going to have to go away to school.'

'Almost certainly not.' His voice was dry.

The pickers had settled at the far end of the field, the pole-pullers were hooking the bines from the wires, ready for stripping. The women—for in this, the fourth year of the war, most of the pickers were women, supplemented by a few older men and a few, maimed, young—settled themselves on the sides of the bins, their backs against the uprights, fingers and tongues flying with equal alacrity. Dogs and children tumbled about them. A cool wind had begun to blow and once more there was the scent of rain in the air. 'They aren't doing this for fun, you know.' Kit's eyes flickered to the pickers and back to hers. 'They're doing it for money. And it's

22

damned hard work. They could probably live for a year on what your Mama and your sister spend on perfume. Security is not to be sniffed at. And, unfortunately, security is money. It's all very well to be a free soul, but even a free soul has to eat occasionally.'

She watched him as he stood, swinging his satchel on to his shoulder. They fell into step companionably, following the rutted cart track that led along the side of the field and back to the footpath. A great, ambling carthorse passed them, pulling a cart with wheels as tall as Poppy. The driver saluted her with his whip and she waved back. She cocked her head, looking up at Kit. 'Have you got any money?'

The typically direct question brought a smothered snort of laughter. After a moment he shook his head. 'No, Poppy. I don't have any money. None at all. Well, not the kind you've got, anyway.'

She regarded him with wide, guileless brown eyes. 'I haven't got any money.'

He nibbled his lip, suppressing his amusement. 'No, I suppose that's true. And that reminds me—' He fished in his pocket again, drew out a coin, 'I owe you a penny.'

She took it. 'Thank you.' The grins they exchanged were the very currency of friendship.

Some ten minutes later they crossed the river by a narrow footbridge and came to the fallen tree where their paths diverged. As had

23

become their habit they paused there, Kit leaning against the huge fallen trunk, Poppy scrambling with his help on to it. Clouds billowed and built in the sky. Something the child had said earlier had recurred to Kit. 'Don't you want to go away to school?' he asked.

'No!' The word was so quick and so vehement that he glanced at her in surprise.

'Why don't you want to go?'

She shrugged, looking down, picking at her fingernails. 'I just don't. That's all.' How to find the words to explain? How to express the terror of finally, and with absolute certainty, losing her freedom? Isobel laughed at her. Isobel told her what fun she would have. Isobel had loved school. Isobel had belonged. Isobel had left St Beatrice's with regret, with everyone's approval, with the undisputed accolade of being the most popular head girl in the history of the school, and with no academic qualifications at all. Her eager accounts of the friendships, the crushes, the small-mindedness and the conspiracies of school life had appalled Poppy. 'I just don't,' she said again.

He shrugged. 'Fair enough,' he said gently.

She looked up in genuine surprise. 'Aren't you going to tell me off? Everyone else does.'

He eyed her, pulled a face. 'Poor Poppy,' he said in mock sympathy, and in a moment she was gurgling with laughter, bouncing on the

24

tree like a monkey.

'Poppy? What on earth are you up to now?'

The voice, light and musical but with an edge of exasperation to it, came from above them, from the top of the grassy slope of the river bank. Both of them looked up. Silhouetted against the angry, billowing clouds stood a strikingly pretty young woman. She was dressed in dark blue, a jacket and skirt of fashionable military cut, the skirt short enough to show the fetching turn of her ankle. The braided jacket was belted round a waist that looked slender enough to be spanned by Kit's two hands. Her wind-blown curly hair, drawn back from her face into a loose bunch on her neck, was the colour of marigolds, and even from where he stood Kit could see that her eyes were the clearest blue: forget-me-nots after rain.

'Oh, Lord,' Poppy said under her breath. 'It's Isobel. Now I'm for it!'

CHAPTER TWO

Kit was the first to recover himself. 'Miss Brookes,' he said, smiling, 'it's nice to meet you. Poppy has told me a lot about you.'

But not that this older sister of hers was a beauty; that the child had omitted to mention.

Delicate eyebrows lifted. Isobel did not

smile. She watched him, gravely and questioningly.

'Kit Enever,' he offered, limping up the slope to extend his hand.

Poppy had hastily slid from the tree-trunk and was surreptitiously dusting at her skirts. 'He's my friend. He's an artist. He hurt his leg in the war.'

Isobel hesitated a moment before, very briefly, taking the proffered hand. 'How do you do, Mr Enever. Poppy, for goodness' sake—I've been looking everywhere for you. Mama's waiting for you. Do come along.' The words were addressed to her sister, but her eyes, wide and thoughtful, stayed upon the young man's face. Though thin and tired-looking it was an interesting face, dominated by clear, long-lashed eyes of gold-flecked brown that now were surveying her with an intentness that, as their fingers brushed, brought a slight and becoming flush to her cheeks. His thick hair, curling at his collar a little longer than was fashionable, was tousled and damp from the rain.

Poppy was standing on one leg, polishing a dirty boot on the back of her already snagged stocking. She looked from one to the other, a slight frown on her small face. 'All right, I'm coming,' she said loudly.

Still their eyes held.

'Well?' Poppy said, a little crossly, 'Come on, Isobel. We shouldn't keep Mama waiting.

You know she doesn't like it.' She was obscurely put out by this encounter, and by the strange way the two grown-ups were looking at each other. Kit was *her* friend. Hers. She didn't want to share him. Especially not with Isobel.

Her words attracted her sister's attention at last. The eyebrows lifted again, faintly exasperated. 'Since when did such things bother you, young lady? You were supposed to be back at the house half an hour ago.'

'It was my fault,' Kit said quickly. 'I've been sketching in the fields. We forgot the time.'

'You didn't know I had to be back, anyway,' said the scrupulously honest Poppy. 'And I forgot.'

Isobel shook her head resignedly. The wind caught a bright strand of hair and blew it across her face. She tidied it back with slender fingers. Her skin was pale and smooth as pearl. Kit found himself wondering if it would be as cool and silky to the touch as it looked. His fingers itched for a pencil. Isobel held out her hand to her sister, who slipped her grubby paw into it. The huge eyes flickered back to Kit. 'Goodbye, Mr Enever. It was nice to meet you.'

'Goodbye.' Again the intensity of his gaze brought the blood to her face.

Poppy tugged on her sister's hand. Isobel ducked her head and turned away.

' 'Bye, Poppy.'

Poppy waved to Kit with her free hand.

27

' 'Bye.'

Kit watched them as they set off towards the house, the older girl tall, slim and graceful, the little one bouncing, small and sturdy beside her.

Poppy turned and waved once more. He lifted a hand.

Isobel did not turn. 'You really are naughty, you know,' she said. 'You know very well you aren't to talk to strangers.'

'He's not a stranger,' Poppy said. 'He's my friend.'

'Is he indeed?'

'He's staying at the Rectory with his uncle until his leg gets better. He's an artist. He was drawing pictures of the war when he got shot. He's been up in a balloon. They send people up in balloons to see what the Germans are doing, and he went up in one and took some photographs—'

'You seem to know a remarkable amount about him.'

'I told you. He's my friend.'

Isobel stopped walking for a moment, turned to survey her young sister with serious eyes. 'Poppy—I'm sorry, but I don't think Mama and Papa would—'

'Oh, no!' Poppy interrupted fiercely, her small face passionate. 'Isobel, no! Please don't tell them. Please! They'd spoil it. I know they would! I'll be good, I promise I will. I won't be late any more and I'll come when I'm called

28

and I'll keep my clothes clean—but please, Isobel, don't tell Mama and Papa about Kit.'

Isobel nibbled her lip, started walking again. Poppy ran to keep up with her. 'Isobel! *Please!*'

Isobel was trying with little success not to dwell on the recollection of a pair of intent, gold-flecked eyes. 'We'll see,' she said.

*   *   *

In the eighteen years of her privileged life Isobel Brookes had seldom been denied anything she really wanted. There were few people she could not beguile into indulging her. Only circumstances had balked her—she hated the war that had killed her brothers and deprived her of the admirers and the bright social life she knew would have been her natural due in more normal times. Her mother's wistful and nostalgic recollections of the parties, the dances, the picnics, the gentlemen callers of her own youth served only to make things worse. Isobel was convinced that life was passing her by, that nothing interesting or exciting would ever happen to her, as it did to the heroines of the romances she loved to read. She was absolutely certain, despite her mother's gentle reassurances, that buried here in the country her looks would fade, her figure thicken before her dream— her only dream—of love and marriage could be fulfilled. Vivacious and self-centred, as

29

warm-hearted as she was light-minded, in common with her young sister she could be remarkably stubborn in pursuit of something she wanted; the difference between them being that Poppy had never acquired the talent—and probably never would—of disguising it behind guileful smiles and pretty words. Isobel felt cheated. She felt that through no fault of her own her life was being wasted. Isobel was bored.

It was a dangerous state of mind for an attractive and impressionable young woman who had just met—and made an impression on—an utterly unsuitable but equally attractive young man.

*   *   *

'Did you get into trouble?' Kit threw a stone into the slow-flowing stream, watched as the ripples widened around the spot where it had disappeared. He had come across Poppy on the stone bridge playing an arcane game of her own that involved dropping sticks into the water, then racing to the other side of the bridge to watch them appear from beneath the moss-covered stone arch, and tossing grass into the fierce wind to see how far it would fly before dropping into the water. He had watched her, amused, for a long time, struck as he so often had been by her single-mindedness, her ability to concentrate totally on what she was doing. Her apparently total self-sufficiency.

She shook her head. 'No. Isobel didn't tell.'

'Didn't tell what?'

'About you. Look, I tell you what—I'll drop the stick, you throw the grass.' She shoved a handful of grass into his hand.

Obligingly he took it. 'Shout when you want me to throw it. What are we trying to do?'

'Seeing if the grass beats the stick. Is the wind blowing faster than the water's running?'

'Ah, I see. I think. What do you mean that your sister didn't tell about me? I thought you'd get into trouble for being late?'

'Oh, no. I'm almost always late. I don't think anyone expects anything else any more, and they've given up telling me off about it. Well, almost. Now!'

Obediently he let go of the grass. It fluttered and fell. 'But you thought you might get into trouble for being with me?'

She cocked her head to look at him solemnly. 'I didn't know. I wasn't sure. But I didn't want to take the chance. Isobel agreed. In the end.'

He grinned and ruffled her hair. 'You're an old-fashioned little thing, aren't you?'

'I don't know. But I think I probably am, because people are always saying so. Have you finished sketching for the day?'

'Yes.'

'Do you like mushrooms? There are some

31

huge ones in the top meadow. Well, there were. The hoppers have probably got them by now but it's worth a try.' There was a week left of the picking season. The year was closing in.

They set off companionably, side by side, along the path. Kit waited for a moment before asking, carefully, 'Did Isobel—say anything? About the other day?'

Poppy had picked a stick from the hedge and was energetically swiping at thistle-heads with it. 'Not much. She said I shouldn't talk to strangers and I said you weren't a stranger, you were my friend. Then I told her about you. Then she said Mama and Papa wouldn't approve and I asked her not to tell. And she said, "We'll see",' exasperatedly the child mimicked her sister's soft voice. 'Why *do* grown-ups always say that? Then she asked—' Poppy stopped in mid-sentence, 'Oh, look! Blackberries. What lovely great big ones! Can you reach them?'

Dutifully Kit pulled the bramble down with the hook of his stick. The blackberries were indeed big, and very sweet. There were a few moments' silence.

'Asked what?' Kit was casual.

'Sorry?' Poppy's fingers and mouth were purple with juice.

'You said Isobel asked something.'

'Oh, yes. She asked if you were married.'

Did she, indeed? Kit's lips twitched a little. 'What did you say?'

32

'I said no.' The child looked suddenly uncertain. 'You aren't, are you?'

'No.' All at once the laughter was gone from his eyes. 'I'm not.'

'Mmm! I love blackberries. Especially in apple pie. Mrs Butler makes lovely blackberry and apple pie. It's a shame we haven't got anything to carry them in.'

'Here.' Kit sorted through his satchel, came up with a tattered paper bag. 'Will this do?' He stretched the stick out to another bramble.

'Golly, thanks.'

'So—that was all?'

Poppy hesitated with a berry poised at her lips, thought a moment, then nodded vigorously. 'Yes. Then I had to go and see Mama. She wanted to hear me play the piano. To see if I had improved.'

'And had you?'

She shook her brown head. 'Of course not. It was *terrible*.'

Kit laughed softly at the depth of feeling in the word. 'Don't you like the piano?'

'I like *listening* to it. I just don't like *doing* it. I can't, you see. Not like Isobel can. That's the kind of thing she's good at. Things that girls are supposed to be good at.'

'And—she hasn't mentioned me since?'

The child directed a sudden, steady look at him. 'No,' she said shortly.

Something in her tone warned him off the subject. In silence he reached for a blackberry.

33

It was later, as they strolled back to the bridge, that he asked gently, 'Poppy? Would you do something for me?'

She was nursing the disintegrating, juice-soaked bag in stained hands. She smiled up at him, nodding. 'Of course.'

He hesitated. She waited.

'Would you—ask Isobel—' He saw the flicker in her face, saw the sudden straightening of her blackberry-stained mouth, but it was too late to stop. 'Would you ask her if she'd let me sketch her? It's what I used to do, you see. I used to paint portraits. Perhaps one day I will again. I'd like to try.'

Poppy marched on.

'Poppy?'

She lifted a shoulder. 'We'll see,' she said.

*   *   *

'Have you seen your—friend—Kit again?' Isobel was arranging flowers. Poppy had hauled herself up on the wooden table and was sitting, small booted feet swinging, watching her. The rain sheeted against the windows in vicious gusts.

Poppy's swinging feet stilled. She cocked her head in characteristic manner. 'What are those? The pink ones?'

'Peonies. There are still some in the greenhouse. Have you?'

'Yes.'

34

Isobel waited to see if her sister might be about to embellish the terse reply. When it became obvious that she would not, she asked, 'Did he say anything?'

'Well, of course he did.' The child was scornful. 'What's the point of seeing each other if you don't say anything?'

Isobel's long eyelashes fluttered. She took a slow, pained breath. 'I mean—did he say anything about—well, about the other day?' About me. About *me*.

'No,' said Poppy. 'We talked about me not being able to play the piano. And picked blackberries.'

Isobel adjusted a bloom, stood back to survey the effect. 'I see.'

Poppy, nonchalantly, swung her feet again. 'I was right,' she said, as a concession. 'He's not married.'

*   *   *

The Germans were finished, and everyone knew it. They had lost more than a million men in a series of disastrous defeats since the spring. Everywhere the Allies were advancing steadily, through drenching rain and in mud that in places was waist deep and voracious enough to swallow a horse. Yet still they fought on, and still men died, needlessly, for a cause long lost.

'Your leg seems a lot better.' Poppy wriggled

impatiently, drummed her heels on the parapet of the little bridge. 'Does that mean you'll have to go back to the war?'

'Yes. Probably.' Kit's pencil stilled for a moment then moved again, quick and light on the paper. 'Keep still, you little fidget. Just a minute longer.'

With elaborate patience she sighed and stilled her movements. A moment later he lifted his head. 'There. Do you want to see it?'

She jumped from the wall and ran to him, craning her neck to look at the sketch. 'It's very good,' she said, approvingly. 'Even better than the mouse one.'

'That was a joke. This is a proper portrait, or at least a sketch for one. Perhaps one day I'll be able to paint you properly.'

'I'd like that. Perhaps Mama and Papa would pay you to do it. They paid lots for the pictures of Hugh and William that Mama has in her horrible Orangery thing—and they aren't as good as you could do,' she added, sturdily loyal.

There was a sudden, small silence. Kit tucked his pencil into a tin box and slipped it into his satchel, folded his sketch-pad.

'Do you know when you'll have to go back?' she asked, reverting to the original subject of the conversation.

He did not answer for a moment. His eyes were thoughtful.

'Kit?'

'Sorry?'

'I asked if you knew when you might have to go back?'

'Oh—no. I'm still under the doctor at the moment. A few weeks yet, I should think.'

'I'll bet you don't want to go.'

'No. I don't.'

'Papa says that it will all be over soon. He says—' Poppy stopped. Kit lifted his head. A tall, slender figure moved gracefully towards them along the footpath. Isobel was wearing a cream linen outfit of similar cut to the one she had worn before, and this time she carried a wide-brimmed straw hat by its pale silken ribbons. Her hair gleamed like spun gold in the October sunshine. The pair on the bridge watched her in silence.

'Well!' The great flower-blue eyes moved from Poppy's face to Kit's, and stayed there. Isobel smiled her most bewitching smile. 'Hello there! Poppy's pestering you again, I see.'

'I'm not pestering!' Poppy said, hotly indignant. 'Kit's been drawing me. He wanted to. Didn't you?'

He ruffled her hair affectionately. 'Yes, I did. And no, you aren't pestering me.' He looked back at Isobel. His eyes were very bright. 'Would you like to see it?'

She half-shrugged, affecting indifference, but nodded nevertheless.

Kit reached into his satchel and handed her

the sketch-pad. She put her hand out for it, and their fingers touched. As she leafed through the pad the pages trembled a little, as if stirred by a breeze. She stopped at the drawing he had made of her sister, and studied it, her downcast lashes shadowing her cheeks.

He watched her.

The lashes lifted. 'It's very good,' she conceded.

'Thank you.'

Poppy had scrambled on to the parapet again and was standing beside Kit, leaning on his shoulder in an exaggeratedly proprietary way that brought an affectionate smile to his face. 'He wants to make a proper picture. A portrait. I said Mama and Papa might pay him for it, like they did for the ones of William and Hugh.'

Once again two pairs of eyes met and held. Kit saw the sudden gleam of something bright and speculative and very close to mischief. For a moment the blue eyes widened even further. 'Do you think they might be interested?' he asked quietly.

Isobel did not answer for a moment. Then she lifted a slim, indolent shoulder. 'I don't know. They might, I suppose.' She swung the hat thoughtfully, long fingers tangled in the ribbon. 'They do already have one of me when I was little—about Poppy's age, in fact.'

'Then perhaps they'd like one of you grown up? And one of Poppy before she grows up?'

She laughed lightly. 'A job lot? The Brookes girls on canvas?'

He smiled. 'Why not? Nice things often come in twos, I find.'

Poppy pushed away from him. She was scowling. They were doing it again. Shutting her out. It was as if they were holding a conversation of which she was no part; saying things that she couldn't understand, despite the almost silly simplicity of the words. Kit noticed the movement, and held out his hand to help her down from the wall. She ignored it and scrambled down alone, grazing her knee in the process. 'I suppose you've come to get me?' she said, gracelessly direct, to her sister.

Isobel shook her head innocently. 'No. I decided to go for a walk, that's all.'

Poppy stared at her. 'You don't go for walks,' she said flatly.

Isobel flushed a little. 'Don't be silly. Of course I do. It was such a lovely day, and after all the bad weather we've been having it seemed a shame to stay indoors.' She settled the hat upon her curly hair, tied the ribbon beneath her chin. Her blue eyes lifted, alight with laughter, challenging and flirtatious, to the young man's face. 'Do you like to walk, Mr Enever?'

Kit surveyed the bright, flawless face for a long moment. Then, 'I do indeed, Miss Brookes,' he said tranquilly.

'It doesn't hurt your poor leg?' Isobel

39

turned and began to stroll along the sheep-cropped bank of the river, Kit falling into step beside her.

He smiled, entertained. 'My poor leg is considerably improved, thank you.'

Poppy stood for a moment, stubbornly still, watching them. Birdsong rang in the sunny afternoon. Isobel threw back her head and laughed, the pretty sound a counterpoint to the birds.

Poppy waited to see if Kit would turn back and wait for her. He did not. Gloomily she trailed after them.

*　　　*　　　*

Over the next few days Isobel took a sudden and remarkable liking to walking—a pastime for which until now she had, to say the least, never much cared. Fortunately the weather remained fair and this new and unlikely interest went unremarked—at least by everyone but Poppy. She would sit in the window of her schoolroom as Miss Simpson droned on about apples at tuppence-ha'penny and pears at three-farthings and watch as her sister strolled apparently casually down the gravelled drive of the house and disappeared beneath the trees towards the gate that led out into the lane and on to the footpath to the river. That Isobel was meeting Kit the child did not for a moment doubt; and in the initial wave of resentment that beset her at what she perceived to be Kit's unkindness she herself obstinately stayed at home. If he wanted to be friends with Isobel and not her, then let him. She didn't care.

But she did. She cared very much. That in staying away from him she gave him no chance to continue their friendship did not occur to her for two or three days; and by then Isobel had started her campaign for the portraits.

*   *   *

They were in the Orangery: Isobel, Poppy and their mother. For all her forty-three years, Elizabeth Brookes was still an exquisitely pretty woman with the same blue eyes and fine-drawn features as her elder daughter. At the moment she was, as she did so often, inspecting the lushly growing plants that were her passion, a small black cat preening about her ankles. Never particularly robust, years of child-bearing had left Elizabeth in fragile health, and the tragedy of two dead babies and the brutal loss of the sons who had been her pride and her delight had given her an air of abstracted and delicate melancholy that Isobel tried in vain to replicate.

In truth there was no real sense in which Elizabeth could be described as strong. Through no fault of her own she belonged to a generation of women brought up in a society so strongly paternalistic that to question its ways and beliefs was tantamount to blasphemy. Marriage to a man whose adamantine opinions left little room for discussion, let alone for disagreement, had meant that she had never learned to think for herself; to be truthful, it could be said that she had never had the inclination. When she agreed with her wrathful husband that the women who were agitating for greater freedoms for her sex should be whipped through the streets it was not simply through docility; she believed it. She did not want the vote. She was certain that she would not know what to do with it if she had it. She could not see what possible difference it could make, except to be a worry, to change a status quo that in fact perfectly suited her; or it had before this dreadful war had erupted and taken away her sons, her visits to London and Paris and most of her servants.

She longed for the slaughter to be over, for things to return to normal—or as normal as they could ever again be. Meanwhile she had her girls, her memories and her beloved tropical plants. She loved the heavy, sweet-smelling air of the Orangery, loved to sit with her needlework or her magazines in the wicker armchair beneath the portraits of her sons that had been carefully protected behind glass from the moist air. She would spend at least part of each day tending the plants, all of them exotic, most of them rare, some of them reaching to the roof, twenty feet above. She touched a pale, gold-green orchid with a gentle finger. The little cat stalked away and settled itself in a patch of sunshine, licking a tiny paw.

Poppy wriggled in her armchair, scowling fiercely at a grubby sampler the execution of which, even to the unskilled eye, quite obviously owed more to motherly coercion than daughterly skill.

'Poppy, darling, do stop fidgeting,' Elizabeth said gently. 'It's most unladylike.'

Poppy's face was as bright as the flower after which she had been named. Sweat trickled between her shoulderblades and her brown hair was lank with it. 'I'm sorry, Mama. It's just so hot in here—'

'You wouldn't *get* so hot if you didn't fidget so much,' Isobel pointed out, irritatingly reasonable. She was sitting at a small glass table writing a letter. The silence broken, she laid down her pen and rested her chin on her long, curled fingers, her eyes wide and artless upon her mother. 'Mama—did I tell you I met Mary Hilden in the village the other day?'

'No, you didn't.' Elizabeth turned, interested. 'How are they? I haven't seen any of them for ages. Have they come back to the Hall?'

'No.' The word was very quick. Isobel picked up her pen and turned it in her fingers. 'They're still in London. They'll be staying

43

there, from the sound of it. Sir Robert's doing
something terribly secret and important in the
War Office. Mary had just come down with
Lady Hilden to check on the house. Her
sister's married, you know.'

'Yes.' Absently Elizabeth reached for a pair
of secateurs. 'Yes, I had heard.'

'I heard it ages ago.' Poppy had lifted her
head and was watching her sister with a
puzzled frown. 'It was all over the village. It
was in the papers. She married a Lord in the
Life Guards or something.'

Isobel's mouth tightened a little and she
shot Poppy a look so fierce that it startled the
child to silence. The cat started on the other
paw.

'She was saying—' Isobel continued
casually,'—that there's a young man staying at
the Rectory who's apparently quite a well-
known painter.' This time the quelling look
came from beneath lowered lids. Poppy, who
had opened her mouth, closed it again, very
firmly. 'Or at least she said she's sure he would
have been if it weren't for this beastly war.
He's—' she hesitated, '—sort of vaguely
connected to the Hildens, I believe. Mary said
he painted a portrait of the two little boys, just
before the war. She says Sir Robert and Lady
Hilden are delighted with it.' She studied the
pen she was playing with as if it were the most
absorbing object in the world; after a moment
lifted her head. 'He's been doing war work,

44

and was wounded.' She sat back in her chair and lifted her eyes to the portraits of her brothers. 'Mary's sure he'll probably be quite famous one day.'

'Really? That's interesting.' Elizabeth's attention was back on her plants. She actually sounded about as interested as might the little cat, that was now sound asleep, whiskers twitching.

Isobel shot her mother an irritated look. Poppy ducked her head, concentrating ferociously on the hated needlework, ears pricked.

Isobel tried again. 'I was just wondering—' She gathered the pages of her letter together and tapped them neatly upon the table '—if Papa might not be interested?'

Elizabeth's attention was at last caught. She turned a puzzled face to her daughter. 'Your father? But my dearest, why ever should he be?'

'Well—' The pen joined the neat pile of paper, set straight and parallel beside the pages. 'You have a portrait of me when I was little. I just thought you might like one of Poppy when—'

Poppy's head shot up. 'I'm *not*—' Two pairs of blue eyes turned upon her sharply, and she subsided, '—little,' she muttered and went back to her needle.

Her mother laughed, a sudden, clear sound, infectious and too little heard. 'Well, you aren't exactly ancient, are you, my darling?' The laughter died. The door had opened and a girl in black uniform and frilled white apron and cap had entered. 'Yes, Lucy, what is it?'

The girl bobbed an untidy and somewhat casual curtsy. 'It's Cook, Mrs Brookes. Says can you come down an' tell her what you want from the butcher. 'E's turned up a day early.'

Very carefully Elizabeth set the secateurs on the table, her sweet-natured face as close to irritation as it ever got. She glanced at her daughters. 'It seems that Cook requires my presence in the kitchen. I shan't be long, girls.' She followed Lucy to the door, turned, sighing, before shutting it behind her, 'This *wretched* war!'

'Mama never could handle servants,' Isobel remarked.

Poppy was staring at her. 'Isobel! What on earth are you up to? I'll bet Mary Hilden hasn't been anywhere near the village for months! Everyone knows they aren't going to open the Hall again. Not for ages, anyway.'

'Well, of course she hasn't. But Mama doesn't know that, does she? And who's to tell her?'

'But what are you *doing*?' Poppy's voice had dropped to a hissing whisper. 'All this business about Hilden connections and portraits—'

'Ssh! Poppy, leave this to me. You want Kit to come and paint your portrait, don't you? Papa would never agree to it if he knew you'd

46

been sneaking out to meet him. He'd be *furious*. You know he would.'

Poppy was staring at her sister in outraged disbelief. 'Me?' she squeaked. '*Me* sneaking out to—'

'Poppy, do be *quiet*! I told you—leave it to me.'

'But—supposing Papa checks with Sir Robert? Supposing he finds that—'

'What he will find,' her sister said witheringly, 'is that what I've told Mama is absolutely true. Well, almost, anyway. There *is* some connection between Kit and the Hildens, but not a close one—second cousin several times removed or something—that's how his uncle got the living. For goodness' sake, Poppy, give me credit for some sense! And he *did* paint a portrait of the two little Hilden boys just before the war, and they *are* very pleased with it.'

'How do you know? If you didn't really meet Mary Hilden, how do you know?'

The pale and lovely face, the forget-me-not eyes, turned to her. They were very wide and very steady. 'Kit told me,' said Isobel, and there was a strange defiance in both voice and gaze.

The child's solemn brown eyes held hers. For the briefest of moments the small lips trembled. It was Isobel's gaze that faltered and dropped before the accusation and hurt in the little pointed face. 'Don't be silly, Poppy,' she

47

said brusquely.

Poppy said nothing, but picked up the battered sampler and bent over it, her lank hair falling across her face.

'Oh, my dears,' Elizabeth said from the doorway, 'what very trying times these are! I never thought the day would come when I'd be required to haggle with a tradesman!'

Isobel jumped up, all concern. 'Come, Mama. Sit down. I'll ring for some tea.'

Elizabeth sank gracefully into an armchair. 'Would you, my dear? Thank you.'

Isobel moved to the bell-push. 'Poppy? Would you like some cake?'

Poppy neither replied nor lifted her head.

Elizabeth leaned forward. 'Poppy? Is something wrong?'

There was a small movement, a quick intake of breath. Poppy lifted a hot, tear-streaked face. 'I pricked my finger,' she said. 'Look.' And watched as the blood dripped, dark and thick, soaking brightly into the pale material of the sampler.

CHAPTER THREE

George Brookes could by no means be described as an indulgent father; on the contrary it was his firm belief that an indulged child was a child spoiled for life. That said, however, he was far from immune to the blandishments of his elder daughter, and as it happened her suggestion that Kit might be invited to paint the girls' portrait was made on a day of uncommonly good temper. Despite the chancy weather the harvest was going well, a recent investment had paid off handsomely, the news from the Front was hopeful. And—a not insignificant point this, as Isobel had already realised—the fact that Kit Enever had painted a portrait for the family at Hilden Hall influenced him further. If the young man had painted the Hilden boys, then why not the Brookes girls?

Kit was duly sent for. Poppy waylaid him in the hall. 'Papa's going to say yes. I'm sure he is,' she whispered, excitedly conspiratorial.

Kit smiled. 'Good.'

'Just one thing—'

'What's that?'

'Don't let him say you're to paint us in the Orangery? Please!' Poppy rolled her eyes. 'I *hate* it in there. I'll die of heat! And the *smell*!'

He laughed. 'Poor little Mouse. I'll try. Where would you rather sit?'

'The drawing-room.' The words came from above them. Isobel stood on the stairs. 'The drawing-room would be perfect. By the French windows. They're west facing. The light in the afternoon is quite lovely.' She ran lightly down the stairs, skirts drifting about her slim legs, and stood smiling up at him. 'Papa's in the

49

office. I'll take you to him.'

Poppy stuck her hands in her apron pocket and hunched her shoulders.

'Hey!' Very gently Kit touched her shoulder. 'What's the matter?'

'Nothing. I've got to go.' She pulled away from him. 'I'm supposed to be learning the dates of the Hundred Years War.'

'Oh, dear.' Kit was sympathetic, but Poppy was gone, scrambling up the stairs in ostentatious and noisy haste. He looked after her. 'What a funny little thing she is.'

Isobel shrugged. 'She's just a baby. Come on, I'll take you to Papa.'

*   *   *

'Why did you run away like that?' Kit asked Poppy later. The deal had been struck, the arrangements made. Poppy had materialised beside him out of the shrubbery as he walked down the drive to the gate.

'Isobel,' she said briefly. 'She spoils everything.'

He stopped walking, stood looking down at her. 'That isn't fair, Poppy, and you know it.'

Poppy said nothing. The small face was mutinous.

Kit took her hands in his and hunkered on to his heels in front of her. 'Things do change, Poppy. They have to. Nothing stays the same. Nothing.' Face and voice were sombre.

'You were *my* friend,' she said.

'I still am.' His slow smile lit his face. 'I always will be. Always.'

'D'you promise?' Her dark eyes searched his face.

'I promise. Do you?'

It was her turn to smile. 'Yes. Faithfully.'

'Well, there we are then.' He stood up and strolled towards the gate. Poppy ran ahead to open it, scooted it open with one foot, clinging to the top bar as it swung. Kit caught it and swung it back. Poppy giggled delightedly. 'We'll get into trouble if anyone sees us.'

'I won't tell if you won't.' He leaned against the gatepost watching her as she scrambled up the bars like a monkey and sat somewhat precariously astride the top one.

'Is it true that you're Sir Robert's cousin?'

He shook his head. 'No, Poppy, it isn't true. My uncle is his cousin, about a dozen times removed. Where that puts me in the Hilden pecking order I have no idea—about on a par with the caretaker, I should think. I'm a penniless artist with a game leg. End of story.'

'But Isobel said—'

He smiled gently. 'Isobel is inclined to romance a little, isn't she?'

'You mean she tells fibs.'

'I mean nothing of the sort. I mean exactly what I said.'

'You like her, don't you?'

He nodded. 'Yes, I do. Don't you?'

The question startled her. 'She's my sister.'

'What's that got to do with it? I asked if you liked her.'

'She's a bit bossy sometimes.'

'Sisters are, I believe,' he said, straight-faced.

She laughed, and slid from the gate. 'I suppose I do like her, really. Yes.'

'And you're my friend?'

'Yes.'

'Then do me a favour.' Kit reached to where a late summer rose rambled through a hawthorn bush and plucked a bloom. 'Give her this from me and tell her that she was right: the drawing-room—and the French windows— are perfect.'

Poppy took the flower. 'When are we going to start?'

'Tomorrow afternoon. I don't know how much time I have—' He stopped.

'—before you have to go back to the war,' she supplied helpfully.

'Yes.' He walked through the gate, pulled it to behind him, and leaned on his elbows on the top bar. 'You'll give Isobel the rose?'

'I'll give it to her.' The child turned and ran back up the drive towards the house.

He watched her go with the clear young voice still ringing in his ears:—*before you have to go back to the war.*

Before you have to go back and face the unfaceable.

52

He dropped his head for a moment, breathing deeply, fighting his demons; then he straightened, turned, and walked slowly away. From her bedroom window Isobel watched with pensive eyes as the slim figure, shoulders hunched, disappeared into the shadows of the trees that overhung the lane.

*   *   *

'You've actually lived in Paris?' Isobel made no attempt to conceal the envy in her voice.

'Yes. For about a year, just before the war. I'm sorry—could you just tilt your head a little? To the right, so—' Kit put a finger under her chin to guide her. The huge eyes were veiled for a moment by the golden lashes before they focused, wide and soft, upon his face.

'Paris,' Elizabeth said longingly. 'Oh, how I loved Paris. We used to visit every year, you know, Mr Enever.' She was seated on a sofa, her hands idle upon the embroidery on her lap. 'Poor Paris,' she added softly. 'Will she ever be the same?'

Kit dropped his hand from Isobel's face; but not before she had sensed the tremor in the finger that had touched her skin. The eyelids drooped again, lashes long and lustrous against the pearl of her skin. She was wearing dark blue, a colour that suited her well, and her hair was dressed softly away from her face.

She looked quite extraordinarily lovely, and she knew it. Indeed, she had gone to great lengths to be certain of it.

'I would think so,' Kit answered Elizabeth, his eyes still on Isobel's face. 'She's been through worse before. Paris is a formidable old lady. She'll survive.' He stepped back, reached for his sketch-pad. Isobel kept her eyes upon his.

'We used to stay in a little hotel near Notre-Dame.' Elizabeth's voice was wistful. 'We always went in the spring. It was always so lovely; the parks, the *Bois de Boulogne*, the river—' she sighed softly.

Kit dragged his attention from Isobel's brightly challenging gaze. 'It will be again,' he said gently. 'Once the war is over.'

'The war.' There was an edge of weary bitterness in the words. 'Will it ever be over?'

'Of course it will, Mama. Don't be so silly,' Isobel said sharply. 'Did you study in Paris, Mr Enever?'

'Yes.' Kit had begun, swiftly, to sketch, his eyes flickering from Isobel's face to the paper. 'In Paris and in Florence.'

'I should like to go to Florence.' Isobel sat, straight-backed and graceful, watching him. 'Tell me—which did you prefer?'

He answered with no thought. 'Florence.'

'Why?'

He smiled a little. 'Because, lovely as Paris is, it has one great disadvantage—'

54

'Oh?'

The smile widened. 'It's in France. For me, there's nowhere to touch Italy. Especially Tuscany.'

'Tell me about it.'

'Isobel—poor Mr Enever is trying to work—'

'It's perfectly all right, Mrs Brookes.' Once more Kit reached to Isobel's chin. 'I'll tell you about Tuscany if you promise to keep your head still,' he said with mock severity.

She smiled, well satisfied.

*   *   *

The sittings continued for the best part of a week, sometimes with one or other of the girls, sometimes both, and always with Elizabeth in attendance as chaperon. And as she sat placidly embroidering, and Poppy, almost unnoticed, quietly sulked, Isobel and Kit talked of Tuscany. November was approaching; the weather had turned dull and damp. For days the sun had not broken through the heavy cloud and mists hovered over the river. The drawing-room fire was lit against the chill. But for Isobel the sunny, romantic landscapes that Kit evoked so vividly as he talked became more real than the fine, drenching rain that drifted so depressingly against the tall French windows; as familiar, almost, as the Kent countryside she knew so well. He delighted her by sketching a couple of little pictures for her; a vista of sunlit hillsides punctuated by the slim dark fingers of cypress trees, a tree-shaded village church with a tower he called a *campanile* and a picturesque jumble of steep tiled roofs.

By the time the easel had been set up and the picture had been blocked in—Isobel sitting upon a velvet-upholstered dining-room chair, Poppy standing beside her—an atmosphere of playful ease had grown between them, teasingly familiar, perilously flirtatious despite Elizabeth's almost constant presence. In fact, for Isobel, the presence of her mother at the sittings if anything actually added to the delicious piquancy of the situation. She knew perfectly well the effect her studied grace and artless, wide-eyed gaze had upon Kit, and employed both quite shamelessly and with growing and coquettish confidence. It was, for the moment, enough that she woke each day knowing that she would see him, that at last her dreams and romances had acquired a focus and her life the longed-for stimulus of excitement. From the moment she had seen Kit he had interested and intrigued her. His enigmatic gold-flecked eyes and the slender vulnerability of his frame fascinated her. Even his limp she found attractive. She watched his capable artist's hands as he worked and was enchanted by the tingling of her blood and the quickening of her heartbeat. In their conversations about Italy she came to a certainty that she knew him, that she was sharing with him a precious part of his life.

'Why do you love it so?'

He hesitated. 'I suppose—quite simply because it's so beautiful. So—inspiring—is the only word. The countryside is utterly lovely, the cities and towns are bursting with life and activity. There are so many pictures that come to mind. A cluster of roofs on a hillside. A shimmering heat haze over dusty fields. A magnificent cathedral. A market square. A village sleeping in the midday sunshine. A peasant hoeing his vines. A quick, bare-legged child. At the turn of a corner, a sculpture or a building that takes the breath away. Italy has a legacy of art and civilisation that is unique in the world. And that's not to mention the wine, the food, the people—' He stopped, shrugging, half smiling at his own enthusiasm.

'Is that all?' Poppy asked, fidgeting grumpily.

He threw back his head and shouted with laughter. 'I'm sorry, Poppy. Are we boring you?'

'Yes,' she said with perfect honesty.

And 'Poppy!' her mother exclaimed, scandalised.

'Sorry, Mama.'

In the second week there were fewer sittings. The sketches made, the double portrait taking charming life upon the canvas, the routine changed. Dangerously. Kit would

57

work alone in the drawing-room. Elizabeth retired, thankfully, to her Orangery; which, as Isobel had been well aware when she had suggested the drawing-room as a setting for the portrait, was at the other end of the house. Poppy each morning was confined to the schoolroom.

'May I come in?' Isobel tapped lightly at the open door.

'Of course.' Kit, absorbed, did not look up.

'I'm not disturbing you?'

'No.'

She slipped quietly into the room and stood behind him. 'How funny,' she said.

'What?'

'Poppy and I. We're so different, yet—there is a clear resemblance, isn't there?'

'You're sisters. It isn't surprising.'

'I suppose not. It just isn't usually that obvious.' She stepped a little closer, in a fresh drift of soap and rose-water. 'Has Papa seen it yet?'

Kit grinned wryly. 'There was an inspection yesterday.'

'And does he like it?'

'It seems so. Do you?'

There was a moment of silence. Then, 'Yes,' she said consideringly. 'Though I think you may have flattered me a little.'

He half smiled, but did not rise to the bait.

She wandered away from him, lifted the lid of the piano, played a few notes one-handed.

Beyond the window a shifting mist drifted, ghostly, a nebulous curtain between the house and the outside world. The fire crackled in the grate.

Isobel executed a gentle ripple of notes. 'It's November next week,' she said inconsequentially.

'Yes.'

'Winter. Dark evenings. Dark mornings. Cold skies. The weather's been really horrible this year. How's your leg?'

'Much better, thank you.' He had stopped work and was watching her.

She bent to the keys and brought her other hand to the keyboard. There was a brief and accomplished flurry of Chopin. She lifted her bright head. 'When it's better, will you have to go back?'

'I suppose so, yes.'

'You haven't spoken about the war.'

'No.'

'Is it awful?'

'Yes.' His smile was lopsided.

Isobel straightened, and closed the lid of the piano with quiet precision. 'Papa says it will end soon.'

'I'm sure Papa is right.'

She smiled, quickly and mischievously. 'Papa always is. It's a habit he finds hard to shed.'

His laughter was genuinely amused.

She walked to him, still smiling, her

cornflower eyes brilliant and steady. 'When it's over, will you go to Italy?'

He shrugged. 'Perhaps.'

'The wine. The sunshine. The mountains. Isn't it what you most want in the world?'

In the mist-enclosed silence that followed the words, he kissed her.

As she had intended that he would.

Footsteps sounded in the hall outside. Kit stepped back, his colour high, his breathing uneven. 'I'm sorry.'

Isobel shook her head a little, smiling calmly, as Lucy came through the door carrying a tray. 'I'm not. Oh, look, how nice— Lucy's brought you some tea.' And with another beguiling smile she left him.

In her room she sat at her dressing-table, chin on hand, gazing into the mirror, studying her own image intently. Her eyes blazed. She was beautiful, and she knew it. He had kissed her. He had kissed her! And he would kiss her again. She would make sure of that.

Humming softly, she jumped up and took a few dancing steps about the room. It had happened; at last it had happened. Life had finally come to Isobel Brookes; and Isobel Brookes was going to make sure that she grabbed it with both hands before it passed her by.

*   *   *

60

The days were short and the weather dull; Kit could work only until about three in the afternoon. Poppy, released at last from lessons and from nursery lunch, joined him in the drawing-room at about one-thirty that day. As the door opened, he lifted his head, sharply expectant, but relaxed and grinned as the small brown head appeared. 'May I come in?'

He beckoned, smiling. 'Of course, Mouse. Come on.'

She skipped into the room. Her straight brown hair had slipped from its fastenings and hung untidily about her face. She came to the easel and studied the half-finished picture. 'You've done a lot of Isobel,' she observed, a little abrasively.

His grin widened. 'I'm saving the best till last.'

The child laughed at that. 'You're teasing.'

He looked at her for a moment, thoughtful and affectionate. 'Perhaps I am. Perhaps I'm not.'

'How much longer will it take?'

He shrugged, bent again to the canvas. 'Three, four days. Something like that.' He hesitated for a second. 'Perhaps a little longer.' The room was very quiet. Fog billowed to the windows. Kit turned his head, listening. Was that a footstep? She'd come back, surely? Wouldn't she?

Poppy threw herself into a velvet-upholstered armchair. 'Have you heard the

61

news?'

He glanced at her. 'What news?'

'The Turks have surrendered. Papa read it from the paper. He says that Germany will have to give up now.'

'He's probably right.'

A companionable silence fell. She watched, engrossed, the movements of his brush. 'I think you're very clever.'

'Thank you. I think you are, too.'

'Me?' The word was a squeal of laughter. 'What do you mean?'

'I bet you can do arithmetic.'

'Well, of course I can. Can't you?'

He shook his head dolefully.

She eyed him suspiciously. 'You're teasing again.'

His grin was non-committal.

Poppy jumped from the chair and wandered to the window, stood peering into the fog. 'What horrible weather. Have you seen Isobel today?'

His hand stilled, and there was a brief moment of silence. Then, 'Yes,' he said. 'She popped in to check on progress this morning. Why?'

Poppy shrugged. 'I just wondered where she was, that's all. I haven't seen her all day. I suppose she must have gone out.'

He was surprised at the strength of his disappointment. 'Oh? On a day like this?'

'She's probably gone to see awful Mary

Seward. She lives in the house at the end of the lane. She's the same age as Isobel. They pretend they're friends.'

Kit cocked a puzzled eyebrow. 'Pretend to be friends? How do you mean?'

Poppy turned from the window, shrugging prosaically. 'They can't stand each other really. The only thing they talk about is those silly books they read. But there isn't anyone else around, you see. It's a bit of a shame. I mean—Isobel's bad enough, but *Mary*—' she rolled her eyes and pulled a face '—she's *gruesome.*'

Kit laughed. 'Mouse, you're priceless.' He applied himself to the portrait again, smiling as Poppy clattered out 'Chopsticks' on the piano, trying to tell himself that it did not matter that a flighty girl had kissed him and run away, apparently not to return. Telling himself that even if she did, it could only lead to trouble, and trouble was something he had quite enough of at the moment.

Trying, unsuccessfully, not to remember the touch of her hand, the yielding of her lips under his. His hand shook a little. 'Blast it!' he muttered, and reached for a rag to repair the damage.

Poppy, however was wrong; Isobel had not gone to see her friend Mary. She was in her room, sitting at her small writing desk, a scrap of paper in front of her. Her smooth, prettily manicured fingernails clicked upon the desk as

63

she drummed her fingers nervously. She could not decide; was she being too bold? Too precipitate? And yet—if she did nothing—might she not regret it for ever? The one thing they did not have was time. Any day now he might have to leave, to go back to France. The thought terrified her, for him and for herself. She reached for a pen.

Kit was tidying his things away when she slipped through the door of the drawing-room. Hearing her, he spun round. Swiftly she put a finger to her lips, enjoining him to silence. He took a step towards her and in a second his arms were about her, his lips on her hair. For a moment she clung to him, then shook her head quickly and struggled free. 'No, Kit,' she whispered. 'Not now. Not here.'

'Then when?' He, too, was whispering fiercely. 'Where?'

She took his hand, folded a small piece of paper into it, turned and sped back to the door. Once there she turned. Her eyes glowed with excitement. She touched her fingers to her lips, blew a kiss and was gone.

For a moment Kit did not move. It had happened so quickly that he had hardly taken breath. He looked down at the crumpled piece of paper in his hand and smoothed it carefully.

The message was simple: *'The summer house. 8 o'clock.'*

*   *   *

The summer house stood on a rise of land some few hundred yards behind the main house beneath a great, spreading copper beech, overlooking the tennis court and facing west to catch the evening sun. On a fine summer afternoon the view was splendid, the distant waters of the river reflecting the sunlight, glinting like a sequined tapestry through the curtain of the riverside willows. The house was a spacious affair, wood-built and with a wide, covered veranda. Elizabeth was fond of taking tea there, George even fonder of surveying his property from its height; before the advent of a war that was to destroy them, a couple of generations of young people had used it as headquarters for tennis tournaments. It was the perfect refuge from a cool spring breeze or from warm summer rain. On a dank and foggy late October evening it gave at least some protection from the chill. Kit, bare-headed, his shoulders propped against the wall, leaned in the misty shadows of the veranda, cupped his hand over the flame of his lighter as he lit a cigarette. It was ten minutes past eight.

The house loomed beneath him, wreathed in fog, its lighted windows glowing muted gold. He could smell woodsmoke in the thickened air. Water dripped from the bare branches above him, splattering on to the wooden roof, surreally loud in the still darkness. Moisture stood in his hair and on the rough fibres of his tweed jacket. The cold was beginning to creep to his bones.

Would she come?

It seemed that he had been waiting for an eternity. It had actually been half an hour. Carefully he lit his lighter again, peered at his watch. Twelve minutes past.

Something rustled on the lawn beneath him. He lifted his head sharply, like a scenting animal, straining his eyes into the shifting, disorientating fog. The glow of the windows dimmed as a particularly thick patch drifted in from the river. Sound was muted. Nothing happened.

How long should he give her? Was this some kind of game? Was she sitting safe and warm beside the drawing-room fire, modest and smiling, knowing he was here, watching, waiting, wanting her? Memories stirred, and he winced. No. Never again. No woman would ever treat him like that again.

'Kit?' Her voice was soft, endearingly unsure. 'Kit, are you there?'

Warmth flooded him. 'I'm here.'

She materialised out of the fog, shrouded in a cape and hood, a ghost in the cold mist. He saw the pale blur of her face as she lifted her head to look at him. For a suspended moment there was stillness. Neither moved. Then he took a step and held out his hand. In a second she had run up the steps to the veranda and was in his arms. He held her, rocking her, holding her fast to him.

'I'm sorry I'm late. I had to say I had a headache—it wasn't as easy as I thought it would be—Mama made a great fuss and insisted I take an aspirin—'

The fog billowed silent and isolating about them. 'Come,' she said and caught his hand, drawing him towards the door of the summer house. It stuck for a moment, then flew open, screeching in the silence. 'Have you got a light? There's a little lamp in here somewhere and in this pea-souper no one will notice if we light it.'

Kit flicked his lighter again. The room was furnished with a wooden table, several rattan chairs and a low two-seater couch. A couple of tennis rackets were propped in a corner. The windows were shuttered, closed for the winter. Upon the table stood a small lamp. As he lit it, it guttered and flared before settling down to a steady glow. Isobel put back the damp hood from her bright hair. Moisture clung to the tendrils that framed her face. The hand he held was cold, and trembled in his. She looked very young and very vulnerable. There was a moment of silence.

'Do you think me very forward?' There was a quiver of trepidation in the words; the eyes that searched his were anxious.

He smiled and drew her to him, bent his lips to hers. The kiss was long and very gentle.

When at last he released her, her eyes were glowing like stars in the lamplight. He slipped his arms beneath the cloak she still wore and held her to him again, laying his cheek upon her damp hair, feeling the trembling of her body, trying to control the growing urgency of his own. She lifted her face to kiss him again, one hand reaching to the soft thickness of his hair. The movement lifted her breasts softly against him and the clean curve of her back and buttocks were under his hands. He tried to pull away, but she clung to him. His hands slid to her narrow waist, and tightened, trying gently to push her away a little. 'Isobel—'

'Kiss me. Please, kiss me.'

He kissed her.

After a long time she drew away from him, her fingers at the fastening of the cloak. It dropped from her shoulders to the dusty floor. The slim-waisted velvet-trimmed corduroy dress that she wore suited her graceful figure to perfection. 'You're beautiful,' he said.

She came to him again. 'Am I? Am I really?'

'You are. Really.'

She leaned back in his arms to look at him, her face lit to a fearful excitement. 'We must be careful. Papa would kill us if he found us.'

He smiled wryly. 'I'm well aware of that, my darling.'

She laughed, softly and delightedly, at the endearment. 'No one's ever called me that before. Well—' she stopped, suddenly shy '—

you know what I mean.' She laid her head on his shoulder, her hands flat against his chest. 'Your heart is beating very fast.' The words were barely a whisper.

He tightened his arms about her. Her hands crept up to slide about his neck. With a strength he could no longer control he kissed her again, fiercely and hungrily. He felt her gasp, struggle a little against him and then suddenly she was kissing him back, as demanding as he. His hand moved to cup her breast. Her mouth opened beneath his.

Somewhere within him the small voice of sanity spoke. What was he doing? What the *hell* was he doing? Then the flood of his senses took over and the voice was drowned. She made no attempt to stop him as he fingered the velvet-covered buttons at the front of her dress and one by one they slipped open. She gasped aloud as he slid his hands beneath the material. Her breasts were heavy, warm and silky. As he bent his head to kiss them she closed her eyes, her long fingers cupping his head against her.

On the table the lamp burned steadily in the rustling darkness.

It was perhaps half an hour later when he said softly, 'You really should go, my darling. It's nine o'clock.'

'Yes.' She did not move. She was lying beside him on the little couch, half covered from the cold by her cloak, her head in his lap, her bared breasts gleaming like pearl in the lamplight. She lifted her great eyes to his, bit her lip a little. 'Kit, if I ask you something—something you might think silly—you promise you won't laugh? I should die if you did.'

He cocked his head a little, his smile gentle. 'Don't be silly. Of course I won't laugh.'

She hesitated. 'What—what we did just now. Is it—' She stopped, chewing her lip again, a deep, embarrassed flush creeping into her cheeks, then finished in a rush '—is it what makes babies?'

There was a moment's startled silence. Then he leaned to her, gathering her to him, burying his face in her hair. 'Oh, my poor darling, no! No, it isn't. We touched each other, that's all. You needn't be afraid.'

'I'm sorry. Do you think I'm stupid?' Her voice was muffled, and on the brink of tears.

'No, my darling, I don't think you're stupid.'

'No one's ever told me—you know—what actually happens.'

He released her, smiling into the blue, tear-bright eyes. 'Do you regret doing what we've done?'

'No! Oh, no! Please don't think that.'

Gently he sat her up, carefully buttoned the front of her dress, bent forward to kiss her lightly. 'Come on. Time to get you safely home.'

They slipped through the fog-shrouded gardens to the back door, carefully skirting the lighted drawing-room window. In the shadows by the door she lifted her face once more for his kiss. 'Kit?'

'Mmm?' Their voices were soft as breath in the misty darkness.

'You do love me?'

A more experienced woman might have noticed the fatal moment of silence that followed the question.

Then, 'Yes,' he said quietly. 'Of course I do.'

CHAPTER FOUR

Isobel was almost frantic with happiness. Far from distressing her, the necessarily clandestine nature of her relationship with Kit actually added to her delight in it. In the house as he worked she teased him with glances and the swift brushing of hand or lip; when they met in the quiet, dripping woodland or in the summer house she was fierce with passion, all the dull and closeted years of her young womanhood a spur to her infatuation. She looked neither forward nor back. She lived only to see him, to touch him, to have him woo her, with words and with the touch of his body.

As for Kit, for all his efforts, restraint was well-nigh impossible. Radiant with love and excitement, by turns demanding and sweetly pliant, Isobel would have tried the virtue of a

71

celibate saint, and Kit was far from that. Though infinitely more experienced than Isobel, even for him the bittersweet tensions of their situation were a heady aphrodisiac; the fact that they were thrown so much together, the knowledge that with each day that passed he was one step closer to returning to the Front, Isobel's eager, high-strung and perilously infectious excitement—all served to create a reckless and total disregard for good sense. The secret lash-veiled glances, the notes tucked into his hand, the hasty, dangerous meetings in the darkness heightened his senses and stirred his body; in the chill whispering darkness of the summer house, three days after that first meeting, he gave in to her pleadings and made love to her. And the seeds of disaster were sown; from that moment neither could stay away from the other. Inexorably the days moved on, and the time for Kit to leave grew closer. Time spent apart was time wasted. They took greater and greater risks, were less and less careful around other people, and though neither of Isobel's parents suspected anything—to them, such behaviour by their cherished elder daughter was quite literally unthinkable—there were sly and knowing glances from the servants and, more dangerously still, a growing and unfortunately unnoticed resentment from small, miserable Poppy.

'Darling, darling Kit. I'm so happy!' Isobel

lay upon the wicker sofa in the summer house, her head in Kit's lap, his hand gentle upon her breasts. She closed her eyes, smiling a little. Looking down at her, at the curve of her lashes against the pale skin, the delicate vulnerability of her face, the supple temptation of her body, he thought he had never seen anything so beautiful. Past traumas, surely, were past; could this not be the future? It was a dull and wet afternoon, the light already fading to an early winter dusk. Isobel had opened the shutters and in the shadowed room her skin gleamed, smooth and cool and shining with life. Languidly she lifted an arm to touch his cheek with her finger. 'Make love to me. Please?'

'Isobel—' He stopped. He didn't have to tell her yet. Not yet.

Outside the window a tree rustled and was still.

'Please?' She slipped her hand behind his head and pulled his mouth down to hers. There was a long moment of silence. When he lifted his head she smiled, suddenly mischievous. 'Am I learning to kiss properly?'

He laughed a little. 'You certainly are.'

'I've had a good teacher.' She stretched, her arms above her head. 'Make love to me,' she said again, softly.

In silence he shifted her weight from his lap and stood up, slipping off his jacket, reaching for his tie. Isobel watched with fascinated eyes as he undressed. Almost always their love-making had been in the dark.

Again there was movement by the window. Neither of them noticed.

Naked, he leaned to her, opened the buttons of her blouse, baring her breasts completely. Her flesh roughened suddenly in the cold, and she shivered a little, laughing.

He took off her small boots very carefully, placed them neatly side by side on the floor, lifted her skirt to reveal dark silk stockings. She moved a little.

'Lie still,' he said softly. 'Let me.'

In the quiet winter twilight beyond the window the leaves trembled slightly and were still.

Isobel bent her long, pale legs and held open her arms to her lover.

Poppy, out in the darkness, gasped in anguish and flung herself from the leaf-veiled window, turned to run blindly back towards the house, sobbing as she ran. 'I hate them! *I hate them!*' She stumbled across the wet grass, tripped and fell, lay for a moment winded and crying before she scrambled to her feet. *'I hate them!'* Within the house, lamps were being lit; the long windows glowed with warmth. The smell of woodsmoke was heavy on the air. Mist lifted from the river. Muddy and sobbing, the child threw herself through the front door and into the hall.

Elizabeth, half-way down the sweeping

staircase, stopped in astonishment, poised, one hand upon the curved banister as her daughter clattered into the hall beneath her. 'Poppy! Why, Poppy—whatever's wrong?'

The child flew to her, slipping on the stairs, sobs choking her, threw herself into her mother's bemused arms. 'Mama! Mama—*I hate them!*'

*　　　*　　　*

Isobel's eyes were tear-filled, huge with misery and affront. 'Why didn't you tell me before? Why didn't you? Do you think I'm a child? Why didn't you *tell* me?'

'I—' Kit shook his head helplessly. 'Darling, I'm sorry. I couldn't. I didn't want to hurt you. To upset you. For Christ's sake—it's bad enough that I have to leave you.'

Isobel was curled beside him on the wicker sofa, his jacket about her naked shoulders. The tears welled over, running down her smooth cheeks almost unnoticed. The smoke from his cigarette wreathed in the cold air. 'When?' she asked at last. 'When do you have to go?'

'In two days.'

'Oh, God!' She caught her breath miserably. In silence he slipped a hand into the pocket of the jacket that covered her, and handed her a handkerchief. She mopped at her tears. 'Two days!'

He took her hand. 'Yes. We still have two

days,' he said gently. 'A lifetime. Until the last moment, a lifetime. Don't spoil it.'

She lifted her head, searching his face in the half-darkness with the drowned, forget-me-not eyes. 'You really have to go?'

'I'm afraid so.'

'But—you'll come back? You promise you'll come back?'

There was a long moment's silence. Then he put a finger to her chin to lift her face to his and kissed her, smoothing her wet cheeks with his finger. 'If it's in my power, my darling, then, yes, I'll come back.'

'Oh, it's too unkind!' She had started to cry again, very quietly.

He turned to her, stopped, his head suddenly lifted.

'I love you,' she said. 'You'll never know—'

'Ssh!' His arm tightened so fiercely about her that she gasped. Then she, too, heard it. The sound of footsteps; heavy, authoritarian, no attempt being made to disguise their swift approach. And with them the glimmering flash of a swinging lantern.

'Jesus!' said Kit.

'*Papa!*' Panic-stricken, Isobel rolled from the little couch and reached for the tangle of her clothes.

'No.' Kit's voice was crisp. 'No time. Put this on.' He slipped the jacket back over her shoulders, buttoning it firmly into place. Before he had finished, the door crashed open.

In the brief silence that followed, Kit, still naked, placed himself between the sobbing Isobel and her father.

Very precisely but with a hand that shook, George Brookes placed the lantern he carried on the table, turned to face them. 'By Christ,' he said, and, like the hand, his voice trembled with anger and outrage, 'the child was right, then! By God, young man, I'll have your hide for this.'

'Papa—' Isobel's voice was a frightened breath.

'*Quiet!* I'll deal with you later, my girl.' The man stepped forward and raised his hand. Kit did not move. The back-handed blow brought blood, which trickled down his chin from his split lip.

'Papa—no! Please!' Isobel slipped from behind Kit and caught her father's arm. 'Don't hurt him. Please!'

He shook her off roughly, and she stumbled. George Brookes hit Kit again, this time with the flat of his hand, rocking his head. Still Kit neither moved nor spoke.

'Well?' Brookes reached out and caught Kit by the hair, bringing his bloodied face close to his own. The lantern flickered and steadied, casting long shadows about the room. 'What have you got to say for yourself, you limb of Satan?' He twisted his hand viciously into the thick hair. 'By Christ, I should kill you for this.'

'*Papa!*' Isobel was crying uncontrollably.

77

Her father threw Kit from him and turned to her. She recoiled, flinching, at the look on his face. 'Slut!' he said very quietly. 'Wanton slut! Get dressed. Now. Get back to the house. Your poor mother is waiting for you. And as for you, sir—' the quiet, venomous emphasis on the last word was the worst of insults '—get off my property now, before I whip you off it. And never—you hear me?—*never* come near it or my daughter again. You will never see her, never speak to her, never mention her name again, you hear? Or, by Christ, I will swing for you.'

'Sir—' Kit's voice was very quiet '—I must protest! Please don't blame Isobel. All of this is my fault entirely.'

'I don't doubt that for an instant,' Brookes said grimly. 'You, sir, are a knave and a scoundrel. You have taken advantage of an innocent young girl. You have ruined her. Ruined her! And as to the harm to which you have exposed her small sister—there are no words for that. There are names for men like you; and I shall make quite certain that both your uncle and your commanding officer hear them all.'

Isobel, sobbing incoherently, was struggling into her clothing. Her father bent to pick up Kit's trousers and flung them at him. 'For God's sake, man, make yourself decent and go. Before I lose control of myself entirely.'

Kit did not move. 'I will go. But not before

I've spoken.'

The other man's face suffused. 'You whippersnapper! Get out! Now!'

Kit's eyes were steady. Dark blood dripped from his chin, staining the trousers he held. 'I wish to apologise. Sincerely. I've already told you, the fault is entirely mine.'

George Brookes made a sound so close to a growl that Isobel jumped and backed away from him fearfully.

Kit's eyes moved to her. 'I also want to say,' his voice was firm, 'that I love Isobel. And I believe she loves me.'

The sound this time was more like a roar. Isobel began crying again, truly frightened. 'Kit—Kit, please go! I don't want him to hurt you again. Please!'

Stubbornly, Kit shook his head. 'He can do as he likes to me. I want a promise that he won't harm you.'

Brookes stepped forward swiftly and surprisingly lightly for such a big man. The fist that caught Kit on the point of his chin sent him reeling and flung him crashing through one of the wicker chairs, splintering it, and on to his hands and knees on the floor. 'Impudent puppy! You'll demand nothing. I'll deal with my daughter as I see fit. Isobel! Come!' He caught her arm and pulled her to the door.

'Kit! *Kit!*'

Dazed, Kit shook his head, like a dog coming out of water, attempted to get up, collapsed and fell, hitting his head as he did so. In the shadowed light of the lantern the last the distraught Isobel saw of him before her father, hand vice-like about her wrist, dragged her, weeping, across the lawns towards the house, was his still, marked face and a long, lax hand, the fingers smeared with blood.

*　　　*　　　*

The disaster was complete. No one in the household was unaffected by it. Isobel, pale, haggard and almost constantly in tears, was confined to her room. Her mother too took to her bed, prostrated, she declared, by a migraine brought on by shock. Poppy crept about the house like the mouse Kit had nicknamed her, crushed by guilt, alternately angry, confused and miserable. It was almost twenty-four hours before, in defiance of her father's orders, she could bring herself to creep to Isobel's door.

'Isobel? Isobel, are you all right?'

'Go away.' The words were flat, Isobel's voice hoarse with tears.

'Please, Isobel—'

'I said, go away.'

Poppy hesitated for a moment, half-turned from the door, then, mouth set in a sudden stubborn line, changed her mind and pushed it open. Isobel stood in her dressing-gown at the window, looking out into the cloudy afternoon.

At the sound, she turned. Poppy gasped. Her sister's face was ravaged, eyes swollen and reddened, skin pinched and pale. Her hair, usually so smooth and shining, was an unkempt mop. A tray of cold, congealing food stood untouched upon the table. 'I told you to go away. I never want to see or speak to you again.'

Poppy was trembling, tears welled in her eyes. 'I'm sorry, Isobel. Truly I am. I was just—' The words trailed wretchedly to nothing.

'You were just poking that stupid nose of yours in where it had no right to be.' The words were vicious with anger and misery.

'I'm sorry—'

'It's too late to be sorry!' Isobel had locked her hands together as if in an effort to prevent herself from slapping Poppy. 'You've ruined my life! I'll never forgive you! Never!' In a sudden paroxysm of tears she threw herself face down on the bed, her face buried in her arms. 'He's going away tomorrow. He'll be killed. I know he will. I'll never see him again! And it's your fault! I hate you!'

'Isobel, don't say that—please don't say that!' The child, too, was crying helplessly. 'What do you mean about Kit going away?'

'He told me yesterday. He's got to go back to France. He told me just before Papa—' Isobel could not bring herself to go on. Her sobs were hoarse and exhausted. Poppy watched in awed and anguished silence. 'He

81

could be dead by next week,' her sister said at last. 'And I didn't even have a chance to say goodbye!' The thought brought a new flood of tears. 'Oh, *go away*, you little monster! I want to die! I just want to die!'

Poppy backed away from the bed and stood for a moment before creeping out on the landing and closing the door quietly behind her.

Ten minutes later, scarfed and gloved and booted against the winter chill, face still tear-stained, she had slipped from the house unnoticed and was running along the muddy path to the village.

*   *   *

'Why, my dear, whatever is the matter? It's little Poppy Brookes, isn't it?' Harold Matthews, rector of the tiny village church of St Peter's, was a tall, thin man with a large, bony nose upon which perched a pair of wire-rimmed half-spectacles over which peered a pair of shrewd, kindly eyes.

Poppy was sobbing for breath. Her small, distraught face was pinched with cold. 'Is Kit here? Oh, please—is Kit here?'

'He is indeed.' The man stepped back. 'Come in, come in. Martha will make tea.' He shut the door and went to the foot of the stairs. 'Kit? You have a visitor.' He turned back to Poppy. 'He's packing. He has to leave tomorrow.'

Poppy, with an effort, remembered her manners. 'I know. And I'm sorry to bother you like this—'

The man put up a hand. 'It's no bother, my dear.' Some two years before Poppy was born, George Brookes had objected vehemently to the then new rector's plans to reorganise the extremely limited seating space in the ancient village church, that would entail doing away with the traditional family pews. No member of the Brookes family had since set foot in the church, preferring to attend the larger St Michael's in the next parish. 'Let me take your coat. Come—there's a fire in the study.' He led the way to a small, comfortable, book-lined room. The leather furniture was cracked and battered, the curtains and rugs faded, but a fire roared in the small fireplace and it was cosily warm. 'Sit yourself down. Kit won't be a moment. Would you care for biscuits with your tea?' Somewhere here, he was certain, lay the explanation of his nephew's grim demeanour and marked face; the laboured story of lost footing in the mud of the woods had been far from convincing.

'Yes, please.' Poppy's voice was a whisper. The thudding of her heart was easing, but tears were still very close.

The kindly eyes were concerned. 'You're sure there's nothing more I can do?' Poppy shook her head. The man patted her shoulder. 'Then I'll go and organise tea. Ah—Kit—' The door had opened. At the sight of Kit's bruised face, Poppy's tears brimmed over again.

'Poppy! What on earth are you doing here?' Kit came swiftly over and knelt beside her, taking her hands. 'What's happened? Isobel—she is all right? Tell me—'

'She hates me—she said she hates me—it's all my fault—I told on you—I looked through the window—'

'Ssh.' He pulled her head on to his shoulder and held her for a moment as the sobs shook her small body. 'Hush now. No one hates you, believe me. Now, tell me what's happened.'

'Isobel can't leave her room and Mama says it has all made her ill, and Papa is so angry he frightens me, and now Isobel says she hates me and wants to die.' The words were all but incoherent. 'And she says you've got to go back to the war and she didn't have a chance to say goodbye—' She raised her head. 'Oh, and look at your poor face!'

He smiled a little grimly and more than a little lopsidedly. 'Never mind about that. Come on now, calm down. You've been a very brave girl coming here. Now—will you be an even braver girl and do me a favour?'

'Oh, yes! Anything.'

He smiled again. 'Let's have a cup of tea. Then, if I write a note, will you take it to Isobel for me? And be very careful not to let anyone else see?'

'Yes. Oh, yes! Of course I will.'

He reached a hand gently to stroke her hair. 'My dear little Mouse.'

* * *

'Do you like me a bit better now?' Poppy asked, eyeing her sister doubtfully. 'I couldn't think of anything else to do to show you I was sorry.'

Isobel turned a tired face to her. Her eyes were almost feverishly brilliant. She held out a hand. 'Of course. I'm sorry. Sisters shouldn't say such things to each other.' The eyes dropped again to the note she held. She lifted it to her lips. 'Will you take a note back for me?' Poppy nodded. 'And—he's given me an address to write to. Will you post the letters for me?'

'Yes.'

Isobel threw herself backwards on to the bed, arms outflung, still clutching the note. 'He loves me,' she said softly.

Poppy hunched her shoulders. 'I know. He told me.'

* * *

Three days later, with Kit still on his way to rejoin his unit, the war that had taken so many souls, that had caused immeasurable destruction and misery, was over. The news transcended even the troubled atmosphere of Tellington Place. A pale, subdued Isobel was allowed downstairs to the celebration dinner and after a bottle of Madeira was emptied, Elizabeth was inclined to tears.

'My poor boys.' She stood in the Orangery before the portraits. 'So full of life. Why did they have to die?'

'For King and country, my dear.' George put an awkward arm about her narrow shoulders. 'For King and country. Never allow yourself to think otherwise.'

In the dining-room, Poppy surveyed her sister with pragmatic brown eyes. 'Why haven't you eaten anything?' She herself had polished off every morsel on her plate. 'The pie was awfully good.'

Isobel's dreaming eyes, too big for her thin face, turned upon her young sister. 'I'm not hungry.'

Poppy dipped her spoon into the trifle. 'Kit will come back now, won't he?'

'Yes.' Isobel's lips twitched to the smallest of smiles.

'Papa will be watching you.'

The smile became wider, and sweeter and was bent full upon her. 'I know,' Isobel said gently. 'But he won't be watching *you*, will he?'

In the event it was a couple of weeks from Christmas before the first word of Kit came, and it was Lucy who brought it. In the intervening weeks Isobel had given everyone cause for concern. She ate little or nothing, spoke hardly at all. Her shining good looks were transposed to a brittle beauty, the sharpness of her bones gleaming through her pale, almost transparent, skin. She was lethargic, constantly tired, and took to spending long hours lying on her bed, eyes fixed wide upon the ceiling. Even her father was moved to a more gentle attitude towards her, but she would have none of it. With the stubborn inflexibility that so often masks weakness, she ignored his overtures. She wanted one thing and one thing only.

She wanted Kit Enever.

'Miss Isobel. Miss Isobel?' Lucy, carrying a coal-bucket, peered timidly through the half-open bedroom door.

Isobel stirred. 'What is it, Lucy?'

The girl came into the room and busied herself with the fire. She glanced over her shoulder for all the world as if the room were full of people. 'It's Mr Kit, Miss Isobel. He's back. I saw him in the village this morning. He wanted me to bring you a letter.'

Galvanised, Isobel sat up. 'Where is it? Give it to me, quickly.'

Lucy straightened, easing her back, and shook her head. 'Oh, no, miss. I dursn't. I told him, I dursn't. If Mr Brookes found out—'

'Oh, you stupid—!' Isobel dropped her face into her hands for a moment, then lifted it again. 'What did he say? How did he look?'

'Same as ever, miss. Hardly limps at all. But I didn't speak much to him. I said, I dursn't. If

Mr Brookes was to find out—' She shrugged helplessly. 'Just thought you'd like to know, miss, that's all.' She picked up the scuttle.

'Thank you, Lucy.' With sudden energy Isobel swung her legs from the bed, reached for her dressing-gown and went in search of Poppy.

*   *   *

Poppy never forgot those following, hectic days. She carried notes and messages. She watched the feverish excitement in her sister's eyes and wondered that her parents could not sense it. Elizabeth, poorly again, and this time in worrying pain, had taken almost permanently to her bed. Miss Simpson left to visit her family in Yorkshire for the Christmas holidays. Nobody checked on a small energetic girl's comings and goings.

Plans were laid.

The Christmas tree went up in the drawing-room. Cook purchased and plucked the goose. Presents were wrapped. Local schoolchildren arrived on Christmas Eve to sing carols at the door. Stockings were hung. It was the first Christmas after the war, and the staidest of souls was intent upon enjoying it.

Only Poppy was unsurprised to wake up on Christmas morning to discover that Isobel, with no word, had gone.

PART TWO

Italy,
Ten Years Later

CHAPTER FIVE

The train jolted, slowed from a walking pace to a crawl and finally—and not for the first time—stopped altogether. Poppy Brookes, dozing in a corner seat, started awake and peered sleepily out of the window. Rolling hills stretched to distant mountainous heights, the vineyards and olive groves that cloaked their verdant slopes lying in almost breathless stillness beneath a cloudless sky. It was very hot. Poppy's close-fitting cloche hat was making her head itch; the height of fashion it might be, but it hardly qualified as the most sensible piece of headgear to be wearing on a stifling and crowded train in the middle of Italy. She took it off, ran her fingers through her short, damp hair, studiously avoiding the interested gaze of the young man opposite who had beamed at her hopefully every time their eyes had met. It had not taken her long to realise that in Italy a young woman travelling alone was something of a novelty; nor that a knee-length skirt that would not raise an eyebrow in London was rather more likely to attract attention here. She glanced at her wristwatch. They were over an hour late. Who on earth had started the rumour that the Fascist government had managed to get the Italian trains running on time? The high

91

excitement with which she had begun this journey had long since evaporated in tiredness and nervous frustration; all she wanted now was to reach Florence, where Kit had promised he would be waiting for her. The arrangements from then on would be up to him, and for all her hard-won—and very real—independence, for once she would be happy to have it so. She only hoped that he did not intend them to travel straight on to Siena. If she didn't get a night's proper sleep soon, she would quite certainly go mad and bite someone.

She could not resist a small grin at the silly thought; the young man's smile widened eagerly. She bent her head, reached into her handbag for a handkerchief to wipe her already scarlet face, and her hand touched the letter. Poppy fingered it thoughtfully. It had arrived at Tellington Place on the day of a particularly bitter row between Poppy and her young stepmother; she could not deny that a desperate need to escape from the young woman who considered her an unwelcome intruder in her own home and made no bones about showing it had greatly influenced her decision to come to Italy to visit Isobel and Kit. But there had been more to it than that. The tone of the letter itself had concerned her, and Kit's brief postscript—'*Poppy—please come—Isobel needs you. K*'—had made up her mind. Not, she thought with a somewhat bleak honesty, that anyone had made any great effort to unmake it for her.

Indeed, her father had taken little persuading to fund the trip. Only little Thomas had shown any sign of upset at her decision to spend the summer with the sister she had not seen for ten years; and that, she suspected was more out of self-interest than anything else. Poppy was the only one in the household who ever bothered to protect her small timid half-brother from the bigger, bullying John, four years his senior. She sighed a little. She had never been able to understand why, after her mother's tragic and painful death from cancer just a few months after the end of the war, her father had so quickly remarried. Nor, no matter how hard she tried, could she see why he had chosen a woman younger than his elder daughter with a spiteful temper and the brains of a flea. Her stepmother Dora, so far as Poppy was concerned, had no single redeeming feature. To be sure she had given George Brookes the two healthy sons that he had obviously wanted, but she had also spent his money, antagonised most of his friends and complained constantly and bitterly about being buried, as she put it, in the country.

She and Poppy had seen little of each other during the early years of the marriage— George Brookes' solution to the problem of having, so to speak, a daughter beyond requirements having been to pack her off to school within months of her mother's death and more or less leave her there. But for the past two or three years, since Poppy had come home, the relationship had deteriorated from bad to impossible. The letter had given her not only a reason to go, but a place to go to, and she had jumped at it. Now Kit awaited her in Florence, where he had been to deliver some paintings to his agent, and would escort her on to Siena. If, that is, this beastly train ever decided to move again—

Just as she thought it, in a protesting shriek of steam the train did indeed begin to move. Poppy sat back in her seat and closed her eyes.

Kit.

What would he be like? Had he changed? She had, that was certainly true, how could it not be? The years between ten and twenty must surely bridge a greater gap than any other ten years of a life? She remembered him so very clearly; and yet she knew from this vantage-point that she had never really known him at all. She suspected that she had been a little in love with him; certainly none of the young—or even of the older—men who had shown interest in her since had borne any comparison with him. And she was honest enough to admit to herself if to no one else that, sometimes consciously, sometimes not, he was the yardstick she had used. In defiance of Dora's—and even her father's—opinion that in a world as short of men as post-war

94

England, she should take the first offer to come along and be grateful for it, she had remained obdurately single. Not, she had to admit that she had been actually overwhelmed with opportunities to do otherwise.

Her father had favoured an elderly widower friend of his who had a business in Canterbury and three married sons all older than Poppy herself. Poppy had declined firmly. A pathologically shy young man from the next village had, to Dora's unflattering surprise, paid court for a little while—if, Poppy thought wryly, a few occasions sitting in virtual silence in the drawing-room whilst the poor boy's acne-marked face turned from fiery red to a death-like pallor and back again could actually be termed paying court—but he, too, to her stepmother's chagrin, had been shown the door. There had been a short and not terribly exciting dalliance with a boy she had met at the tennis club and another with the son of one of her father's friends. Not once had a spark ignited in her. Sometimes she almost came to believe that it never would. She knew what she wanted, or thought she did. She wanted not Kit, but what he had somehow come to represent to her. The trauma of what she had seen in the summer house she had buried deep. In the unutterably miserable school years that had followed she had remembered only his gentleness, his teasing smile, his kindness to a rather awkward child.

His elopement with her sister was the absolute embodiment of romance. If she couldn't have that, she didn't want anything.

She had followed their wanderings around Europe through the cards and drawings that Kit had regularly sent to her—from Honfleur, from Paris, from Rome, from Florence and finally from Siena—and from the occasional letter that Isobel had penned. They had settled in Siena four years ago when Isobel had been pregnant with their son, Robbie. When Poppy had tried to inform her father of both facts, he had turned stonily from her. Isobel's name was never mentioned in the house.

Behind closed lids Poppy tried to conjure her brother-in-law's face, and could not. She could produce only a recollection of thick, curling brown hair, sharply sculptured cheekbones, a straight mouth that crooked when it smiled. Would she even recognise him when she saw him again? On that slightly unnerving thought she dozed again.

*   *   *

In the event it was he who found her. A lone English girl standing by a fair-sized pile of luggage in the seething mass of manic activity that was an Italian station did, after all, she realised later, stand out like the proverbial sore thumb. Hot, nervous and dog tired, she stood watching the noisy activity about her

96

when a quiet voice spoke beside her. 'So here you are. At last. My little Mouse, all grown up.'

She turned. He was not as tall as she remembered him, neither did she recall that he was so slender; but it came to her immediately that she would have recognised his face anywhere. For one faintly awkward moment they stood smiling at each other. Then he opened his arms and she flung herself into them. 'Oh, Kit, Kit! It's so lovely to see you! How's Isobel? And little Robbie? Are they both well? Oh—I am just dying to see them!'

He put her from him, laughing. 'They're both fine. Fine. Let's worry about you for a moment. How was the journey?'

Poppy rolled her eyes. 'Gruesome. There was a hurricane in the Channel and I was seasick and it seemed to take at least three days to get through France and I missed the connection in Milan and had to wait for *hours* and a horrible little man wanted to buy me dinner and I had to be *very* rude to him to get rid of him—' She ran out of breath.

'A hurricane?' he asked, the gleam in his eye belying the amazement. 'In the Channel?'

She laughed. 'Well, nearly. I swear it. And now this wretched train has taken—' she consulted her watch'—three and a half hours to make a two-hour journey. Make me a promise.'

He beckoned to a porter. 'Anything.' His

face was alight with laughter.

'Don't tell me that the train that's leaving from platform nine in ten minutes is the only train for Siena for three days. If I don't stop going along for at least half an hour I swear I'll die.'

'You can do better than that.' He bent to help the porter with the luggage, and straightened, smiling. 'As it happens, the next train for Siena isn't until tomorrow. I've booked us in to a small hotel, the one where I usually stay when I have to come to Florence. It isn't the Ritz, but the food's good and the beds are comfortable, it doesn't cost an arm and a leg and it's near the Ponte Vecchio.' The crooked grin she remembered so well flashed. 'Are you going to put that hat on?'

She glanced down, half-surprised, at the crumpled thing she held in her hand. 'No,' she said. 'Probably never again, actually, daft thing that it is. Would you like to say that again?'

'I said, Are you going to put that hat—'

'No, don't be silly! The bit about good food. And comfortable beds.' Poppy tilted her head back, shaking it, closing her eyes. 'I'd forgotten there were such things.'

*   *   *

'Better?' Kit surveyed her across the table, smiling.

Poppy pushed her empty plate away with a

sigh of contentment. 'Much.' She leaned her elbows on the table and rested her chin on her hands, watching him. 'There's so much to talk about,' she said after a moment. 'So much to catch up on. It's hard to know where to start, isn't it?'

He nodded, leaned forward to replenish her glass from the jug that stood on the table between them. 'Let's start with "How are things at home?" ' His voice was gentle.

She held his gaze for a moment, then shrugged a little and her eyes dropped. Absently she played with the crumbs on the tablecloth, pushing them into tidy piles with her fingertip, flicking them apart with her nail. There was a noticeable moment of silence. Then, 'Best not to talk about it, really,' she said, glancing up at him with a quick, too-bright smile. 'I'd hate to make you cry into your wine.'

He was watching her with sympathy in his eyes. 'Poor Mouse. Is it really that bad?'

She pulled a funny, self-deprecating face. 'Only Mondays to Fridays. Weekends are worse. Anyway—' she continued briskly before he could speak again—'that wasn't what I wanted to catch up on; I know quite enough about it already. It's you and Isobel—and little Robbie, of course. And your painting, and where you live, and whether you like it, and—'

'Whoa!' Kit held up his hands, laughing.

'I've kept every single one of the cards and

little paintings you sent me. I used to take them out and look at them—imagine the romantic life you were leading. The only distinction I ever achieved at that beastly school that Papa sent me to was through having a sister who'd run away to Paris to marry an artist! The girls all imagined that you looked like Rudolph Valentino.'

He raised amused eyebrows. 'I trust you disabused them?'

Poppy opened large, innocent eyes that gleamed with mischief. 'Of course not. It would have spoiled the fun entirely.' Her laughter died. She regarded him for a moment, steadily and soberly. 'Why did Isobel write to me?' she asked then. 'Why was she so desperate for me to come? And why did you say that she needed me? Is something wrong?'

He did not for a moment answer, but picked up his glass, turning it in his hands, his face impassive. Then he looked at her. 'It hasn't been easy for Isobel. Right from the start it hasn't been easy.'

She waited, watching him.

He sipped his wine. The small dining-room was full. The sound of conversation and laughter rose and fell about them like the ebb and flow of water. A child cried fractiously. 'There are some things you don't know,' Kit said.

'Tell me.'

He drew a long breath. 'Isobel and I ran

away together because she was pregnant.' He closed his eyes for a moment as if in a spasm of pain. 'I'm sorry. I put that very badly. What I mean is that if she hadn't been, things might have been different.'

'How—different?' Poppy was staring at him.

'Your father might have come round. We might have been able to lead a more—shall I say conventional—life. A more comfortable life, certainly. It might, I think, have suited Isobel better if we had. However—' He shrugged a little, ran a finger around the top of his glass.

'What happened? To the child?'

'Isobel miscarried. In Paris, two months later. Some few months before your mother died.'

'You didn't tell me.'

He reached to touch her hand. 'You were too young to be told such things. And no one else cared. That's what Isobel found so hard. She was so sure—' He stopped.

'What? What was she so sure of?'

'She was so certain they would forgive her. In the beginning, for her, it was almost make-believe—running away with me—getting married in Paris—she was living a fantasy. It didn't occur to her for a second that your father wouldn't forgive her. That in a few weeks, a few months perhaps, he wouldn't be begging her to come home. There had never been a time, until then, when Isobel hadn't got

101

her own way—' Kit took another sip of wine, his eyes distant. 'It was difficult for her. And the miscarriage and the blow of your mother's death left her weak for quite a long time. I'm not sure she ever really got over it, either physically or mentally. She was very poorly when she had Robbie—'

'And now she's pregnant again.' Poppy's voice was sharper than she intended.

He looked at her very steadily. 'Not intentionally,' he said quietly.

Poppy felt a flood of warm colour rise in her face. 'I'm sorry. I had no right to—'

'You have every right.' Kit put his elbows on the table and leaned towards her, his face intent. 'Poppy, I'm worried about her. She's being—' he hesitated '—very difficult. And physically she isn't strong. I'm sure that having you around will buck her up no end.'

'I hope so. At the very least I can help her with little Robbie.' Her lips quirked to another small, self-deprecating smile. 'I'm good at looking after other people's children. It's the only thing Dora ever found me useful for.'

He leaned back, returning her smile. 'You and she don't get along.' It was not a question.

The smile widened to a grin. 'The devil and holy water come to mind.'

Kit cocked his head quizzically. 'Are you suggesting your young stepmother is the devil?'

Poppy opened her eyes wide in mock

outrage. 'And are you suggesting that I'm wet?' she asked offendedly.

He gave a little yelp of laughter.

Poppy tapped her nose knowingly. 'Scarlet by name, scarlet by nature, that's me. You ask Dora. She knows.'

He reached to take her hand. 'Oh, Poppy, Poppy, I am so very glad you've come. You're going to be so enormously good for us all.'

'What happened to "Mouse"?'

He studied her for a very long time, long enough to bring a small flush of colour to her cheeks. 'It doesn't suit you any more,' he said softly.

*   *   *

The following day, rested and restored, Poppy was eager to see as much of Florence as possible before they left for Siena. Kit was more than ready to oblige.

The city, dressed in her early summer best, enchanted Poppy, and Kit delighted in her enthusiasm. They visited the Duomo, with its spectacular and gloriously spacious interior and breathtaking works of art, marvelled at the magnificence of the intricate bronze doors of the Baptistry, the so-called 'gates of paradise' and strolled through the famous Piazza della Signoria at the heart of the city, dominated by the massive Palazzo Vecchio with its great crenellated tower. Poppy was wide-eyed and infectiously excited as a child. 'I've never seen so many lovely sculptures! And the fountain—it's perfectly beautiful—'

Kit smiled, and glanced at his watch.

'Oh—we don't have to go yet, do we? There's so much to see!'

He laughed. 'You don't have to see everything at once, you know. We can come back another time. But no, we don't have to leave just yet. We've time for a flying visit to the Uffizi if you'd like. And then, if you don't mind before we go back to pick up your luggage, I'd like to pop into a shop just over the Ponte Vecchio. It's a small gallery. The proprietor takes a few of my paintings. She may have sold one or two. Is that all right?'

'Of course.' She slipped her arm through his, gazing at the busy, sunlit scene around her. 'Oh, Kit, I am so very pleased I came!'

He smiled into the bright, excited face. 'I'm glad.'

In the event the treasure-house that was the Uffizi all but overwhelmed her. 'It's no good. I can't really take it all in. I feel like Alice in Wonderland,' she confessed at last.

Kit turned from his contemplation of a Madonna and Child. 'It's a bit much to expect you to. Come on. As I said, we can always come back another day if you'd like. And time is getting a little tight. I promised Isobel we'd be back in good time today. She doesn't much like being left alone.'

Out in the narrow, shadowed Piazzale degli Uffizi, the heat hit them immediately. Glimpsed through the arches that led to the embankment, the Arno flowed, sluggish and ill-smelling. Kit laughed as Poppy wrinkled her nose. 'Don't worry. You'll get used to it. Most Italian rivers smell like that.'

Poppy was fascinated by the ancient and picturesque Ponte Vecchio that arched, crowded with small, overhanging buildings across the river, as once, she supposed London Bridge had over the Thames. Once over the river, Kit guided her down a tall canyon of a street to a small gallery. As he pushed open the door a dark, well-dressed woman who was seated at a desk looked up, smiling delightedly as she saw who the visitor was. 'Kit! *Buon giorno! Come sta?*'

Kit responded in easy and rapid Italian. Poppy caught her own name and Isobel's. The woman smiled at her. *'Piacere, Signorina.'* She turned back to Kit, speaking quickly, illustrating her words with gestures of her well-shaped hands. Poppy looked around. The place was a good deal larger than she had expected, the walls completely lined with pictures. Leaving Kit and the woman to their business, she wandered, interested, about the room, inspecting the paintings. Not unnaturally most were of the city itself, or of the surrounding countryside, the exception being a small group of portraits, some in oil,

105

some in watercolour and some simple pencil sketches. Poppy's attention was caught by a charming sketch of a child's head; fair-haired, wide-eyed, his pretty mouth looking as if it were about to curve in a mischievous smile. A faintly familiar face, the long-lashed eyes direct and ingenuous. She knew before she reached it whose signature it would bear. This, then, must be her nephew Robbie. She studied it with undisguised pleasure. The little boy looked a delight, and Kit had captured perfectly the grave innocence of childhood. There were two more sketches by the same hand; both of a woman, strikingly handsome, dark hair pulled sleekly to her head, with narrow, slightly slanted eyes veiled and enigmatic.

'I see you've found him.' Kit had come up behind her.

'It is Robbie, then?'

'Yes, it's Robbie.' His voice softened upon the name, his eyes lit with a smile. 'It's rather a good likeness, actually.'

'He looks as if he's about to burst out laughing.'

'He always looks like that. He's a darling. You'll love him.'

'I'm sure I shall.' As they turned away, she asked, 'Who's the other one? The woman?'

There was a moment of silence. Then, 'An acquaintance,' Kit said stiffly. 'Just an acquaintance.'

106

So different was his tone that Poppy glanced at him, surprised. 'She's very beautiful.'

'Yes.' Again the word was short, off-hand, uninviting of any further discussion. 'Right, young lady, let's get a move on.' He was suddenly brisk. 'In the unlikely event that it's going to leave on time, the train goes in an hour and a half. We'd best get back to the hotel for your luggage.'

*   *   *

'I don't think I've ever seen such beautiful countryside. No wonder you love it so much.' Poppy was looking out of the carriage window, over the changing panorama of green cypress-dotted hills and blue skies, of tiny villages, hilltop fortresses, of grand houses set among their vineyards and lemon groves. 'Oh, look—there's another castle—'

'It's a fortified village, actually. There are quite a few in this area. They haven't changed for centuries. Very little has.' Kit, sitting opposite her, surveyed her with affectionate eyes. He had not of course been foolish enough to believe that there would be no change in her; but then again he had not been quite prepared for the extent of the change. This was no little Mouse with untidy hair and a dirty apron, but a surprisingly self-confident young woman, tall, long-legged and very slim, the shining cap of her hair stylishly cut. The

107

boyish fashions of the times suited her well. Her skin was creamy and, like her sister's, flawless. Only the soft velvet eyes were exactly as he remembered them. While attractive, she had little of Isobel's obvious beauty, yet the sparkle of her energy, her easy, friendly smile and ready laughter would turn heads equally quickly. And possibly keep them turned for longer.

She leaned forward, eager to talk. 'Tell me about the house. Is it really grand?'

He threw back his head in laughter. 'Not the word I would use! Crumbling is more like it. Dilapidated. Parts of it are more or less derelict. Oh, it was grand once—but over a hundred years of neglect will reduce any building to a virtual ruin. Most of it's shut up. We live in only a few rooms.'

'Who does it belong to?'

'An old Siena family, the Gordinis. They deserted it a couple of generations ago to live in the city, though they still work the estate. They rent it to us for next to nothing. It's a perfect place to work.'

'It stands alone?'

'Sort of. There's a small village a little further down the hillside. Most of the estate workers live there.'

'Is it very old?'

The enthusiastic persistence of her questions amused him; for a moment again he found himself remembering the little girl he had met on the river bank in Kent ten years before. 'Yes, many centuries old. The original building is a tower in the woods behind the house. That was built sometime around the eleventh century. The house was built in more settled times and has been added to over the years. You'll see it soon.' He nodded towards the window. 'We're nearly there.'

*   *   *

Siena station was outside and below the magnificent city's walls, which had stood almost unchanged since the thirteenth century. Whilst Kit organised her luggage, Poppy walked outside and gazed about her, entranced. The massive red-brown walls crowned the hillside above her, and beyond them she glimpsed the splendid spires, domes and bell-towers within. The gentle wooded hillsides that surrounded the city lay tranquil in the bright afternoon sunshine. Here and there a small village, set amongst terraced fields, dozed in the heat of the day. The soil, too, was red. The city looked as if it had grown from earth and rock, at one with its surroundings. She thought she had never seen anything so perfect in its setting.

'Your carriage awaits, my lady.' Poppy turned to find Kit behind her, smiling. With him was a small, gnarled gnome of a man with one shoulder hunched higher than the other.

109

His face was brown and lined as a walnut. 'This is Umberto. He's come to fetch us.'

'*Buon giorno*, Umberto.' Poppy extended a hand.

'*Signorina.*' With a smile of astonishing sweetness he took it, bowing a little. He reached only to Poppy's shoulder.

'This way.' Kit led the way to where a pony and trap stood. Poppy's luggage was already stowed in it. With remarkable agility the little man swung himself up and took up the reins.

Poppy laughed delightedly. 'A *real* carriage! How lovely!'

'It's called a *calesse*. Everyone uses them around here.' Kit handed her into the trap. The seats were worn, upholstered in scuffed and battered leather, but they were sprung, and comfortable. Kit pulled up the hood to shade them from the sun, then climbed aboard and settled himself beside Poppy. 'Nearly there. An hour or so and we'll be home.'

Umberto swung the pony around and set off at a good pace, away from the city, into the fertile valleys and the green folds of the hills. The *calesse* rocked over the dirt road. Dust hung in the air. Donkeys ambled along the roadside with fatalistic patience, their loads swaying as they moved. In the villages, children watched the little trap as it passed, waving shyly. A great church loomed, limned sharply against the bright sky. A river sang beneath a bridge shaded by huge spreading chestnut trees. Tilled red fields reflected the heat. Meticulously trained and clipped vines absorbed it.

It had been a very long journey and, in spite of the roughness of the track, the movement of the vehicle was almost hypnotically soothing. Despite her best efforts, Poppy's head nodded on to Kit's shoulder, and she slept.

She stirred and woke an hour or so later, at Kit's voice in her ear. 'Poppy. Poppy? Time to wake up. We're nearly there.'

'Oh, good Lord!' She straightened, rubbing the sleep from her eyes. 'Oh, I'm sorry—'

'Don't be silly. You're worn out, and no wonder. We're coming to the village. I thought you'd like to see it.'

They were climbing a winding track through woodland. The pony had slowed to a plodding walk. Ahead, Poppy could see a scattering of rudimentary stone houses. The smell of woodsmoke was strong in the air. From the quiet woods a cuckoo called, again and again.

'There, you see? There's the house.' Kit was pointing upwards. Looking up, Poppy caught a glimpse of roofs, and beyond and above them a tall, crumbling stone tower. Then they were lost in the trees again.

She straightened up and ran her fingers through her hair. 'I must look a complete sight!'

'You're fine. You look—' He stopped.

Poppy glanced at him, followed the

111

direction of his gaze. They were passing a small whitewashed house with a rickety wooden veranda running its length on the first floor. A woman leaned on its rail, watching them, unsmiling. As she caught their eyes, she lifted a hand in grave greeting. She was tall and neatly built, dressed in a white shirt and wide, floppy trousers, a belt about her narrow waist. No Italian peasant woman, this. The smoke from the cigarette she held between long slim fingers rose straight in the still air. Poppy stared. For a moment her sleep-bemused mind refused to work. Why did she feel she had seen this woman before? Sleek black hair was drawn severely to a bun at the nape of her neck. Her eyes, that from this distance looked oddly light and reflective, were slightly slanted. There was a distinctly, almost an exotically, foreign look to her. The one thing that was undeniable was her beauty.

'You look just fine,' Kit said calmly, and lifted a hand to return the woman's greeting.

Poppy's brain started to work again. 'Kit, wasn't that the woman in the sketches? That I saw in the gallery this morning?'

He turned his most amiable smile upon her. 'Yes, it was. Her name is Eloise. Eloise Martin. As I told you, she's—an acquaintance. A friend of Isobel's. You'll meet her soon, I have no doubt. But look—here we are.' The little vehicle had swung on to a side track and through a set of huge, rusty wrought iron gates that hung askew upon massive brick pillars. Both gates and pillars were covered in ivy and waist high in weeds, bracken and even small saplings. The air of neglect was palpable. In the distance the tower reared against the dark background of the trees. A little closer, tiled roofs and shuttered windows glinted in the sunshine.

Kit laid a hand upon hers. 'Welcome to *Tenuta di Gordini.*'

CHAPTER SIX

At first viewing, despite what Kit had said, the house did indeed look grand. As they turned a curve in the overgrown driveway, Poppy gave a small gasp of surprise. From this vantage-point the place stood like a fortress, three or four storeys high, four-square, the peeling stuccoed walls massive, the windows long and narrow. The ancient iron-studded door stood within a huge archway approached by a flight of wide, shallow steps. There were stables to the right and a run of barns and outbuildings to the left, forming an open-sided courtyard. It was only as they drew closer that the real state of the place became apparent. The windows were blank and dirty, some glassless, the walls not simply flaking but, in places, so badly neglected that the mortar had fallen

113

completely away to reveal the rough stone beneath. Weeds and nettles choked the courtyard. The steps that led to the door were cracked and broken, the heave of the ground beneath tilting them to perilous angles. The great door itself looked as though it had not been opened in a hundred years; an impression that Poppy later discovered to be the simple truth. An ancient, abandoned *calesse*, one shaft broken, rested in waist-high grass in one corner of the yard. Most of the outhouses were derelict, doors hanging off or missing altogether, tiled roofs holed. Chickens scratched about the courtyard and outbuildings and a solitary cat sat upon a crumbling wall, watching them with detached condescension. As the cart rolled to a halt, the rasping chirrup of cicadas was suddenly loud on the warm, thyme-scented air, as was the hum of the bees that clustered about the wild flower heads. Beyond the house the dark-shadowed, bright-dappled woodland, fern-carpeted and trackless, started again, the ground sloping gently upwards.

'It's like—' Poppy stopped, shook her head a little, laughing '—it's like Sleeping Beauty's castle! Apart from the hedge of thorns, that is.'

'If it weren't for Umberto we'd have that, too, believe me,' Kit said wryly. 'I'm sorry. I did warn you.'

'Don't be silly!' Poppy's dark eyes were shining. 'I think it's absolutely enchanting.' She stopped as a tiny figure, laughing and babbling excitedly, almost tumbled around the corner of the house and flung himself towards the trap. 'Daddy! Daddy!' Clamped under one arm was a knitted woollen toy, so battered that its identity as a dog could only just be discerned.

Umberto was out of the *calesse* in a flash and had scooped the little boy up, squealing with laughter, to be deposited upon his father's lap. 'Hello, sunshine!' Kit hugged him, burying his face in the tousled fair curls. The child struggled free, flung his arms about his father's neck, smacking great wet kisses all over his face. Poppy, watching, laughed delightedly. Her little nephew turned his head to look at her, fair brows drawing together for a moment before, suddenly shy, he hid his face in Kit's shoulder.

'Hey!' Kit was gentle, shaking him free. 'Come along, little man. Look—here's your Aunt Poppy come all the way from England to see you. At least say Hello.'

The blonde head shook, the softly pretty face still hidden.

'Robbie, don't be silly—'

'No, don't force him.' Smiling, Poppy put out a hand to touch the silken curls. 'There's plenty of time.'

'*Signorina*—' She turned. Umberto stood beside the trap, courteous, work-hardened hand outstretched. When she took it, she was amazed at the strength of its grip. Trying to

115

reveal as little leg as possible—not an easy task—she scrambled with rather more speed than elegance to the ground. Kit handed the still bashful Robbie down to Umberto and jumped down beside her. A flash of movement caught her eye. A figure, moving heavily and carefully, had come around the corner of the house. For a moment, sun-blinded, Poppy blinked. Then, with only one fleet moment to register the changes in her sister, she was in her arms, hugging and rocking, laughing and all but crying, both speaking at once.

'Isobel—darling—how are you?'

'Oh, Poppy, Poppy, I am so very pleased to see you! Was the journey too awful?'

'It's been such a long time!'

Robbie, watching perplexed from Umberto's arms, did the safest thing and burst into tears. Isobel immediately pulled away from Poppy and turned to the child, arms outstretched.

'No, no.' Gently Kit restrained her. 'You know you shouldn't carry him. I'll take him. There's absolutely nothing wrong with him. He just wants a share of the attention. Come on, let's get Poppy in out of this heat. The poor girl's exhausted. She couldn't keep her eyes open on the way out here.'

Isobel slipped an arm through Poppy's and they followed Kit and the now pacified Robbie round towards the back of the house. Poppy was shocked at how thin and tense was the arm

116

that was linked with hers, at how heavily Isobel leaned upon her. When her sister asked with sudden urgency, 'Poppy?' she almost jumped.

'Yes?'

'Tell me something—' the blue, beseeching eyes held hers anxiously '—you *did* remember to bring the tea?'

*   *   *

The practical Poppy had indeed, of course, remembered the tea—Lipton's best—that her sister had requested; she had added for good measure marmalade, Marmite, tomato ketchup and custard creams. Isobel was absolutely delighted, Kit amused. 'You haven't come to Outer Mongolia, you know!'

'I know it perfectly well.' Poppy cocked her head to look at him. 'But, tell me, what were those feathered things that I saw scratching about out there?'

He grinned. 'Chickens?' he ventured.

'Exactly. And how can you eat a nice fresh soft-boiled egg without Marmite soldiers?'

He shook his head, laughing aloud. 'You're priceless.'

'So you've told me before, if you remember. And if you laugh at my Marmite, I won't give you this—' She held up a bottle wrapped in paper.

'The Marmite,' he said, 'was an excellent idea. Pity you didn't bring two.'

117

'I did. The other one is buried in another case somewhere.' She handed him the bottle. 'And now—' she rumpled through the case she had opened on the vast kitchen table, her head all but buried behind the lid '—ah!' A square biscuit tin appeared. She levered off the lid to reveal bags and boxes of sweets and a bundle of lollipops.

'Are those for me too?' Kit asked, straight-faced but still barely able to conceal his amusement.

'Only if you let Robbie have the Scotch,' Poppy said, 'and that doesn't seem too good an idea. Can he have one now?' The little boy was snuggled on his mother's lap, his head resting on her shoulder, thumb in mouth, watching the proceedings with warily interested eyes, the knitted dog still tucked comfortably under his arm. Poppy extracted a lollipop, unwrapped it, offered it to him. The thumb stayed firmly put. Poppy hunkered down in front of him. 'Robbie? It's for you. Don't you want it?'

The small, bright head shook stubbornly.

'Oh. All right, then. May I have it?' She made as if to put the sticky thing to her own mouth.

That did it. Out came the thumb; a plump, dimpled hand was outstretched. Smiling, she handed him the sweet. He took it shyly, touched it with his tongue, then, eyes wide with pleasure, sucked on it with noisy enthusiasm.

'Robbie?' Isobel said gently. 'Aren't you going to say thank you to Aunt Poppy?'

For a moment the child concentrated on the sweet. Then he took the lollipop from his mouth, smiled the sweetest—and the stickiest—smile Poppy had ever seen, and said, 'Ta.' Then he added carefully, 'Pop.' And Poppy was enslaved.

She straightened, turned back to the case, rooted in it again, turned with two large brown paper parcels in her hand, which she gave to Isobel. 'These are for you.'

Kit could restrain his laughter no longer. 'No wonder that damned thing was so heavy!' He leaned to take his son from Isobel's lap so that she could unwrap her presents.

'Poppy! Oh, Poppy, thank you! How marvellous of you!'

'They're only a few books,' Poppy said, bending to receive her sister's kiss of thanks. 'I bought every Mills and Boon I could find, and then a few others. Are they all right?'

'Perfect! They're perfect! It's absolutely years since I've had anything decent to read.'

Poppy smiled gently. 'I'm glad you like them.' She turned back to the case, only to find that Kit, Robbie riding contentedly on his arm, was shutting it firmly.

'Oh, no, you don't. Anything else you've got in there can wait. You're exhausted, and you must be hungry. Come on. I'll show you your room. You can wash and brush up, then we'll eat. After that, I'll show you the rest of the house. Which cases do you need?'

Poppy pointed. 'The little one will do for now.'

'Right.' Kit handed the child back to his mother, who took him and bounced him absent-mindedly on her knee. She was already riffling through one of the books absorbedly. Kit led the way out of the vast room, with its high, rustic beamed ceiling and huge cast iron range, through an arch that led into another, smaller kitchen—that nevertheless, Poppy thought, was half as big again as the one that as a child she had always thought so cavernous at Tellington Place—and up some steps that led to a corridor. 'We only use the back of the house, and then only part of it,' Kit said over his shoulder. 'I know it seems confusing at first, but you'll soon get used to it.' He led on up a set of narrow stairs, along more corridors. 'This is our bedroom.' He indicated, as they passed, a heavy door that stood half open. Poppy glimpsed an enormous unmade bed, a chair with clothes tossed untidily across it. Heavy curtains were haphazardly half-drawn. Poppy felt suddenly uncomfortable, obscurely embarrassed, as if she had inadvertently invaded her sister's privacy. 'And this is Robbie's.' Kit pushed open the next door. Again the room was untidy and ill-kept. The little boy's cot was unmade, there was a heap of bedclothes tossed into the corner, presumably awaiting the wash. As in the previous room, the walls were flaking and there were water-marks on the ceiling. 'I put you along here.' Kit set off again to the end of the corridor and turned a corner. 'If you'd rather be closer to us, then of course you can pick any room you wish. But I thought you'd enjoy the view.' He pushed open the door. 'What do you think?'

Poppy's small exclamation was one of pure delight. The vista, framed by a pair of high, narrow, floor-to-ceiling windows, drew the eye the moment the door was opened. To the right the tree-clad hillside sloped upwards, gently at first and then, suddenly more steeply and ruggedly, to the clear blue bowl of the sky. Half a mile or so away the ancient tower that had been the first habitation on the site rose tall from the encroaching woodlands, honey-coloured in the sunshine, a crumbling finger of masonry studded with small shadow-dark windows, silent and secretive observer of the centuries. To the left, beyond the slope of the hillside the window looked along a fertile valley to yet another range of hills that shimmered in the heat haze. In the middle distance, on a small rocky outcrop amid the tilled and tended fields of the valley floor, a church stood, massive as a fortress, surrounded by a huddle of tiny houses, its bell-hung campanile dominating the countryside around.

'It's absolutely lovely!' Poppy said. She walked to the open windows and leaned over the waist-high iron grille that protected them. Below, more chickens scratched around a paved yard, a substantial corner of which was protected from the sun by a sagging pergola that appeared to all intents and purposes to be entirely supported by the ancient grapevine that scrambled up and over it. Directly below, next to a door that she presumed must lead to the kitchen, was a heavy iron pump. A few shallow steps led to a small and extremely neat vegetable patch and a grove of olive and lemon trees, the scent of which drifted headily through the window and filled the room. Incongruously, in the centre of the vegetable garden, a life-sized, lichen-covered statue of a girl with a dove settled upon her outstretched hand leaned precariously, as if imminently about to fall. From an iron gate in a high wall, that like everything else had obviously once been impressively substantial but now appeared to be held up more by brambles and ivy than by the crumbling mortar between its stones, a rocky track led into the woodlands in the direction of the tower.

'There are deer in the woods.' Kit spoke from behind her. 'Deer, porcupine, foxes too, of course. And wild boar. They're the ones you have to look out for, especially if they have young. The Gordinis still occasionally come out here to hunt them.' He touched her shoulder, then turned to walk to the door. 'Right, then. If everything's all right, I'll leave you to it for a while. Come down when you're ready and we'll have a bite to eat. Only bread and cheese, I'm afraid. We eat our main meal in the evening, when the day cools down a little.'

'That'll be fine. Thank you.' Poppy turned from the window.

'You can find your way back downstairs?'

She grinned. 'It did occur to me that I should have done a Hansel and Gretel and dropped some crumbs, but yes, I think I can find you.'

He smiled his crooked smile. 'I'm afraid they wouldn't last for long if you had. We've got a small army of mice about the place. You can always yell if you get lost. See you later.' He closed the door quietly behind him.

Poppy surveyed her surroundings. In scale with the rest of the house the room was vast, as was the high bed. The walls were painted, but the pattern was so faded and flaked that it was impossible to discern. An oil lamp stood upon a table, one foot of which was propped up with folded newspaper on the uneven floor. The ceiling was stained and dark with smoke. Touchingly, there was a small bunch of wild flowers on the washstand beside a massive china bowl and jug. Beside the tall window, shutters were folded back to the wall. For the moment, there was no need for them. The room faced east, and the sun had already moved to the front of the house. The yard below was in shade. Poppy moved back to the window, stood for a quiet moment, enveloped by the scent of the afternoon. Even the cicadas had fallen quiet. Not a blade, not a leaf stirred. She ran her fingers through her bobbed hair, lifting it from her damp scalp.

A confusion of impressions and memories suddenly invaded her mind, the events of the past couple of days, that had seemed so endlessly long, suddenly snapped short, like the closing of a telescope. The awkward farewell to her father at Victoria station. The excitement, despite the foul weather, of crossing the English Channel for the first time, and on her own at that. The equally exciting, if tiring, experience of watching the French countryside—so very different in character from the countryside that she knew, so very *foreign*—stream past the train window. The enveloping warmth and softly scented air of the south, growing perceptibly and beguilingly stronger as she travelled. The impossibility of sleep, except in snatches; the anxious moments, the missed connections. And then Florence, and Kit. The towering walls of Siena. Now—

She leaned on the wrought iron balustrade. Now—this. A great, mouldering house to whose romance and atmosphere she was already warmly attracted. A hillside woodland guarded by an ancient tower and inhabited by deer, wild boar, and goodness only knew what else.

A sister so changed that she could not, for the moment, bring herself truly to think about it. Pregnancy, she supposed, did change people. But—that much?

Briskly she turned, slipping off her jacket, stepping out of her travel-crumpled skirt. It was, after all, to help Isobel that she had come. Everything would be all right now.

*   *   *

After a lunch taken under the vine-covered pergola, and which inevitably, with so much news to be exchanged, stretched well into the afternoon, Kit and Poppy left Isobel and little Robbie resting in the quiet heat and embarked on a tour of the house. The place was built, off centre, around a courtyard, on one side of which was the massive front door, on a second a high brick wall against which was situated, unexpectedly, a well with a wrought-iron cover. Next to this was a small arched doorway that led out of the side of the house to where a tiny church stood, dilapidated as the rest of the buildings. The living accommodation—or what had been the living accommodation—comprised the other two sides of the courtyard.

125

'Some members of the family still occasionally use the rooms on this side—' Kit pushed open a heavy door, stood back for her to pass through '—only rarely, for hunting trips, or if they feel the need to cast an eye over the estate. Careful. It's a bit dark.'

Poppy had stopped, wide-eyed. 'Goodness me!'

Behind her, Kit laughed quietly.

It was a room from another age: heavy furniture, tapestries, portraits and dark oil paintings on the walls. A rug of faded splendour on the flagged floor. Kit walked to one of the long windows and opened the shutters. Light glinted on tarnished silver, reflected from stately damp-stained and fly-specked bevelled mirrors. Almost the whole of one wall was lined with bookshelves upon which stood rank upon rank of leather-bound volumes. A mahogany desk big enough to play table tennis on was neatly laid out with blotter, paper, pot of ink, two quill pens and a small pen-knife.

'It's—' Poppy stopped, shrugging helplessly.

'—incredible.' Kit supplied. 'Isn't it? Wait till you see the bedrooms.'

An hour or so later they were back in the kitchen. Even with the windows and doors open, and shaded by the ancient grapevine, at this time of day the stove made it uncomfortably warm. 'Let's sit outside,' Kit suggested. 'How about a glass of wine?'

'Wonderful. Thank you.' Poppy wandered out into the yard and sat down upon a battered but comfortable wicker chair. Movement caught her eye. The diminutive, unmistakable figure of Umberto, dark skin and faded clothing almost blending with the colour of the dry soil, was working in the neat vegetable patch, moving with slow patience along the rows with a hoe.

'There—village special, but very drinkable, I promise, providing you aren't too picky. It could be that I've just got used to it.' Kit placed a large glass of red wine in front of her. For himself he had brought the bottle of whisky and a small glass. He settled down across the table from her, splashed the amber liquid into the glass, tossed it back and poured another. 'That's a rare treat. Thank you.'

She smiled, looked back to where Umberto leaned for a moment upon his hoe. Kit's eyes followed hers. 'He's a treasure,' he said, 'an absolute treasure. I don't know what we'd do without him.'

'Does he live here in the house?'

Kit shook his head. 'No. He lives down in the village. He has a wife about three times his size and a gaggle of daughters who nag him silly.'

Poppy's eyes moved to his face. 'And you? Where do you work? Do you have a studio in the house?'

'Not exactly. I've converted one of the

127

stables. I'll show it to you later, if you'd like. I had initially intended to use the tower—' he nodded his head towards the wooded hillside '—but it turned out to be too inconvenient. And it would have cost a fortune to convert. And, to be honest, Isobel didn't like the idea of my being so far from the house. She gets— nervous.' The hesitation before he used the word was infinitesimal, but noticeable.

'She's changed,' Poppy said, with straightforward candour, her eyes steady upon his face. 'She isn't well, is she?'

Kit looked down into his drink, tilting his glass a little. Then he lifted his head to meet her eyes. 'I did try to explain. She's had a very difficult time—'

Poppy shook her head thoughtfully. 'It isn't only that. She seems—' she shrugged a little '—overwrought—unhappy,' she finished, gently.

There was a long moment of silence. Then Kit again tossed back his drink in a swallow and set the glass with some care upon the table. A small wry twitch of a smile touched his mouth. He did not deny the word. 'I'm sure having you here will go a long way towards changing that. Now—would you like to see my studio?'

She followed him out of the yard and round the corner of the house, passing the tiny dilapidated chapel. Poppy caught a glimpse of the inner courtyard of the house as they passed the arched doorway and then they were at the front of the building. Kit led her across the overgrown paving. 'Mind you don't turn an ankle. It's all a bit rocky.' Three or four chickens flurried away from them, then settled down to strut and peck officiously some yards off. The cat still sat upon its wall, grooming itself. It stilled and watched them with lambent, disdainful eyes as they passed. 'Here we are.' Kit pushed open a door.

The room, which reached to the beams of the tiled roof, was spacious, light and very untidy. All vestiges of its previous use had gone, except for the channels and drains in the brick-paved floor and a single metal manger attached to one wall and filled with a careless collection of jars, brushes and paint-stained rags. Canvases, finished and unfinished, were stacked everywhere. On an easel was a half-finished landscape. A big table stood in a corner, its surface entirely engulfed in more jars, books, papers and several empty wine bottles. The light streamed through two huge windows that had been set into the back wall of the room. Poppy moved to look through the windows at the rolling countryside beyond. 'What a gorgeous view!'

'These are the only windows in the house that ever get cleaned.' Kit came to join her. 'Umberto cleans them religiously, every week. I think he rather likes being in charge of an eccentric English artist.'

Poppy had wandered off, pausing every now and then to study a picture or leaf through a book. She shot him a quick grin. 'And are you?'

'What?'

'Eccentric.'

He laughed. 'No more, I think, than I ever was.'

Poppy had stopped by a collection of pictures stacked against the wall. The first was yet another study of Robbie. She looked at it with pleasure. 'I think Umberto is very fond of you,' she said. 'Devoted, even. And to Robbie.'

Kit acknowledged the comment with a small nod of his head. 'We're very lucky. To be honest, I think the only thing that takes precedence so far as Umberto is concerned is the Palio.'

Poppy, in the act of leaning the half-finished portrait carefully against her leg in order to look at the next picture, turned her head. 'That's the horse race, isn't it? I read about it when I knew you were going to come here to live.'

Kit shouted with laughter. 'You'll get yourself lynched if you go around here calling the Palio a "horse race"!'

She raised surprised brows. 'Isn't that what it is?'

'Strictly speaking, yes, I suppose so. But to the Sienese it's more. Much more. It's a way of life, no less.'

'Oh?' Poppy moved on to the next picture.

'It's—' he paused '—it's a tournament. An old-fashioned, honest-to-God medieval tournament. A combination of circus, religion and quite deadly rivalry.'

Poppy, still flicking through the paintings, did not notice his sudden stillness. 'It all sounds terribly Italian. I say, I like this one.' All at once she became aware of the sudden tension in the atmosphere. And at the same moment she realised that the door behind her had opened. She turned.

Silhouetted against the light stood a tall, slim figure in shirt and soft, loose trousers. Cigarette smoke wreathed about her and she carried a large leather shoulder-bag. There was a moment of silence. Then, 'Eloise,' Kit said, his voice expressionless.

The woman was looking not at him, but at Poppy. For the moment her face was in shadow and Poppy could not make out her features. It was only as she sauntered forward into the room that the severe, almost cold, beauty of her came into focus. In contrast to the dark hair her eyes were the palest green, luminous against her smooth olive skin. There was, as she studied Poppy, a glint of something close to amusement in her face. 'So,' she said. 'The little sister.' Her English was easy, but quite heavily accented; not, Poppy was surprised to hear, Italian accented, but unmistakably French.

Poppy glanced at Kit, nonplussed.

He took a stiff step forward. 'Poppy, this is Eloise Martin. Eloise—' he gestured '—Poppy Brookes. Isobel's sister.'

'Of course.' The very smallest of smiles flickered.

'How do you do?' Poppy stepped forward, hand extended.

For a startled moment she thought the other woman would ignore the gesture. Then, languidly, Eloise briefly took the hand in hers. Her grasp was dry and firm, surprisingly strong. 'I am very pleased to meet you, Ma'mselle Brookes. Isobel has told me so much about you.'

Whereas no one has told me anything at all about you. Why not, I wonder? Poppy felt it impolitic to voice the thought. She smiled, politely noncommittal.

Eloise turned to Kit. 'I came to tell you that Michel arrives in two days. He will bring Peter with him as arranged. Will you tell Umberto, please? Peter stays with me, of course, but as you know since the house is so small, the arrangement is made that Michel will lodge with Umberto and his wife.'

'Yes,' Kit said a little brusquely. 'He mentioned it yesterday. I'll tell him.'

The woman nodded, eyes veiled. She looked back at Poppy. 'You stay for the summer, I understand?'

'Yes.'

'Ah. How very pleasant for us all.' The mockery, not gentle, was barely disguised. Poppy found herself flushing a little. Again she glanced at Kit, who avoided her eyes. 'So.' Eloise looked from one to the other, her hand resting lightly on the leather bag that swung from her narrow shoulder. 'I will have a word with Isobel before I go.' Her cool, pale gaze rested upon Poppy. '*Au'voir*, Miss Brookes. We will meet again. Quite soon, no doubt.'

Poppy smiled, said nothing.

Eloise Martin, without another glance at Kit, left them.

'What an extraordinarily—' Poppy stopped, searching for the word '—odd woman,' she finished a little lamely.

Kit had turned away, absent-mindedly tidying the table. 'She's all right. One gets used to her.'

'To be frank, I'm not sure I want to,' Poppy said, honest as ever. 'Who are Peter and Michel?'

'Her son and her brother. Peter's at school in England. Michel teaches French there.'

'Is there a husband?'

Kit shook his head briefly. 'No.'

Poppy's curiosity, as always, was getting the better of her. 'Was there ever one?'

'Oh—yes. He died. In the war.'

'How old is the son?'

Kit thought for a moment. 'About ten, I suppose. Yes. He's ten.'

133

'Poor little scrap, with a mother like that.' Poppy cocked an eyebrow at Kit's quick, rueful grin. 'Well, she doesn't exactly emanate warmth and motherly love, does she? Or is the youngster a chip off the old block?'

'I don't know. I've never met him. Eloise only arrived here six or seven months ago. Peter's been at school all year.' Kit with a quite obvious effort pushed himself away from the table. His face was strained.

'Peter,' Poppy said. 'And an English school. Was the father English?'

'Yes, I believe he was. They met during the war. Anyway—' In a clear attempt to change the subject, he stacked a book precariously on a pile. 'Let's get back to the house, shall we?'

'Yes, of course. What's she doing here? Eloise, I mean?'

'I believe she's suffered from ill health over the past couple of years. It was recommended that she came to Italy for convalescence.'

'She looks perfectly all right to me.'

His hand on the door-latch, he turned, and his laughter was quite genuine. 'Oh, Poppy, Poppy, I'm so glad you've come. You're quite priceless.'

'That's the second time you've said that!' Poppy's voice was faintly and cheerfully aggrieved. 'And I've only been here since lunch-time.'

He put an arm about her shoulders as they strolled off across the front of the house.

'What I mean is—you're a breath of fresh air.'

'Well, that's all right, then. I don't mind being that.' Poppy stopped and turned, gazing beyond the gate down the woodland-cloaked hillside into the valley. A mile or so away woodsmoke rose, marking the position of the village. The smoke drifted to their nostrils, pungent and evocative. Tranquillity lay across the scene like a veil of gossamer. 'It really is beautiful,' she said softly.

'Yes. Come—I'll show you the chapel before we go in.'

The chapel, compared to the faded splendour of the house, was something of a disappointment. Everything had been stripped from it except what was immovable: the ancient stone altar, the faded, damaged frescos on the walls, a couple of plaques. To Poppy it smelled mustily of sadness and desertion, and she was glad when they stepped back out into the sunshine.

Isobel was in the kitchen, sitting in an armchair, her feet upon a stool, a book open on her lap. She looked up with an oddly dreamy, almost secretive, smile as they came into the room. Robbie, sitting at the table industriously scribbling upon a sheet of paper, jumped from his chair and ran to Kit. 'Daddy!'

Kit lifted him, kissed the tender curve of his cheek, set him back upon the chair, ruffling his fair hair.

Isobel, Poppy was pleased to see, looked

better for her rest; more relaxed, less tense, though in the gloom of the kitchen her bright eyes looked curiously darkened. She held her hand out to Kit. He took it, bent to kiss her hair. She tilted her head to look at him, a gesture that had somehow something of defiance in it. 'Eloise was here,' she said. 'She just left.'

Kit looked at her with enigmatic eyes. 'Yes,' he said. 'So I see.'

And Poppy, for the life of her, whilst quite clearly recognising it, could not fathom the depths of bitterness in his tone.

CHAPTER SEVEN

'So—tell me about this horse race that isn't a horse race.' Poppy and Kit were strolling through the woodland at the back of the house towards the tower. 'When is it held? Will I be able to see it?'

'It's actually run twice a year, on the second of July and the sixteenth of August. And yes, you certainly will get to see both of them if you want to. I always go. It's an extremely—' he flicked a quick smile at her '—colourful occasion, in every sense of the word. It's run in the Piazza del Campo, the town square.'

'I read about it before I came. The tradition goes back centuries, doesn't it?'

'Yes. It really is quite unique.' Something rustled in the woods to their right. Kit turned his head, watching for a moment. When nothing further happened, he resumed his slow pacing, his hands in his pockets, head bowed, watching his feet scuffing through the leafmould and pine needles that carpeted the woods. His hair flopped over his eyes. Poppy smiled a little. 'Putting it simply, the city is divided into various quarters, called *Contrade*. There are seventeen of them. Each *Contrada* has its own traditions—its own symbol, its own colours, its own banners. They have their own saints' days, their own festivals. You'll see. The whole life of Siena revolves around the *Contrade* and the Palio—and not just in the summer but all year. It's all very passionate; very Italian. The parades and ceremonies before the races are as spectacular as the races themselves. The rivalry is intense—almost literally cut-throat.' They were approaching the tower. It was bigger than Poppy had expected, rearing from a massive, brick-built base. They stopped, looking up at it. To Poppy's own surprise—she was not usually given to such flights of fancy—she found something menacing in the huge thing.

'It's a bit creepy, isn't it?'

Kit laughed. 'I suppose it is; something to do with the age of it, perhaps. There's a splendid view, though.' He led her through the door.

In the shadowed interior she stopped in surprise, then shook her head firmly. 'Not a view I'll be seeing,' she said. The building was a shell, all the wooden floors long collapsed. Dazzlingly bright fingers of sunlight struck through the narrow windows. Poppy jumped as a pigeon swooped from the rafters. She pulled a face. 'You wouldn't get me up there for all the tea in China, thank you very much, view or no view.' A flight of dangerously decaying stone steps, very narrow, led up to a wooden platform, from where a rough wooden staircase—almost a ladder—zigzagged up the wall to a tiny lookout point in a window embrasure high overhead. 'It makes me feel dizzy just to look at it!'

'You don't like heights?'

She grinned, shrugging a little. 'Let's just say I prefer my little flat feet to be on the ground.' They walked back out into the warm sunshine. Poppy rubbed her bare arm. 'What a peculiar place. I've come out in goose bumps.'

'Isobel doesn't like it either. That's why she didn't want me to build a studio up here.'

'I don't blame her a bit. Now, tell me some more about the Palio. Do you support one of these—what did you call them—?'

'*Contrade*. Oh, yes, I have to. Or Umberto would have my head on a plate! I tell you, you just don't understand the passions the Palio arouses in the Sienese.'

They strolled back to the house, talking

easily. Isobel, watching them from the kitchen window, ran her hand through her tangled, sweat-damp hair tiredly. It had been strange to discover that the small, brown child that Kit had so appropriately nicknamed 'Mouse' had become this bright, capable and unnervingly modern young woman. Strange, and a little daunting. But then everything seemed to be nowadays. Strange. And daunting. Between one second and the next, helpless to prevent it, she felt her fragile composure slip from her; felt, as she all too often did nowadays, the burning of tears—pathetic tears, she knew; childish, demoralising, futile, unnecessary— she had heard all the words from the occasionally and she supposed justifiably exasperated Kit and from the gently chiding— gently mocking?—Eloise.

Eloise.

Isobel closed her eyes for a moment; saw the perfect, subtle face, the slender, elegant body. The little phials that she so— apparently—reluctantly produced at Isobel's begging.

Clenched against tears she turned suddenly and with a small sob slammed her open hand painfully hard upon the table; her left hand, upon which the dull gold of her wedding band gleamed, loose and heavy; for as her body swelled and distorted, the rest of her flesh shrank. Through blurred eyes she stared at the ring.

'Mummy?' Robbie stood in the doorway, the shabby woollen dog that had been his lifelong sleeping companion tucked under one arm, his blue eyes wide and worried. His bottom lip, soft as a ripe berry, wobbled a little. 'Mummy?' he said again.

Isobel clung to the table for a moment, steadying herself. 'It's all right, darling. Mummy has a headache. That's all.'

A headache with no cure. The laudanum Eloise had brought her yesterday had gone frighteningly quickly; she had been unable to resist the temptation to slip those few extra drops into her wine. And yet the period of relief it afforded—relief from the nightmare of doubts and fears, the terror of what was to come—seemed to get shorter every day.

The little boy leaned against the door jamb, his thumb in his mouth, small forefinger stroking the side of his button nose.

'Don't suck your thumb, Robbie,' she said automatically; a plea rather than an order, even she could hear that.

'Want to.' He spoke around the thumb, his fair, stubborn brows drawn together.

Isobel bowed her head. In this state she could not even attempt to control her own child.

Outside she heard voices, Poppy's laughter.

'Daddy,' Robbie said very softly.

Isobel lifted her head.

'—so to Dora's absolute fury I decided that

140

the shelf was a rather more desirable place to be than—' Poppy stopped as she caught sight of Isobel, her laughter dying, her face concerned. 'Isobel? Are you all right?'

Isobel nodded, avoiding her eyes. 'Yes. I've got a bit of a headache, that's all.'

'You ought to sit down and put your feet up. Look at your poor ankles—' Poppy hurried to her sister's side, put an arm about her to lead her to a chair. 'Let me make you a cup of tea.'

'Robbie hasn't finished his nap. I really ought to put him back to bed for half an hour or so.' Nevertheless Isobel allowed herself to be fussed into the chair, leaning her head back tiredly and closing her eyes.

'I'll see to that.' Kit swooped his son from the floor, settled him, crowing delightedly, on his arm. 'Come on, old chap. Back to bed for a little while.'

'Story,' the child said, with through the golden veil of his lashes, a small, cautious glance at his mother. 'Want story.'

Isobel did not even open her eyes.

'Then a story you shall have. Which one would you like?'

He considered solemnly. Then a broad beam lit his face. 'Pirates,' he said firmly, and back went the thumb.

Kit laughed. 'What a bloodthirsty little wretch you are! All right, then, pirates it will be.' Father and son left the room, Kit's voice fading as they went into the shadowed

141

labyrinth of the house.

Poppy busied herself at the stove for a moment, putting on the kettle, rinsing out the teapot.

'Poppy?' Isobel asked from behind her, her voice barely audible.

Poppy turned. Her sister was still half-lying in the chair, her feet upon a stool, her head tilted wearily upon the cushioned back. The light showed the bruise-like shadows beneath her closed eyes; gleamed too upon the film of perspiration on her forehead and the tears that slid down the thin cheeks, trickling into the bright tangle of her hair.

'Isobel!' Poppy hurried to her, dropped to one knee beside her. 'Darling, what is it? What's the matter? Don't you feel well?'

The drowned blue eyes opened. Isobel turned her head a little on the cushion to look with sudden, tearful intentness into her sister's face. 'Tell me the truth,' she said abruptly. 'Do you think Kit and Eloise are having an affair?'

The question was so unexpected that for several moments Poppy could not speak. She stared at Isobel, her eyes round and startled.

Isobel sat up, knuckling the tears half-angrily from her cheeks. 'Tell me the truth,' she said again, insistently.

Poppy shook her head, 'Isobel—' She shrugged helplessly, at a loss for words. 'What makes you think such a thing?' she asked at last, lamely.

The sudden caustic and self-mocking gleam in the look her sister threw her was an answer more eloquent than words. 'Poppy, I may not be as bright as some, but neither am I entirely stupid. You've seen them together. Haven't you sensed anything between them?'

Poppy nodded. 'Yes,' she said, quickly and frankly, 'but—I'm not sure what it is.'

'What do you mean?'

Poppy sat back on her heels, again half-shrugging and spreading her hands. 'To be honest, I don't think Kit really likes her. Or she him, come to that.'

'Since when did that matter?' Isobel's words were quite shockingly bitter. 'I didn't ask if you thought they *liked* each other.' She reached into her sleeve and pulled out a crumpled handkerchief, blew her nose loudly.

Poppy watched her for a moment, a small frown on her face. 'Tell me about Eloise.'

Isobel sniffed. 'I don't really know very much. She's French. She was married to an Englishman who was killed at the end of the war. She has a son who was born after his father's death—he's ten now. He'll be here soon; his uncle's bringing him—'

'Tomorrow. Yes, I know. Tell me more about Eloise. What's she actually like? What's she doing here? How did you come to meet her?'

Isobel was twisting the handkerchief in her fingers. She lifted her eyes to Poppy's,

143

genuinely surprised. 'Hasn't Kit told you?'

Poppy shook her head. 'Not very much.'

'You mean he doesn't talk about her?'

'No. Hardly ever. And, when he does, he doesn't really say anything.'

Isobel's eyes went back to the handkerchief as if it were the most fascinating object in the world. 'She's—well, she's a contradiction, I suppose. Sometimes she's really kind, and then sometimes—' she trailed off, shrugged. 'She's very intelligent. And very beautiful.'

'I had noticed.' Poppy's voice was dry.

'Perhaps that's it. Kit is an artist, after all. He loves beautiful things.' The tears welled again. Isobel dashed them away with her fingers.

There was a long moment of silence, then, 'Kit said something about her having been unwell, and having come here to recuperate,' Poppy prompted.

'Yes, that's right.'

'She doesn't *look* as if she hasn't been well.' The words were thoughtful. Isobel shrugged. 'How did you meet her?'

The handkerchief was twisting again, the curly head bowed miserably. 'Kit met her walking in the woods a few months ago. He brought her back to meet me. She said she wanted us to be friends. That we had a lot in common, and that she'd help Kit look after me. There's precious little company around here, as you can imagine. I wasn't feeling very well—' Once again she trailed into silence, biting her lip. 'It was peculiar,' she went on at last. 'Even then I felt—something. I couldn't put my finger on it, but there was *something*. I did wonder if they'd been meeting for some time. Whether this was just a way for them to be together, to prevent me from—well, from becoming suspicious—'

'Kit wouldn't do that.' The words were quick and firm.

Isobel glanced at her. 'No, of course he wouldn't.' Her voice was lifeless.

The kettle danced suddenly on the hob. Poppy jumped to her feet, splashed water into the pot to warm it, then spooned in the tea, waiting until she had made the brew and tucked it under a tea cosy before she turned and said gently, 'Isobel—don't you think you're being a little silly? Why torment yourself like this? Why not ask Kit outright? I'm sure you'll find there's nothing—'

'*No!*' The word was fierce. 'No, I can't. He'd only deny it. Of course he would. But he might get upset. Or angry. I couldn't stand that. I really couldn't. Poppy—please—don't say anything to him? Please? I couldn't bear any unpleasantness.'

'Of course I won't.'

Isobel dropped her face into her hands. 'I shouldn't have said anything. I know I'm being stupid. I know it! But I can't help it!' She lifted her head to look at Poppy. 'It's this wretched pregnancy,' she whispered. 'I get—' she hesitated, searching for the word '—fraught when I'm pregnant. When I was carrying Robbie I spent almost the entire nine months crying because I was convinced Kit was going to leave me. I promised him—*promised* him—I wouldn't do it again. Please don't tell him.'

'I've already said of course I won't.' Poppy crossed to her, put a hand on her shoulder, feeling beneath her palm the knotted tension of her sister's body. 'Look, darling, this is awfully bad for you, you know. And for the baby, too. Why don't you pop up to bed for a rest? I'll bring your tea up to you.'

Isobel gestured vaguely around the kitchen. 'There are things to do—'

'I'll do them. That's what I'm here for. Just go up and rest. Go on. Off you go.'

'I am tired.'

'Then go. I'll be up presently with the tea. Could you eat a biscuit with it?'

Isobel, dragging herself to her feet and easing her back with her hands, shook her head. 'No, thank you. Just tea would be lovely.'

Poppy watched her to the door. 'Isobel?'

Isobel turned.

'Tell me—if you feel like that about Eloise—though I still think you're wrong— why do you let her come here so often? You seem so friendly?'

Isobel's eyes slid from hers. 'We are,' she said. 'Truly, we are. Please forget what I said.

146

I'm just being stupid.'

She left the room, walking awkwardly, her hand still at her back. Poppy looked after her, a small puzzled line creasing her brow, then she reached into the cupboard for a cup and saucer.

*   *   *

'Is Umberto about?' Poppy's bobbed brown head appeared round the door jamb of Kit's studio. 'He picked a lovely bunch of flowers for the kitchen. I wanted to thank him.' Her eye fell upon the half-finished portrait of Eloise that leaned against the wall, and she looked away. In the time since her conversation with her sister the day before she had, despite every effort, found herself more than once thinking about what had been said. Was there any seed of truth—however small— in Isobel's fears? She did not want to believe so. *'Kit's an artist, after all. He loves beautiful things.'* But no; whenever the words came back to her she recalled the couple of times she had seen them together and mentally shook her head. Whatever there might be between these two, it was not love. She was certain of it.

Kit was working on the landscape on the easel, and did not look round. 'He's gone into the city, to pick up Eloise's brother and son.'

'Oh, of course. I forgot.' Seeing him like this reminded Poppy so strongly of those childhood

147

days at Tellington Place when he had painted—or rather half-painted—the portrait of herself and Isobel that for a moment she could almost see and smell the place; see the hall with its curving staircase, smell the too-sweet scent of the hothouse flowers her mother had loved that had always pervaded every room, and that she, Poppy, had so disliked. She watched him for a moment. 'Papa put the portrait you almost painted of us up in the attic,' she said, apparently inconsequentially.

His long mouth twitched wryly. 'I'm not surprised. You could hardly expect him to do anything else. Except, perhaps, to burn it.'

'No, I suppose not.' She came further into the room, stood watching him, head cocked. 'But I'm glad he didn't do that. I went up to look at it, before I left. It really was very good.'

'I've got a couple of sketches somewhere, if you'd like to see them? They're in a box up in the attic, I think.'

'Really? Yes, I would.' She watched him for a moment longer. 'Tell me; which do you prefer to paint—portraits or landscapes and things?'

'Portraits.' The word was patient. He leaned to the canvas. 'They're more demanding. And more satisfying. A portrait—a good portrait— is not just a picture of a person. It's the essence of that person. The more complicated the character, the more difficult it is to capture

148

and the more rewarding if you manage it, even in part.'

Her eyes flickered to the half-finished portrait propped against the wall. 'Is that why you like to paint Eloise?' she asked, and even as she said it winced—as she often did—at her own unthinking outspokenness.

'Yes.' The word came with no hesitation.

She had the grace to blush a little. 'Sorry. You know me. Where angels and Poppies fear to tread and all that. It's none of my business.'

'It's all right.'

She opened her mouth to say more, caught the faintest exasperated movement of his head. 'I'm sorry,' she said again. 'I'm disturbing you.'

His mouth twitched to a smile, but he said nothing.

Poppy stuck her hands in the pockets of her slacks and pulled a self-deprecatingly apologetic face. 'I think perhaps I'd better go and play pirates with Robbie. I promised him I'd walk the plank. It seems to be his favourite game at the moment.' She waited for a second, but he made no effort to prevent her leaving.

'I'll see you later,' he said, already engrossed again.

*   *   *

Robbie had quite got over his shyness with his young aunt. He was a sunny child with an

149

enchanting smile, an infectious laugh and enough energy to run even Poppy off her feet. Isobel, drained as she was, could not keep up with him and was more than ready to hand over his care almost entirely to her sister. Poppy for her part grew fonder of the child every day and was more than happy with the arrangement. Already they had spent hours together inventing games and stories, building complicated edifices with the brightly coloured multi-shaped wooden bricks that Kit had made for his son, messily painting huge and colourful pictures or playing a Robbie-invented game of hide and seek in which he always hid in the same place, giggling noisily and excitedly as Poppy consistently failed to find him, then jumping out upon her with a loud 'Boo!' and squealing with laughter at her dramatically exaggerated fright. He had soon got used to the fact that it was Poppy who tucked him into bed for his daily sleep, Poppy who sat him at the table for his afternoon tea, Poppy who took him walking in the surrounding fields and woodlands. This afternoon, after leaving Kit in his studio, she took the child out into the sunshine of the field at the side of the house to play ball and then to pick a bunch of flowers for his mother.

They were still there when Umberto drove the empty *calesse* up the drive and into the courtyard at the front of the house. Poppy waved, and the little man waved back. So

Eloise's visitors had presumably arrived safely. Poppy wondered—or was it more truly hoped?—if the little household might see less of the woman with her own family around her. She saw Kit come out of his studio and exchange a few words with Umberto, though she could not hear what was said.

'Pop,' Robbie said, pulling impatiently at her shirt. 'Come play.'

Smiling, she stooped to pick him up and dropped a quick kiss on his hot, plump little cheek. His small hand clutched at the bedraggled flowers, squeezing the stems so hard that they drooped already. His curls were damp and springy in the heat. 'No more play, little man. Let's take these flowers in to Mummy and then it's time for your rest. No, no—' she kissed him again, lightly, on the forehead as he opened his mouth to protest '—we'll have more games later. It's getting too hot now. Come on, off we go.'

She left him, half an hour or so later, thumb firmly in mouth, Dog tucked in beside him, long lashes drooping, and went back downstairs to find Isobel sitting at the table drinking tea. As she entered the room, yet again Poppy was struck by the shadowed fragility of her looks. 'He's well settled,' she said. 'Are you all right?'

Isobel gave her a smile so palpably false that it could more be described as a grimace. When she spoke, her voice too held a spurious brightness. 'I'm fine. Truly I am. As a matter of fact—' she hesitated, dropped her eyes from Poppy's '—as a matter of fact, I was thinking of going for a little walk.'

'A walk?' Poppy dropped into the chair opposite. 'Are you sure?'

'Oh, yes.' Still Isobel did not look at her. 'Oh, yes, honestly. I'll be all right. I just—fancy a drop of air, that's all.'

'It's very hot,' Poppy said dubiously. 'Don't you think you should leave it until later?'

'No.' Isobel's softly pretty mouth, so like her son's, set in the stubborn line that Poppy had already learned to recognise in Robbie's. 'I want to go now. I might not feel up to it later.'

'I don't think you should go alone. I'll come with you.' Poppy stood up.

'No.' The word was quick. 'Please, Poppy, don't fuss. I want to go on my own. Just down to the village and back, that's all. And anyway, someone has to stay with Robbie.'

'Umberto's back,' Poppy said. 'He'd listen out for him if I asked.'

There was an odd moment of stillness. Isobel lifted her head to look at her. 'Umberto? Back already?'

'Yes. I saw him just now. Isobel? Is something wrong?'

'No. Nothing.' Isobel's voice was dull. 'So they're here, are they? Eloise's visitors?'

'I assume so. Isobel, I really would rather you didn't go out alone.'

Isobel's shoulders slumped a little. 'All right, I won't. I suppose you're right—it was rather a silly idea.'

'Leave it till later. Rest for the afternoon. Read one of your books. And when it's a bit cooler perhaps we could all go for a stroll together? You're right—you should get some exercise, and you have been cooped up here for a long time. I just don't think you should go out in the heat of the day, that's all.'

'You're right. Of course you are.' Isobel put a hand to her head. 'If you don't mind, I think I'll lie down for a little while. I feel a headache coming on. No, it's all right—' Her smile this time was faint but genuine as Poppy had made a move to help her up. 'For goodness' sake, Poppy, I'm not actually an invalid, you know. I can put myself to bed.'

'Can I get you anything?'

Isobel shook her head. 'No. Nothing. Thank you.' She turned to the door.

'Shall I wake you when I get Robbie up?'

'I doubt I shall actually sleep, but yes, just let me know and I'll come down.' She walked slowly and heavily out of the room. Poppy sat and listened as the sound of footsteps faded and the quiet of the house settled again like a shroud about her. It really was very hot today. She crossed her arms on the table and laid her head upon them, listening to the drowsy sounds of the afternoon as they drifted through the door.

She was dozing when she heard the voices. She straightened, blinking, as a shadow fell across the bright rectangle of the doorway.

'Poppy?' Eloise's voice. 'Where is everyone?'

Poppy rubbed sleep from her eyes. 'Isobel and Robbie are resting. Kit's in his studio. I'm here.' With some difficulty she suppressed a yawn. 'I'm sorry—I was almost asleep.' She rubbed her eyes again, narrowing them against the light.

Eloise was not alone. She came into the kitchen with her arm about the shoulders of a child, and a tall, slim man followed, for the moment nothing but a dark silhouette against the sunlight. Sleepily Poppy scrambled to her feet, the chair-legs scraping noisily against the tiles of the floor. Eloise walked the child forward. 'Poppy, this is my son, Peter.'

The boy extended a hand. 'How do you do.'

Poppy shook hands. The boy was, she judged, about ten years old, a grave, handsome lad with a shy smile. The most immediately eye-catching thing about him was his hair; heavy, and shining, cut to a neat, thick cap about his face, it was the colour of burnished chestnuts and fell across his wide forehead in a soft wave. Poppy knew several girls who would have killed for such hair. Even in the dimness of the kitchen one thing was certain; the boy's looks were inherited not from his mother but from his father. Here was none of Eloise's

154

slender elegance—the boy was well and strongly built—neither had he inherited those strange, pale eyes. His were bright and direct, a sparkling hazel, a deep green-gold as he turned his head to the light.

'And this is my brother Michel.'

The man stepped forward, smiling, and he too shook her hand, acknowledging her in a light, melodious voice. 'Ma'mselle.' The first thing Poppy noticed was how like his sister he was; and the next, somewhat confusingly, how very unlike. His face was longer, the features less regular, the clear eyes a less remarkable green. His dark hair receded from a lofty forehead and the hand that held hers was bony, long-fingered and strong. But the main contrast between brother and sister was the genuine and open friendliness of the smile. Her own smile broadened in reply. Inasmuch as she had bothered to think about Eloise's brother at all, she supposed she had expected something close to a mirror-image of the woman, cool and disdainful; the relaxed warmth that this young man exuded was a surprise of the pleasantest kind.

'You say Kit is in the studio?'

Poppy turned to Eloise. She was a little startled to see a slight flush of colour in the alabaster cheeks, a glitter of excitement in her eyes. She had never before seen the woman's composure ruffled; the thumb of the hand that still rested upon the boy's shoulder stroked rhythmically, almost nervously, on the cloth of his navy blue blazer. Poppy nodded. 'Yes. He's working.'

Eloise smiled her most dazzling smile. 'Then come—we will introduce my two handsome young men to him.' To Poppy's astonishment, she slipped an arm in hers, drawing her towards the door. 'Robbie—' she began.

Eloise lifted an elegant shoulder. 'Isobel will hear him if he wakes. Come. I warn you—' her voice was almost teasing '—I have told my Michel all about you and promised him you will help me to make his stay here a happy one.'

Poppy found herself blushing to the roots of her hair; which, mortified, she suddenly found herself realising must still be tousled from her afternoon doze. She hastily and ineffectively ran the fingers of her free hand through it. Eloise saw the gesture and smiled. 'Come,' she said again.

Kit was standing at the window when, with no ceremony, Eloise pushed the door open and led the way into the room. He turned, startled. 'Eloise? What—?' His eyes moved from the adults' faces to the child's, and he stopped. There was a strange, suspended moment of silence. Eloise was watching him intently. Poppy looked from one to the other, puzzled. Kit appeared to have frozen where he stood. She would have sworn that his tanned face had actually paled. The look on the woman's face was one of almost rapacious expectation. Even the lad felt the moment of tension. Like Poppy, he glanced from Kit to his mother in enquiry; but it was indeed only a moment, and it passed so quickly that Poppy thought she well might have imagined it. With a quick, spontaneous smile Kit stepped forward, hand outstretched. 'Well, hello, young man. You must be Peter.'

The boy relaxed, took the hand. 'Yes. How do you do, Mr Enever.'

'Kit. Call me Kit. Welcome to *Tenuta di Gordini*. And this must be Michel?' He turned to the other man and they too shook hands. Poppy was so busy noticing once again what an extremely attractive smile the young Frenchman had that she almost missed the look that Kit shot at Eloise as he said, 'How very kind of you to bring your guests to meet us so soon.' Almost, but not quite; for so fierce was the sudden flicker of bitter hostility in the normally smiling light-brown eyes that it astonished her.

'I promised I would,' Eloise said, relaxed now, her voice openly amused, 'And you know, Kit, that I always keep my promises.' She seemed to Poppy positively to be glowing with delight. 'Are you not going to offer us a glass of wine? Come—' Laughing aloud she slipped her arm through Kit's, as she had through Poppy's earlier, and almost danced him out of

157

the door. 'We should celebrate, I think. Let us go and find Isobel and small Robbie. Everyone must be introduced.'

Peter had followed his mother and Kit out into the courtyard. Poppy, left alone with Michel, to her own surprise found herself, almost for the first time in her life, completely tongue-tied. There was a small but not uncomfortable silence. He stood smiling down at her; a smile, Poppy found herself thinking bemusedly, that would most certainly charm the most reluctant of birds from its perch. 'Poppy,' he said thoughtfully, in that quiet, musical voice. His accent, like his sister's, was slight. Why did she find it infinitely more attractive? 'What a very pretty name,' he added after a moment. 'It suits you.' The words were as unselfconscious and as candidly friendly as if they had known each other for years.

She found her missing tongue. 'Kit used to call me Mouse.'

He chuckled; and to her utter astonishment her heart quite literally skipped a beat. Another first. 'Now that,' he said, amused, 'doesn't suit you at all, I think.'

She smiled, briefly, turned to lead the way out to the others, suddenly and exasperatedly aware that she was in some danger of behaving like a character in one of her sister's dafter novels. Don't be silly, she scolded herself as she followed the little party into the house;

158

he's tall and he's dark, but you could hardly describe him as handsome.

Could you?

CHAPTER EIGHT

Considering his circumstances—or some might well think even because of them—Michel Brosette was an exceptionally well-adjusted young man; easy-going, intelligent and slow to anger, though his temper, once roused, could be as fierce as any. Half-brother to Eloise, born to a young second wife who had died bearing him, he hardly remembered the father who had hatcd him for being the cause of her death. Brought up by a distant and penurious relative who, though kindly enough, took him in as much for the money his father was prepared to offer as for any desire to care for a child, he had very early on in life developed a temperate self-sufficiency that had stood him in good stead ever since.

His aunt Jeanne, with whom he had spent most of those first formative thirteen or fourteen years of his life, had been a worn, quiet woman married to an even quieter man; a schoolteacher whose only loves in life were the books that he scraped and saved to buy, and hoarded in a tiny boxroom in the attics of the house in a nondescript village by the River

Somme in which they lived. From the time of his first memories Michel had always loved what he still thought of as 'the book room'. The schoolteacher, though reserved to the point of aloofness, had nevertheless recognised in the boy a quick intelligence and eagerness to learn that he was more than willing to encourage. Certainly Michel, when he thought about it—which was, truthfully, not that often—considered him to be far more a father than the stern and unsmiling man who visited occasionally, put the fear of God into the small child who barely recognised his blood kinship to the gentleman he called 'M'sieur', and then left again. The one real relationship that had lit up his young life had been with Eloise, the younger, softer, vividly beautiful Eloise that he remembered from those pre-war years. Eloise it had been who insisted that her small half-brother accompany her for the summer months that she spent in the glorious countryside of the Lot valley where her maternal grandmother's house was set, Eloise who had cossetted and played with him, bandaged grazed knees and wiped away childish tears. An Eloise of warmth and laughter, of a gay and restless energy that had drawn the world to her and coaxed it to smile. As a child, he had adored her. It had been the war that had changed her.

But then, the war had changed everything.

Before Michel Brosette had reached his

sixteenth birthday, what world he had was taken from him; his father's business ruined and the man himself dead of it, the schoolteacher's house with its dusty silences and its 'book room' swept away in the tide of war, the two people who, staunchly conscientious, had cared for him since the day of his birth, crushed to death in its ruins, himself evacuated to yet another unknown and distant relation, this time in the far safety of England.

And Eloise—where did Eloise go in those years? He knew she had worked as a nurse. Knew too of her passion for an English war correspondent, Peter Martin, who had been killed towards the end, in 1918. In the confusion of the war and its immediate aftermath, Michel had lost touch with her. She had turned up in his life again late in 1919, arriving in England with no warning, a child of perhaps six months in her arms, the posthumous son of the man she had loved, who already showed traces of the likeness to his father that was to become so marked as he grew older. The English relatives, their only son dead in the trenches of Ypres, had happily welcomed yet another extension to their family, and the Martin family, too, once contacted, had been overjoyed at the discovery of a grandson they had not known existed and had readily agreed to help support and educate him. Michel, by this time training to be a teacher himself, was the only one to recognise the extraordinary changes that had occurred in his sister; but, then, there could hardly be any surprise in that. Who had come through those unprecedentedly terrible years unchanged? Now, teaching French to the boys of St Edmund's School near Chichester, the boy, his nephew, was amongst his pupils.

It had surprised him, but only mildly, when Eloise had announced her abrupt decision to come here to Italy for the summer; it was not the first time she had unexpectedly disappeared for a few days or a few weeks, though never for so long before. On her grandmother's death she had inherited a sum, not large, but enough to support her and to preserve her independence. She was a restless soul, and sometimes, he knew, grew homesick for her native France. Why she had chosen Italy this time was beyond him—and, questioned, true to form she had smiled and said nothing—but he was content nevertheless. The prospect of a summer here, in the drowsy warmth of the south, had always been a pleasant one. Now it was more so. Standing at the window of his small rented room in Umberto's house, listening to Umberto's women folk squabbling and laughing in the kitchen below, he smiled to himself. The English girl in the strange old house on the hillside had attracted, warmed and amused him. He looked forward to getting to know her better.

* * *

'Good morning.'

Poppy jumped, and turned from the shallow marble sink where she was working her way through washing a pile of Robbie's cot sheets. The kitchen smelled dank and soapy. She was hot, untidy and had managed to soak the front of her light summer dress in suds. One of the shoes she had kicked off lay under the table, the other had landed near the kitchen door.

Smiling, Michel bent to pick it up.

'I—good morning.' Poppy tried to push her hair from her eyes and only managed to smear her face with soapy water. She squeezed her eyes shut for a moment against the sting of it. 'Blast!'

Michel reached for a small towel that hung by the sink and handed it to her.

'Thank you.' She buried her face in it for an unnecessarily long time, trying to regain her composure. 'Blast it!' she repeated to herself, silently, 'Oh, *blast* it!' And it was not her sore eye that she cursed so vehemently. Ever since her first meeting with this young man a couple of days before she had been at first surprised, then a little irritated and finally downright embarrassed at how absurdly often she had found herself thinking about him. Laying no claim to sophistication, even she knew that

163

there was more to a man than a pleasant smile, an attractive voice and a way of looking at you as if you were the only person in the room. But no matter how she castigated and mocked herself, she could not deny how much she had looked forward to seeing him again as, surely under the circumstances, she must. And now look! Red-faced, bare-legged, soaking wet! 'Oh, blast!' she muttered again, aloud, the words still muffled by the towel.

'You've hurt yourself?' His voice was concerned.

She forced herself to come out from her hiding-place. 'No, just got soap in my eye, that's all. It does sting so, doesn't it?'

He smiled his wide, friendly smile and, helpless, she smiled back.

'I came out for a walk,' he said after a moment. 'Eloise said it would be all right for me to walk up to the tower. I was passing the door—' He shrugged, the movement so eloquently Gallic that despite her mortification Poppy almost laughed aloud. 'I thought just to say hello, but I see you are busy—perhaps another time?' He half-turned to the door.

'No—' Even to Poppy's own ears the word came out with a positively embarrassing haste. The colour in her already fiery cheeks deepened. She gave up all hope of dignity and rubbed her wet hands on her skirt. 'There's no need to go—I was just about to put the kettle

164

on. Won't you stop for a cup of tea?'

He hesitated, glancing at the washing that sprawled in a sloppy, dripping heap upon the draining-board, waiting to be rinsed.

'Oh, don't worry about that!' She made a dismissive gesture. 'I was beginning to wish I'd never started the beastly job anyway. There's the rest of the day not touched. It can wait.'

'Well, if you really don't mind?'

'I'm positively grateful.'

He laughed. 'Then I'd be delighted.'

'Good. I'll tell you what—why not sit outside, out of this horrible smell? I'll bring the tea out in two minutes.' She hesitated. 'Is tea really all right? You wouldn't prefer something else?'

'Tea will be absolutely fine.' He was gravely courteous, but there was an amused gleam in his eyes. She turned quickly to the kettle. If her cheeks got any warmer they might well burst into flame.

A few minutes later she joined him outside at the shaded table, with a tray of tea and a plate of custard creams. At the sight of it he could not resist laughter. 'We might be in the drawing-room of an English country house!'

She grinned and reached for the teapot, glancing at him interestedly. 'Your English is incredibly good.' She wrinkled her nose a little. 'You should hear my French. Or, rather you shouldn't.'

He laughed again. 'There's no surprise in

that. I've lived in England for half of my life.'

'Do you like it?'

He smiled at the frank question. 'Very much. I think of it as home.' There was the shrug again. 'Insofar as I think of anywhere as my home.'

Poppy leaned her elbows on the table and her chin upon her cupped hands, head cocked intently. 'What a strange—what a sad—thing to say. I'm sorry, I'm afraid you'll think me incredibly nosy, and I don't mean to pry, truly I don't—but please, do tell me why you should feel like that?'

*   *   *

The tea had long cooled and they were still absorbedly talking an hour or so later when the sound of footsteps on the gravel distracted them. A moment later the sturdy figure of Eloise's son appeared around the corner of the house, dressed in open-necked shirt and shorts, a leather football under his arm. He stopped, a little hesitant, when he saw them.

'Peter.' His uncle held out a hand to him. 'What are you doing here?'

'I came up to find the little boy.' The child smiled diffidently at Poppy. 'I thought he might like to play.'

'He's gone for a walk with his mother. I'm sure they'll be back soon.' Poppy picked up the plate and offered it. 'Would you like a biscuit?'

166

'Yes, please.' He chose one carefully. 'Thank you.'

Poppy patted a chair encouragingly. 'Come and sit down while you wait.'

The boy glanced at his uncle, who nodded, smiling.

'Are you enjoying your holiday?'

'Very much, thank you.' He was softly spoken, gravely polite. 'Do you think Robbie would like to play football with me? I know he's littler than me, but I'd be very careful.'

'I'm sure he would.' Her voice was warm. 'The poor little lad doesn't have any proper playmates. It'll make a lovely change for him to have someone a bit closer to his own age to play with.'

'I'll take care of him.'

She smiled at the earnest words. 'I'm sure you will. Ah—here they are.'

The small figure that had scampered, laughing, around the corner flung himself breathless into Poppy's lap. 'Hide from Mummy! Hide from Mummy!'

It was an oft-played game. 'Quick. Under the table.' Poppy spread her skirts.

Robbie scrambled under the table. 'Tuck your leg in, soppy,' Poppy said, and the child giggled delightedly.

A moment later Isobel appeared and stood looking in mock concern about her. 'Has anyone seen Robbie? I can't find him anywhere. Hello, Michel. How nice to see you.

167

And Peter—have you seen little Robbie?'

Solemnly they all shook their heads. From beneath the table came another stifled giggle.

Isobel sat down heavily, carefully avoiding putting her feet under the table. 'Well, I can't go looking for him just now. He's quite exhausted me, the little tinker. It's a shame he isn't here—he could have had this last biscuit. Oh, well. Perhaps I'd better eat it for him.'

'Boo!' The table rocked precariously as Robbie scrambled from beneath it. 'Robbie's here! Robbie's here!'

Isobel stopped with the biscuit half-way to her mouth. 'Where on earth did you pop out from?'

'I hided,' the child said proudly.

Smiling, Isobel reached for him and pulled him to her, handing him the biscuit, laying her cheek on the fair curly head. Robbie's bright eyes, however, had found the football that Peter held in his lap. He wriggled free, stood looking hopefully, if a little shyly, from the ball to the older boy's face.

'Would you like to play?' Peter asked, a straightforward question with no touch of condescension.

The smaller child hesitated for a moment, then nodded warily.

'Come on, then. Let's go out into the field.' Peter held out his hand. 'There's more room there. We don't want to break any windows, do we?'

Robbie beamed suddenly, the thought clearly intriguing him. 'Yes,' he said.

In the laughter that followed, the older boy took the younger's hand. 'We'll only be half an hour or so,' he said politely to Isobel. 'I won't tire him out.'

'I wish you would.' Isobel's words were heartfelt and provoked more laughter. As she watched the two children walk away, she turned to Michel. 'What a charming child.'

'Yes. He is.' He shrugged. 'A little old-fashioned, perhaps. A little too serious for his age. He's an extraordinarily sensitive child. One has to handle him carefully. His feelings run very deep for one so young; he's very easily hurt.'

'I think he's lovely.' Poppy looked at her sister. 'Would you like me to make fresh tea?'

Isobel shook her head. 'I don't feel like tea. I think perhaps I'll have a glass of milk and lie down for a while.'

Michel stood up, looked down at Poppy. 'Do you feel like a walk? Would you care to show me the way to this tower that I have heard so much about?'

Poppy hesitated, glanced towards the kitchen door. 'The washing—' she said lamely.

Isobel looked from one to the other, dark-ringed eyes gleaming in sudden, amused interest. 'Don't be silly, Poppy. You sound like Cinderella! The washing can wait. Off you go.' She hauled herself up from the chair, and sent her sister a sly glance before turning away, 'Just make sure you're back before midnight. I'm sure Michel is much too sensible to want to go through all that glass slipper nonsense!' As she looked back before she went indoors she had the unexpected satisfaction of seeing her normally down-to-earth sister blush every bit as brightly as her namesake.

*   *   *

'Please, Eloise.' The soft-voiced plea echoed dully in the warm shadows of the bedroom; the bulky figure on the bed moved restlessly. 'Please,' she said again.

The long-boned, elegant woman who stood silhouetted by the window did not turn. 'Where is everyone?' Eloise asked in casual curiosity, as if the words had not been spoken. Smoke wreathed to the ceiling.

'Peter's playing football with Robbie in the field beside the house—didn't you see them? Kit's working, I think. And Poppy and Michel have gone for a walk. Eloise—'

This time Eloise did turn. 'Have they indeed?' Her voice was musing, amused.

'Eloise!'

The other woman reached out to an ashtray on the windowsill and, with elaborate care, extinguished her cigarette. Then at the foot of the bed, she stood looking down at Isobel. The younger woman's hair was tangled and dark

170

with sweat, her face drawn.

There was a long silence. Then, with no word, Eloise very slowly undid the large buckle on her shoulder-bag and felt inside it. Bright blue eyes watched her feverishly. The narrow hand stopped for a moment. In apparent doubt, the sleek head shook slightly. 'I don't know if—'

'*Please!*' The single word was the embodiment of desperation.

Eloise shrugged, extracted a small phial from the bag. 'Isobel, my dear, I did warn you from the first—'

'I know. I know!' Isobel's eyes were fixed on the phial. 'But please—for now—I need it! Eloise, you don't know how I feel without it! It helps me so. I'll give it up. I promise you. After the baby. But for now—'

Eloise took a long, spuriously sorrowful, breath. A gleam of light caught the pale, translucent eyes. She held out the phial.

Isobel took it in a trembling hand, clasped it to her breast, her eyes closed.

'Try not to use it quite so quickly this time,' Eloise said, gently but not kindly.

The eyes didn't open. 'I will. I promise,' Isobel said.

Eloise smiled.

The house was dark, shuttered against the sun. Eloise stopped at the top of the steps that ran down to the kitchens to light another cigarette. She was still smiling. Lightly she ran

171

down the steps, through the smaller kitchen and into the suffocating warmth of the large one.

'What are you trying to do, Eloise?' The quiet voice arrested her movements as suddenly as if a switch had been thrown. 'Destroy her? Destroy us? Destroy me?'

The silence that followed the words was profound. Outside, the cicadas rasped, and a dog barked sharply. Kit was sitting at the table. He learned back in his chair, tilting his head to look at her. For a long moment she stood, perfectly still and poised, watching him. 'It helps her,' she said.

'No, it bloody well doesn't!' The chair-legs scraped as he came to his feet, and his long-fingered hand smacked the table. 'You know damned well it doesn't!'

She was completely unmoved. Her smile was pleasant. 'Then stop her.'

He sat down again, dropped his head into his hands. 'What the hell is it that you want, Eloise?'

He felt her move closer to him, felt the soft touch of her hand on his hair, smelled the distinctive, musky perfume of her. 'Nothing you can give me, Kit,' she said softly. 'What I want I must take. In my own good time. When I decide how to take it.' Her quiet footsteps crossed the kitchen floor and receded into the afternoon's silence.

Kit did not lift his head.

'Umberto is taking us to the city tomorrow.' Michel swiped with a stout stick at some brambles that had encroached upon the path ahead, held them aside for Poppy to pass. 'Peter and me, that is. I wondered—would you like to come with us?'

'Oh, I'd love to! I haven't been yet. I only saw it from a distance on the day I arrived. Kit did say he'd take me soon, but he's been very busy, and I don't think he's happy about leaving Isobel on her own—I didn't like to ask.'

'We're leaving at nine. Can you get down to the village by then? Or would you rather we came to pick you up?'

'No, of course not. I can meet you at Umberto's at nine. What an absolutely lovely idea. Thank you.' Poppy all but skipped along the path behind him. The sun-dappled woodland was very still. They had entered a grassy clearing that was carpeted with wild flowers. Poppy made a small, delighted sound and stilled, eyes bright with pleasure at the sight. Michel, turning to glance at her, stopped; and for a suspended, intimate moment their eyes held, warm and steady. Then the beguiling smile that had been the first thing she had noticed about him lit his face and he held out his hand. With no word she took it, and still enveloped in the sunlit,

173

enchanted silence of the woodland they strolled together through the flowers, hand in hand and content, for all the world as if they had known each other for ever.

That night, unexpectedly, there was a storm, the thunder rolling from hillside to hillside, great sheets of lightning flickering and crashing over a world drowned by torrential rain. Poppy watched from her window, enthralled. Unlike Isobel, who had been touchy and restless all evening as the thunderheads had built, she had always liked storms, enjoying their drama and the sense of power unleashed. She looked out into the drenched darkness that every now and again was lit brighter than day by the lightning, and hugged to herself the small secrets of her afternoon. She could still feel Michel's firm, large-boned hand in hers, still see the warmth in his eyes as he looked at her, still feel the briefest touch of his lips on her cheek as he had left her at the kitchen door, reminding her—as if she had needed reminding!—of their arrangement for the following day. Thunder crashed directly overhead and she jumped a little, blinking at the fierce streak of lightning that followed. Trees stood stark and black for a moment in the glare and the tower was silhouetted against a threatening sky.

In the house behind her she heard Robbie call out plaintively, but before she could move, Kit's voice answered, and a door opened and closed. Poppy went back to her reverie. Tomorrow, at last, she would see Siena—and, better, would see it with Michel. Although this was his first visit to the city, too, he appeared to have made a real study of the place and knew far more of its character and traditions than Poppy had managed to glean. She had at first been a little worried that Kit might have taken affront at her agreeing to go with Michel and Peter instead of waiting until he had time to take her himself, but on the contrary he had been enthusiastic about the idea—even, she suspected, a little relieved.

'What a splendid idea. You'll be quite safe with Umberto and Michel. I'll look you out a map later on, mark some interesting places for you to visit.'

'Oh, for heaven's sake, Kit!' Isobel had been irritable. 'I'm quite sure that Michel's perfectly capable of finding his own way around, and Umberto knows the place like the back of his hand. He was born here, for God's sake!' Even in her own happy preoccupations Poppy could not help noticing a certain tension between the two of them; indeed when she had first returned to the house she had wondered if they had quarrelled, so odd was the atmosphere. For once, however, she had had overriding concerns of her own to think about, and had not pursued the question, even when, as the first ominous rolls of thunder had begun Kit had gone across to the studio to make sure all was secure against the weather, leaving her alone for a few moments with her sister.

Isobel had sat, great shadowed eyes on the untouched plate of food that lay before her, her silence so obviously unhappy that even Poppy's bright spirits were a little blighted.

'You really ought to try to eat something,' she had said gently.

With an effort the long lashes had lifted and the blue eyes had met hers. In the shadows of the storm-darkened kitchen the pupils had been huge, the gaze unfocused. 'I can't,' Isobel had said, and flinched as lightning suddenly streaked in the sky. 'I can't. Oh, God, I hate storms. I really hate them.'

Now, with the elements raging apparently directly overhead, Poppy found herself wondering a little guiltily if she should not check that Kit, in very properly reassuring his son, had not left Isobel alone and frightened. On impulse she pulled on her dark silk dressing-gown, tugging the belt tight about her waist, and reached for the small lamp that burned steadily beside the bed.

As she passed Robbie's room, in a momentary lull in the pyrotechnics outside she could hear the reassuring murmur of Kit's voice, mingled with the light voice of the child. Kit was, then, with the little boy; just as she thought it, the thunder crashed again, so violently that she fancied she could feel it through the fabric of the house.

She tapped on Isobel's door, which stood a little ajar. 'Isobel? Are you all right?' Both sounds were completely lost in the noise of the storm. Rain lashed at the windows in torrents, as if intent upon drowning the world. Poppy pushed the door open wider. A lamp burned upon the table. Isobel stood next to it, a glass to her lips, the bulk of her distorted body silhouetted against the light. Poppy stepped into the room. 'Isobel?'

With a small shriek Isobel turned, and the glass slipped from her fingers, crashing on the marble top of the wash-stand, splintering to shards. Isobel stood trembling, hands cupped about her face, staring at her sister in fright and in dawning anger.

'Oh, Isobel, I'm so sorry! I didn't mean to startle you like that.' Instinctively Poppy stepped towards her sister.

'Look what you've done! *Look what you've done!*' Isobel stared down at the broken glass. 'No!' she added quickly, sensing her sister's movement. 'Stay where you are. There's glass everywhere. You'll cut your feet.' In clumsy haste she reached for the basin that stood on the wash-stand and began to sweep the shards of glass that still lay upon the marble into it.

'Isobel, please—let me help.' Poppy picked her way carefully across the floor and bent to pick up the bottom of the broken glass that had rolled beneath the bed. As she did so, she was aware, almost without noticing it, of a very

177

faint, sickly-sweet smell hanging on the air.

'*No!*' Her sister turned upon her as she straightened. 'Poppy, just—' she paused, obviously fighting for composure, physically wincing as thunder crashed again, '—just go back to bed. I'm all right. It wasn't your fault. It was—' another infinitesimal pause '—it was only a glass of water. It's just a nuisance to have broken it, that's all.' She held out her hand for the shard that Poppy held.

'Isobel? Is something wrong?' Kit had appeared at the door, lamp in hand. 'What's happened?'

'Nothing. I was drinking a glass of water. Poppy startled me, and I dropped it. That's all.'

'I'm terribly sorry—' Poppy began.

Her sister shook her head tiredly, all anger gone. 'Don't be silly. It wasn't your fault. Go back to bed, Poppy. Kit will help me.'

Poppy picked her way to the door. As she passed Kit he smiled reassuringly. 'Good night. Sleep tight.'

She dropped a quick kiss on his cheek. 'Good night.'

Back in her room she walked once more to the long window, stood for a moment looking out into the night. The storm was receding a little, the lightning less fierce and less frequent, and the rain had eased. Tomorrow would be fine, she was certain. Tomorrow! Suddenly, hugging herself, she took a couple of dancing steps towards the bed, dropping her dressing-gown on the floor as she went—tomorrow would be the best tomorrow ever, no matter what the weather did. 'So there!' she said aloud, and jumped on to the huge old bed, bouncing a little, covering her mouth with her hand to stifle childish laughter; and then stopped, surprised, sniffing at her fingers. There it was again: the faint, almost nauseous, sweetness she had smelled in Isobel's bedroom. And this time a memory stirred, distant and elusive. She had smelled something very like this before. Puzzled, she sniffed again, wrinkling her nose, but the memory would not be recaptured. Shrugging, she reached out to turn off the lamp.

Moments later she was asleep, as the storm growled its way into the distance and the softer rain of its passing pattered through the branches of the trees, a lullaby in the darkness.

CHAPTER NINE

'I like Kit.' Peter braced his small, sturdy figure against the bouncing of the *calesse*, swinging his legs to the regular rhythm of the pony's step. 'He's really nice. And he knows some smashing things.' The boy was dressed immaculately in white shirt and khaki shorts, a floppy sunhat shading his face and neck.

Michel smiled, amused. 'What sorts of things?'

'He knows about birds, and animals. And he knows how Michelangelo painted that ceiling in Rome. Did you know that wasn't his real name? His *real* name was—' the child paused for a moment, concentrating '—was Michelagniolo di something or other Buonarroti and he didn't really want to be a painter at all. He just wanted to be a sculptor. Kit told me.'

'It must be true, then.' Michel was teasing.

Bright, serious eyes met his. 'Oh, yes. I'm sure it is.'

'Perhaps I could persuade Kit to come back to school with us? It sounds as if he has a talent for teaching that some of us haven't acquired.'

Still Peter refused to be drawn by his uncle's laughter. 'Oh, no. He doesn't *teach*. That's boring.'

'Thank you.' The words were dry. Poppy chuckled.

'He *talks* to you. Explains things. He makes things interesting.'

'That's true, actually.' Poppy nodded. 'I remember it myself. When I was a child—just about your age, in fact—I adored him.'

The clear, hazel eyes widened. 'I didn't know you knew him when you were a little girl?'

'Oh, yes. It was through me he met Isobel,

and they ran away together to get married. It was all very romantic.' She smiled a little. 'Quite like something you might see at the cinema, in fact.'

Michel had turned his head and was watching her interestedly. 'I didn't realise that, either. How did that come about?'

Poppy firmly refused to allow herself to be distracted by the warmth in the eyes that held hers so steadily. 'I met him by a river one day. It was towards the end of the war. We became friends. As Peter just pointed out, he's extraordinarily good with children. Then Isobel met him and persuaded Papa to let him paint our portrait—Isobel's and mine—and while he was painting it they fell in love with each other. Papa was furious. They ran away before the picture was ever finished. Funnily enough, I mentioned it to Kit the other day. He said he still has some of the sketches. He's going to find them for me. It'll be very strange, I think, seeing myself at ten years old.'

Peter cocked his head. 'That's interesting. When he finds them, could I see them, too, please? I'd really like to.'

Poppy could not help smiling at the grave politeness of the question. 'Of course. I'll ask him when we get back, if you'd like.'

'As a matter of fact I'd rather like to see them myself.' Michel's own smile, that so transformed his face, was quick. 'If you don't mind, that is?'

181

'Of course not.'

'Kit was in the war,' Peter said. 'Like my father.'

'Yes, he was. He was wounded. That's how I met him. He'd come to England to recuperate.'

'I didn't know that. He didn't tell me. He told me about going up in a balloon, though, to sketch the enemy lines. And how one of the balloons broke loose and drifted absolutely *miles*—though luckily the wind was in the right direction, or he'd have been captured by the Germans.'

The child chattered on. Poppy leaned back in her seat, enchanted by the moment. As she had thought it would, the storm had cleared the air and the morning sparkled about them. The sun, not yet high, was pleasantly warm and a gentle breeze stirred the leaves of the woodland. The overnight rain had freshened everything and on every rocky outcrop and beneath every gnarled tree's bole the lichens and wild flowers had bloomed anew. The smell of woodsmoke hung in the air, and high above them swallows and swifts swooped in a crystal clear sky not yet overburnished by the heat of the day. They were on the last slope of the hills and approaching the valley that Poppy could see from her window, with its terraces and low stone walls, its olive and lemon groves, its huddled clusters of houses and its huge, dominating church.

They passed an old man, riding side-saddle on a plodding donkey, the animal's hooves splashing in the occasional puddles that reflected the bright sky. Umberto returned his civil greeting, and the man answered Poppy's smile with a courteous inclination of his head. As Umberto swung the *calesse* on to the wider, flatter track that followed the valley, a house came into sight surrounded by paddocks in which grazed several milk-white horses, sturdy, graceful beasts with flowing manes and tails that glinted silver in the sun. As the trap passed, one of them trotted to the rail, neck arched, head tossing, whinnying gently. Poppy smiled delightedly, turning in her seat to watch as they passed.

Peter was still talking. 'Kit said that long ago the people in the towns around here used to live in towers. The higher the tower, the more important you were. So the towers got higher and higher, and they built these walkways between them, and the families had vendettas and used to fight each other—'

Suddenly sensing Michel's eyes upon her, Poppy turned her head to look at him. He was watching her, the pale, clever eyes for once unsmiling, closely studying her face. His hand, lying relaxed upon the worn seat was very close to hers. After a long moment he smiled, and, very gently, his fingers closed upon hers.

'—so they made them pull them down. Though there are still a few left, Kit says.

There's a place called San Gimignano not far from here. Kit's been there. He says it looks like a trial run for New York.'

How, Poppy found herself wondering, bemusedly, could the simple touch of a hand be so physically exciting? Just a few days before she had not known of this man's existence. Now it seemed that he had bewitched her.

Peter curled his legs under him and turned to face the way they were travelling, bouncing a little on the leather seat. 'I think Robbie's really lucky,' he said, 'to have a smashing dad like Kit.'

*   *   *

The city of Siena, unique in the world, stood within her encircling walls, as she had for six centuries, a medieval masterpiece that lived and breathed. Within those great walls her people, descendants of those who had established her, defended her and often died for her, had fiercely and jealously preserved her ancient rites and traditions, not as a museum preserves, nor as an insect may be preserved in amber, but in vivid and colourful life. At every turn of the steep and narrow streets, canyon-like in the Chianti sunshine, there was evidence of her singular history. A great colourful banner streaming from a rooftop or a balcony. A strangely embellished fountain, an emblem upon a wall. A panther, a she-wolf, a unicorn. The sound of a trumpet or a drum, echoing, in practice for the pageants to come. The sight of a small boy, tutored by his father or an older brother, learning the fanciful intricacies of handling a *Contrada*'s silken flag. The first Palio of the year was ten days off, and the city was in a fever.

As Umberto ushered them through the warren of narrow alleys, fountained squares, busy, cobbled lanes and flights of steps that led to the centre of the city, Poppy thought it was much like being in a maze—a hilltop maze constructed of more churches than she could ever have conceived gracing a single city, of palaces, of tall, shuttered houses, of abbeys and nunneries and sudden, unexpected tree-hung rock-faces brooding with pigeons. They toiled up a steep hill, turned in to a wider shop-lined thoroughfare that Umberto told them was the Via del Città, one of the main thoroughfares. And still she did not realise where she was until the little man led them down a steep flight of steps between two towering buildings, and there it was: Il Campo. The heart of the city. The huge, paved, almost circular arena in which so much of the city's turbulent history had been made; and in which, twice a year, the honour of the seventeen *Contrade* was tested in a horse race that was not a horse race.

'It's glorious,' she said.

Michel spoke with her. *'C'est magnifique.'* She smiled. She had never heard him resort to his native French before, but had to admit that the words were truly fitting. Peter, for a change, said nothing, but his eyes widened as he looked about him. They had entered the Piazza opposite a massively elegant building of brick and stone that dwarfed the by no means small buildings that surrounded it. Its beautifully proportioned façade was punctuated by rows of tall mullioned windows, the crenellations of its roof standing stark against the bright sky. But what caught and drew the eye was the slender column of the tower, brick-built and topped by an ornate stone bell-chamber. It was, Poppy estimated, perhaps three hundred feet high and dominated the great Piazza that it overlooked, yet, like the building itself, so perfectly proportioned was it that the overall effect was of sheer grace, a kind of perpendicular harmony that took the breath away.

Umberto watched their reaction with satisfaction. 'Il Palazzo Pubblico,' he said, pointing at the great building.

'Can we go in it?' Poppy asked. And 'Can we go up the tower?' Peter asked in all but the same breath.

Laughing, Michel spoke a few words to Umberto in Italian. The little man nodded emphatically. *'Si, si—'* He spoke volubly for a moment, then turned and pointed to another

186

of the narrow entrances to the square, at the far end from where they stood. Michel listened, nodding, to what, judging from the expressive hand movements, were a set of directions. He reached into his pocket and produced the map Kit had given them. The man's short, stubby finger traced a route. While they consulted, Poppy glanced with eager interest around the *Campo*. Like the palace, most of the buildings, four and five storeys high, were of brick, and all of them that brownish terracotta colour to which the city had lent her name. Even the most part of the great open space that the buildings encircled, which sloped gently down towards the palace, was paved with bricks, the whole divided, fan-like, into nine separate areas by the different herringbone patterns in which the bricks were laid. Not far from where they stood, water splashed from the walls of a stone pool. Shops and cafés, sheltered by awnings of the same colour as the buildings, lined the square. The whole place bustled with life, truly, obviously, the very centre of the city. She turned. Umberto was lifting a hand in salute. *'Arrivederci, Signorina Poppy. A più tardi.'*

She smiled her goodbye, watched as the little man ran swiftly down the last of the steps to the square and pushed briskly off through the crowds.

'Right.' Michel waved the map. 'We're to meet Umberto at his cousin's house at four o'clock. That gives us five and a half hours. What do we do first?'

Peter was standing, head tilted back, looking up, wide eyed, at the great balustraded bell-chamber of the tower. 'What I'd like best,' he said, 'is to go up there.'

Michel turned to look at Poppy, eyebrows raised, amusement gleaming in his face.

Poppy shook her head very firmly. 'I'm sorry to have to tell you this, young man, but I'm afraid "going up there" is probably the very last of my priorities.'

Peter's face dropped a little. Michel laughed. 'I'll tell you what we'll do. Let's find the Duomo first. It's apparently one of the most beautiful cathedrals in Italy, and that's saying something. We can take our time there, and then come back here for lunch. Then—' he laid his arm across his nephew's shoulders in an affectionate gesture '—Poppy can pay a nice low-level visit to the Palazzo Pubblico and you and I can go up the tower. How's that?'

'Great.'

'You're both mad,' Poppy said amicably.

*　　　*　　　*

The cathedral, just a short walk from the square, was indeed a spectacular and beautiful building. Constructed in black and white marble, its façade with its three magnificent arched doorways was as florid as a wedding cake. The same black and white marble had been used in the huge, columned interior— 'It's a bit like being inside a zebra, isn't it?' Poppy asked, irreverently—and the inlaid marble floor was a marvel in itself. They wandered around in silence, overawed by the sheer opulent magnificence of the place. Altars gleamed with gold and with silver, statues decked in precious stones stared, sightless, down the long centuries of their lovely but lifeless existence. The lamps of the sanctuary flickered, and soft light fell through beautiful stained glass that had defied its own fragility to last through more than six hundred turbulent years. Above them the roof, as studded with stars as the midnight sky, soared in vaulted splendour. They blinked, all but blinded as they came out into the brilliant sunlight of midday. Poppy stepped back, shading her eyes to look up at the dozens of statues that adorned the façade.

'You're very quiet.' Michel was beside her.

She sucked her lip thoughtfully. 'I noticed in Florence. With Kit. These places make me feel—' she hesitated, searching for the word '—odd.'

'In what way?'

'Oh, I don't know. On the one hand the excesses of it all, all that money spent on a place of worship that could have been used to alleviate misery. It might be cynical, but it's hard not to wonder exactly to whose glory this place was really raised. And yet—one can't help but be moved by the kind of dedication that embarks on such a task, knowing it will take hundreds of years—several generations—to complete. Or by the genius of the artists who brought it to completion. Or, more than anything, I suppose, by the knowledge of the hundreds of thousands of people who have worshipped there, true believers—' she broke the solemn mood with a quick, wry flash of a smile '—at least I suppose some of them must be. If these places illustrate anything, to me it's the triumph of faith over common sense. And as you've probably gathered by now I tend, to a fault, to err on the side of common sense.'

In a gesture so natural that even Poppy herself hardly noticed it he drew her hand within his crooked arm. They stood for a moment in silence, studying the building. 'It should have been even bigger, did you know?' Michel asked.

She shook her head.

He pointed. 'Over there. You see? The great arches across the street? They were supposed to be the façade to a new aisle. The original building—this—' he gestured, encompassing the Duomo with a sweep of his arm '—was to be simply the core of the church. Those arches are all that is left of a construction that would have at least doubled the size of the cathedral.'

'What happened?' Peter had joined them.

'Mostly it was the Black Death, in the fourteenth century. So many people died, there weren't enough craftsmen, enough stonemasons, enough workmen so the project had to be abandoned. It happened all over Europe.'

'Decimation,' Peter said with some relish. 'The population was—' he paused, and pronounced the word with a child's dramatic impact, '*decimated*! Kit told me all about that the other day, when we were talking about the Romans. If a legion was cowardly, or mutinied, they executed every tenth man, just like that, whether they had done anything wrong or not. Not very fair, really.'

'I'll bet it worked, though,' Poppy said with a grin. 'So, what's next?'

Michel pointed. 'The building over there, next to the arches, is the cathedral museum. Kit said we shouldn't miss it. Apparently it's a real treasure house.'

It was about ten minutes later that Peter disappeared. He wandered off whilst Poppy and Michel were looking at a particularly beautiful collection of marble statuary, and apparently simply vanished.

'Where can the little monkey have gone?' Poppy was not greatly concerned; she was certain the boy would not go far without them.

'He was interested in the Treasure Room. It's up those stairs, I think. Perhaps he's gone ahead.' Michel led the way to the stairs. But

191

the Treasure Room with its staggering collection of silver and gold, of jewelled vestments and reliquaries was empty; there was no sign of Peter. At Poppy's prompting, Michel asked the custodian of the room if he had seen the child. The man shrugged, shook his head. No child had come in to the room alone; he would certainly remember if he had.

Puzzled, they retraced their steps to where they had first noticed he was missing. 'Do you think he got bored and went outside to wait for us?' Poppy asked, a little uncertainly.

Michel shook his head a little, frowning. 'He shouldn't have done. Not without telling us. It's not like him to be naughty.'

'Well, there isn't a lot of point in both of us standing around here. I'll tell you what—you stay here in case he comes back. I'll slip downstairs and see if he's waiting outside.' She wagged an admonishing finger at him. 'And don't move! I don't want to lose you, too!'

She moved swiftly from room to room and downstairs to the door. There was no sign of Peter. Truly concerned now and fighting the urge to shriek his name at the top of her voice, she made her way back, slowly this time, searching each room thoroughly. There were a thousand places for a mischievous child to hide—behind cabinets, statues, great slabs of carved marble—she'd give him what for when she found him, that was certain.

The small door, when she found it, was

standing slightly ajar, above it a pointing finger and the word *Panorama*. She put her head around it. Steep stone steps led up through the thickness of the wall. She felt a warm blast of air on her face. 'Peter?' she called tentatively, 'Peter, are you up there?'

No reply.

The stairs were so narrow that she could touch each wall as she climbed. Sunlight gleamed above her, reflecting around a curve in the wall. She stopped for a moment, called again. 'Peter?' She heard the tremor in her voice; her heart thumped against her ribcage. And still there was no reply. She desperately did not want to go on; even here, safe within the stone, she could sense the height. Just a few more steps—if he were not around the corner she would go back to find Michel. She laboured on upwards, turned the corner into the sunshine and a wind in her face.

She froze. She had stepped on to some sort of parapet. Around and below her stretched the ancient tiled roofs of Siena. To her right loomed the great black and white structure of the cathedral; the dome at eye level, the huge bell-tower soaring to the sky, the movement of white, fluffy cloud behind it making it look for all the world as if the massive thing were about to crash to the ground. Vertigo clenched in her stomach and spun in her head. Trembling, she clutched at the wall; she felt as if the solid stone upon which she stood was shifting beneath her feet.

But that was not the worst of it; the spot where she stood was reasonably sheltered, and surrounded by sturdy walls of almost shoulder height. Ahead of her, however, stretched a long, narrow walkway that spanned the square far below and the parapet that edged it was very much lower; only waist height to the child who stood in the centre of it staring, white-faced and fascinated, down to where people moved, ant-like across the marble paving. She knew now where she was; on the lower of the two huge arches that Michel had pointed out when they had left the cathedral; the arches that had originally been intended as the façade to a great new cathedral that had never been built. A gusty wind blew, hot and airless. To her horror, Peter swayed a little, still staring down. Very carefully, without taking her eyes from the child, she dropped to her knees.

'Peter! Peter?' She willed the tremor from her voice, kept it very low, afraid of startling him. 'Peter, darling, please come away from there. I don't think it can be very safe.'

At first he did not move. Then slowly he lifted his head to look at her, blinking as if waking from sleep. His eyes were huge and very bright in his pale face.

She held out a hand encouragingly. 'Why don't you crawl, darling? It'll be easier, I think.' She clenched her mind against the knowledge of the abyss beneath him, against

194

the spiralling, physical sickness that rose in her at the thought of it. Her skin, slick with sweat, was as cold as the stone upon which she knelt.

He shook his head. 'It's all right. Truly it is. I'm not afraid.' His voice was high and clear, yet there was a breathy edge to it that terrified her.

'Please, Peter.' She trod the fine line between supplication and authority very carefully. 'It's very naughty of you, you know. We've been looking everywhere for you. Poor Michel is terribly worried.'

'Oh, I'm sorry.' For the first time his eyes truly focused upon her. He took a step forward. 'I really am sorry. I didn't think.' As he moved, there was another sharp gust of wind that caught at the wide brim of his sun-hat, lifting it from his head. To Poppy's horror he made a wild grab for it. Too late. It flew into the air and spun into the space beneath them. For a moment he teetered, watching it, his balance gone. She heard him laugh, high and shrill.

'Peter!' She was shaking uncontrollably now. 'For God's sake *will you get down*!'

He hesitated for one more moment before, sobering, obediently he dropped to his knees.

'Now get back here. At once! You hear me?' Poppy's panic flared into anger. 'I told you— your uncle will be worried sick about you!'

'I'm coming.' Calmly he crawled towards her.

195

The moment he was close enough she reached out to catch hold of his shirt collar and hauled him into her arms, clutching him to her. He looked at her in real astonishment. 'I'm sorry. I really am. The door was open. And I wanted to see the panorama. I didn't mean to frighten you.'

'Whether you meant to or not, you managed it pretty well!' She still could not quite control her voice. 'Now for goodness' sake, come on. Poor Michel must think we've both been kidnapped or something.' She pulled herself up to stand on legs that shook like jelly. For a moment she could not trust herself to take a step. 'You go on down. I'll follow you.'

He turned to the door, hesitated. 'Poppy?' His voice was suddenly uncertain.

'Yes?'

'You won't tell Kit that I did something naughty, will you?'

She took a long breath, then shook her head. 'No, of course not. As long as you promise me—faithfully!—never to do such a thing again.'

His smile was beatific. The colour had come back into his cheeks. 'I promise.'

The rest of the day passed off with no more upsets. Peter, truly sorry for the trouble he had caused, behaved impeccably, and Poppy, with her feet once more thankfully and firmly upon the ground, could not continue to be cross with him for long. They met Umberto at his

196

cousin's at four, as arranged, and by half past were heading back out along the valley road to the Tenuta di Gordini. With the long day of sightseeing behind him, it was not long before Peter's head nodded on to Poppy's shoulder, and he slept. She eased him down more comfortably on to her lap, stroking the shining cap of russet hair gently, touching the smooth curve of his cheek with a curled finger. 'He's nothing like his mother, is he?'

Michel was sitting on the seat opposite, watching her. 'I've always supposed he looks like his father.'

'You didn't know him?'

He shook his head, his eyes on the sleeping child's face. 'No.'

Poppy's ever-lively curiosity was stirring. 'Has Eloise told you much about him?'

'Hardly anything. To be truthful I don't think she can bear to talk about him, even now.'

'She must have loved him very much.'

'Oh, yes. There's no doubt about that.'

Poppy touched the child's face again. 'It's strange. She doesn't strike me—' She stopped, her eyes flying suddenly to Michel's face and she flushed a little. 'Oh, I'm sorry, I don't mean to be rude, truly I don't.'

He smiled a little, finished her sentence for her. 'She doesn't strike you as being the kind of woman to love in that fashion?'

'Well—no. She doesn't.'

'Ah, but that is because you only know the Eloise of today. The Eloise of yesterday was very different.' He stretched his arms along the back of the seat, relaxing. The sky was reddening in the west, the dipping sun gleaming fitfully through streaky cloud. 'The Eloise that I knew as a child was full of love. Full of warmth. Full of sunshine. Full of laughter. Oh, I know you may find that difficult to believe, but it's true.'

'What happened?' Poppy asked bluntly, throwing, she realised, any pretence of tact to the wind.

Michel shrugged. 'The war. Losing the man she loved. Struggling to support a fatherless child. None of it has been easy.'

'No, I suppose not.' She looked down at the sleeping child again. 'Oh, by the way—I forgot to tell you—I promised Peter that we wouldn't tell Kit about the escapade at the cathedral. Is that all right?'

'Of course.'

'He can't bear the thought of Kit thinking him naughty.'

'A touch of hero-worship there, I think. He's of that age, of course. And he could do worse than Kit, I think.'

Poppy shifted a little, settling Peter more comfortably on her lap. He stirred, sighed, settled. 'It probably comes of not having a father of his own.'

'Only a boring uncle who teaches.' His smile

198

was wry.

She looked at him with suddenly pensive dark eyes. 'I can think of a lot of things you seem to me to be,' she said after a moment, very collectedly. 'But I must say that boring isn't one of them.'

The silence that followed was thoughtful, but by no means difficult.

'Perhaps I'll ask you for a list later,' he said at last, straight-faced. And their quick, shared laughter was quiet, so as not to disturb the boy.

*   *   *

It was later that evening that Poppy remembered her promise to ask Kit for the sketches he had done for the portrait ten years before.

'Good Lord, I'd quite forgotten about them,' Isobel said, trying to prevent Robbie from upending his supper dish on to the table. 'Robbie, do stop that and get on with your supper like a good boy. It's nearly time for bed.' She looked back at her sister. 'They're up in the back attic, I think. There's a trunk of Kit's bits and pieces up there that's followed us about from pillar to post for years. Now I stop to think about it, I'm sure they're in there. Why don't you go and have a look? I'd rather like to see them again myself.'

'Would Kit mind my rooting about in his things? Shouldn't we wait?'

199

'Oh, no, of course not. Why should he? Robbie, *will* you stop playing about!'

'Dog wants supper,' Robbie said, and this time the bowl well and truly went over, the contents spilling on to the table. With great concentration the child picked up a piece of meat and fed it to the knitted dog that was, as usual, tucked firmly under his arm.

Isobel sighed exasperatedly, and began to struggle to her feet.

'It's all right. I'll do it.' Poppy jumped up. 'What a naughty boy you are!' she said to Robbie, her tone so indulgent that the child, totally unchastened, beamed happily up at her. 'How do I get in to the attic?' she asked as she mopped up the mess.

'There are some stairs round the corner from Robbie's room. You'll have to take a lamp. There's all sorts of rubbish up there—centuries-worth of it, I should think. But the trunk's right near the door. You can't miss it. Oh, do go on. It would be fun to see them again.' There was a small note of wistfulness in Isobel's voice. 'It all seems so very long ago, now, doesn't it?'

*　　　*　　　*

The attic, as Isobel had said, was indeed cluttered with what looked like the cast-offs of several hundred years. Chests and boxes, furniture, carpets, children's toys, all shrouded

200

in cobwebs and dust. Just inside the door, however, stood a cheap-looking, battered trunk plastered with peeling labels that was obviously a more modern addition to the jumble. Poppy set her lamp beside it and threw back the lid. Inside were two or three rolls of stained canvas, a few old tubes of paint, squeezed almost flat, and a couple of ancient paintbrushes. She lifted them out and laid them on the floor. Underneath them was an untidy mass of paper and some cardboard folders, carelessly tied together with string. There were a lot of dog-eared sketch-books, several half-finished sketches, scribbled notes, what looked like a collection of old bills. Again, carefully, she gathered these together and then reached for the folders; but, as she picked them up, the string gave and before she could prevent it the things had slipped out of her arms, spilling some of their contents as they did so. Sketch-books, drawings and watercolour pictures slithered on to the dirty floor.

'Oh, damn it!'

She sat back on her heels, then leaned to gather them together, flicking through the folders as she did so; and to her delight almost the first thing she came across was the very thing for which she was looking—a folder containing several sketches of a radiantly pretty young woman and a small, solemn child with eyes as dark and round as pennies. She gazed at them, fascinated. For a moment the years between vanished; she could have been that child, playing by the river with Kit, watching with painful jealousy the expression on his face when he had first set eyes upon Isobel—

She tucked the sketches back in their folder and set it aside, then started to tidy the others and put them back into the trunk; as she did so, another couple slipped from the pile. She grabbed at them and, in doing so, only succeeded in scattering the contents of one of them. Tutting at herself she began to pick them up; and then, as she saw, suddenly, what she was holding, her movements stopped. She sat very still for a very long time, looking at the small drawing that she held. Then, slowly, she reached a hand for the others that lay beside her. Some were drawn in ink and some in pencil. All were on poor quality paper; some had faded badly, but others, protected by the folder, were quite clear. Some were dated; *10/1/18, 14/4/18, 10/6/18.* They were all of the same person: a young woman in her twenties, a girl of mischievous vitality with black hair thick and loose about her face, her high cheekbones and light slanted eyes giving her a look of exquisite, almost fey, beauty. The artist—and it could only have been Kit—had captured her every mood. What had Michel said that afternoon on the way back from the city? *The Eloise I knew as a child was full of love. Full of warmth. Full of sunshine. Full of laughter. The Eloise of yesterday.*

The implications of what she had found were unequivocal. And damning. She piled the folders back into the chest, keeping back both the one that she had come to find and the one that she wished that she had not. She went downstairs by way of her bedroom, and entered the kitchen with a jacket over her arm.

'You found them!' Isobel took the folder and sorted through the sketches. 'Oh, Lord—did I ever really look like that? And oh, look at you! You really did look like a little mouse! I love this one. I'm going to ask Kit to frame it for me. It would look lovely over there on the mantelpiece. Oh—' she straightened in surprise, looking at the jacket '—are you going out?'

Poppy nodded. 'It's such a lovely evening, I thought I'd get some air before the sun goes down. I shan't be long.' She turned and left her sister absorbed once more in the pictures.

Kit was sitting at one of the tables in his studio, framing a watercolour. He looked up as she came in. 'Poppy, hello. Is it dinner time already?'

She did not reply, but walked straight to the table, took something from beneath the jacket over her arm and laid it very carefully on the table before him. 'Kit,' she said after a moment into the shocked silence, 'isn't it time that you told at least someone the truth?'

203

CHAPTER TEN

You admit, then, that you did draw them?'

'Yes.'

'In 1918.' Her words were a statement rather than a question.

'Yes.'

Poppy, who, unable to remain still, had been prowling like a caged cat up and down the room, spun on him. 'Kit, that was ten years ago! So why—*why*?—this charade of not knowing one another? Why pretend? And why did she come here in the first place? Was she looking for you? It couldn't have been coincidence that she arrived here, in the middle of nowhere, surely?' She spread her hands upon the table, leaning upon them, watching him. Eyes and voice were passionate. 'Kit, what's going on?'

Kit, still sitting at the table with the sketch in front of him, dropped his face into his hands.

Poppy stepped towards him. *'Kit!'*

He was still for a long moment, then with an abrupt movement he flung away from her to the window, stood with his back to her, shoulders hunched and hands in pockets, looking out into a spectacular sunset that lit the sky above the hills as with the fires of retribution.

Poppy waited. She saw him take his cigarettes from his pocket, heard the sharp snap of his lighter.

At last he turned. 'All right.' His voice was very quiet. 'I do owe you an explanation.'

The austere line of her mouth did not soften. 'Actually—' her eyes were steady upon his '—I wouldn't say it was to me that you owed the explanation?' She emphasised the pronoun very slightly.

His sudden movement, the quick lift of his head, was fierce. 'Isobel? Poppy—you haven't shown Isobel these pictures?'

She shook her head. 'Don't be stupid, Kit. What on earth do you take me for? Of course I haven't.' She paused for a moment before adding, quite deliberately challenging, 'Yet.'

Kit walked to a cupboard. A moment later he was back at the table with a jug and two glasses. Poppy watched, expressionless and silent, as he poured the wine, dark and glittering in the bloodied light that flooded the room. He sat down, made a small gesture with his hand. She picked up the glass he had indicated. 'Please,' he said, 'won't you sit down?' He smiled, slightly and ruefully. 'It's awfully hard to talk to you while you're towering above me like that.'

She dropped into a chair. 'I've never towered above anyone in my life.' He had turned his face a little from her. The light gilded the thick, soft hair and the long sweep of his lashes, limned the austere lines of his profile in fire.

He tilted his head back, his eyes distant, drew on his cigarette. There was a long moment of silence. 'I was twenty years old when I first met Eloise,' he said at last. 'She was—is—four or five years older than I. It was the summer of 1917. In France.' Another silence. 'I loved her—was infatuated with her—from the very first moment I saw her. Before I had ever spoken to her. Before she had even looked at me or smiled at me. When she did, I was lost entirely. I was young, exhausted, disillusioned, afraid. She—She was a light in darkness. Beauty in the midst of almost unendurable ugliness. A shield of kindness and grace against the squalor of fear. Of death. Of cowardice.' The word was spoken so softly that it was almost inaudible. He turned his head to look at the silent girl; smiled with wry affection. 'Dear, practical little Poppy. I don't suppose you believe in love at first sight, even in the most extreme of circumstances?'

'I—' She shrugged a little, did not continue, for a moment unable to meet his eyes.

He did not appear to notice her unwonted discomfiture, but leaned forward, took her hand in both of his, willing her to look at him. 'Poppy, you must try to understand,' he said, fiercely intent. 'I don't want you to think badly of her. Or of me. But you have to understand what it was like. The war. The sheer insanity of it; a world turned upside down. The bloody shambles of mud and death. The knowledge that nothing was safe or certain any more; that each day, each hour, each moment might be the last.' He let go of her hand and steepled his fingers, resting his forehead on them for a moment, his eyes closed. When he spoke, his voice was bleak. 'Unless you have seen it, you have no idea what shreds of red-hot metal can do to flesh and blood. Unless you have heard it, you cannot conceive of the sounds a man makes as the mustard gas billows over him. Unless you have lived through it, you can't imagine what it is like to lie at night in a sodden hole not fit for a dog and hear the screams, the pleading, the agony of dying men strung upon the barbed wire of No Man's Land like linen on some devil's washing line—' He lifted his head, and she almost flinched from the look on his face. 'They turned the world into a lunatic asylum. And I? I drew it. I painted it. I pictured it for them.'

'You were doing a job,' said Poppy. 'And at least you weren't killing.'

His smile was bleaker than his voice. 'No. There were others to do that for me. You think I didn't know that, too?' He picked up his glass and swallowed the wine at a draught, reached again for the jug. 'Anyway, it's enough to say— and I'm sure you'll understand—that under such circumstances one doesn't always find oneself necessarily acting, or reacting, in a rational way. Emotions are heightened; there's little or no time to think, or judge.'

She smiled a little, thoughtfully. 'Are you sure that you can describe love as a rational emotion under any circumstances?'

His own fleeting smile acknowledged the gentle barb. He poured more wine. 'I met Eloise in a small town on the banks of the Marne. Not that a lot of the place was still standing by the summer of '17, but there was a small French military hospital where Eloise was nursing. She's beautiful now; she was beautiful then—but it wasn't simple beauty that made her what she was. Through all the horror—through all the hatred and the fear—she had somehow kept herself whole; God alone knows how. In the midst of that carnage she had not lost her love of life. Her belief in the fundamental humanity of man. In a disillusioned world she was a beacon. She brought laughter and warmth, I suppose you could call it a sense of joy, to everything she did.' He cocked his head, watching her. 'Hard to believe?'

Poppy sipped her wine pensively. 'As a matter of fact,' she said, 'Michel said much the same, if a tad less effusively, this afternoon.'

'It's exactly true what I said. I fell in love with her between one second and the next across a ward full of injured and dying men. There'd been an unexpected push. There was

208

huge influx of wounded. I'd been doing some drawings; I was co-opted to help. And—there she was.'

'The lady with the lamp?' Poppy suggested, a mite caustically, and then, catching his quick glance, made a small gesture of apology. 'I'm sorry.' Almost despite herself she found she was intrigued by this story of love and war. 'Go on.'

Kit got up and wandered back to the window again. The light was dulling, the embers of the sunset glowing in the sky. Shadows lengthened and the air was still. In the studio it was growing perceptibly darker; the man's slender figure stood sharply silhouetted, wreathed in smoke. For the first time and with some slight surprise Poppy realised that he still stood a little crookedly, favouring the injured leg. 'I pursued her with the single-mindedness of a man in search of salvation. I couldn't get her out of my mind, not for one minute, day or night. I would have done anything, gone anywhere, to be with her. Oh, I wasn't the only one, of course. The circumstances again; I don't think there could have been a man that passed through that hospital that wasn't at least a little in love with her. But I was quite, quite certain that no one could love her the way I did. And I was determined to prove it to her.'

'And—did you?'

'At the time I think I did, yes. She laughed,

and teased at first, as she did with everyone. She was friendly and she was kind. She flirted a little. But right from the start I had an advantage over the others.'

'What was that?'

He slanted a quick, faintly amused look over his shoulder, turned for a moment away from his memories by the entirely ingenuous question. 'My irresistible good looks?' he suggested, 'My sparkling personality?'

'Don't be silly!' She refused to be drawn. 'You know what I mean.'

He stubbed out his cigarette, immediately and unthinkingly produced the packet from an inner pocket and extracted another, standing and tapping it abstractedly on his thumbnail. 'She loved me to draw her. It fascinated her that I could make her come alive on paper. I persuaded her to sit for a portrait.'

'In the middle of a *war*?'

He laughed a little. 'War, much like life, I suppose, tends to have its peaks and troughs. It isn't one long rattle of guns and sabres, you know. Yes, I painted her portrait in the middle of a war. If one can't occasionally do something sane in the middle of such insanity, then all reason can be lost entirely.' He looked down at the cigarette he held as if surprised to find it in his hand. He looked around.

'It's here.' Poppy picked up his lighter from the table and tossed it to him.

'Thanks. I smoke too much.'

'I think you probably do. So, you painted Eloise's portrait. Then what happened?'

He lit the cigarette with unnecessary deliberation, avoiding her eyes. 'We were young, and the times were dangerous. I was totally infatuated by her, and perhaps she was a little flattered by that. Or perhaps I'm being unfair to myself. Perhaps for her, too, it was more than simply the situation, the circumstances—' He paused for a moment. 'Anyway, she smuggled me into her room for the sittings.' He stopped.

Poppy, for once, was ahead of him. 'I see,' she said composedly.

'Once we had made love—' Kit shrugged a little '—I was utterly obsessed. I had thought I was in love before.' His words trailed to silence, and in the quiet a bell tolled its mellow tongue through the shadowed valley.

'But you don't love her now.' There was a total certainty in Poppy's voice.

'No, I don't.'

'Then why—?'

'Poppy, please. You asked me to explain. That's what I'm trying to do.'

'I'm sorry.'

'Later that year, in the autumn, we both managed to get leave and went to Brittany for a few days, as man and wife. We stayed in a little house on a cliff top. It was utterly idyllic. I asked her to marry me.' There was a long moment of quiet. 'She wouldn't. Not then, she

211

said. Not while the war was still on. Not while things were so uncertain. I should have guessed then, I suppose, that her feelings were not as strong as mine, but I didn't. Perhaps I didn't want to see it. When we got back, it was to find that I'd been recalled to England for a few weeks. They were the longest weeks of my life. I was distraught with worry for her. Then, by a stroke of luck, I managed to get myself attached to a French Observation Corps, and I went back. But this time I wasn't alone. An old friend—a best friend since school days—came with me. He was a war correspondent, and a good one; attractive, highly intelligent and totally fearless. I think he was occasionally used by the British Intelligence people. You can probably guess his name.'

'Peter Martin.'

'Yes. The funny thing was, I was delighted. He was enormously good company and a very, very good friend. We'd been on assignments together before. As a matter of fact, a year or so earlier, on the Somme, he'd saved my life— or at the very least my liberty. I'd been knocked unconscious by a shell blast. He crawled through a minefield to get me, carried me back to our lines, and then behaved as if it were all a great junket, a bit of fun. I'd talked to Eloise about him many times. As you can imagine—' for the first time there was an edge of real bitterness to his words '—I couldn't wait to introduce my best friend to my best

212

girl.'

Poppy sat in silence, watching him. After a long moment he spoke again. 'No need to go into the gory details. I didn't see it then but I guess what happened to me when I met Eloise happened to both of them when they met each other. I was still totally blinded by my own infatuation. I didn't see what was going on right under my nose. Oh, I don't blame either of them. Not any more. Eloise never did love me the way I wanted her to—perhaps even the way she wanted to. And Peter tried desperately to stay away from her, but couldn't. Who am I to blame him for that? And, ridiculously, it was I who kept throwing them together, at first. I wanted them to like each other. I wanted them to be friends.'

'How did you find out—what was really going on?'

His face was deep in shadow now, his quiet voice almost disembodied. 'I found them together. In bed.'

Poppy bit her lip. 'What did you do?'

'I hit him. The only time I have ever hit anyone in anger. And he let me.' He took a long, slow breath. 'He made no attempt whatever to defend himself, he just stood there and let me. I might have killed him, I think, if Eloise hadn't stopped me. I was so hurt, so bitter. It was like a physical pain. Worse. I remember it still.' He came back to the table, stood looking down at the picture that still lay upon it. 'From there on the whole thing was a nightmare. Peter and I hadn't finished our assignment. He moved in with Eloise and I was left alone, but we still had to work together. A few weeks later he was killed. Eloise was demented. I've never seen grief like it. I think she would have killed herself if it hadn't been for the fact that she had just discovered that she was pregnant with Peter's child. He never knew that. He died before she could tell him.'

Poppy was frowning a little. 'But that still doesn't explain—'

'—why she hates me—hates me still? Why, when she saw some pictures in a Paris gallery and recognised them as mine, she tracked me down, via Florence, to here? It's quite simple. She believes it was my fault that Peter died. I was with him, you see, when it happened. She convinced herself that I could have saved him. She thinks I deliberately left him to die.'

'And did you?'

He took no offence at the straightforward question. 'No. We had taken one risk too many, as we often did. The Germans broke through unexpectedly and we were trapped. There was fierce fighting around the farmhouse where we went to ground. It was chaos; most battles are. There was an abandoned truck. We waited till the fighting died down a little and made a dash for it. I made it. Peter didn't. I tried to help him, but it was too late. It could just as easily have been me. The fortunes of war.'

'Was his body ever recovered?'

He shook his head. 'No. It was weeks before the Allies retook that ground, so Eloise didn't even have a grave to tend. By that time I'd been sent north, to Ypres. It was there that I was wounded.' Absently he rubbed his leg. 'I didn't see Eloise again until the day I met her in the woods here.'

'But what does she *want?*'

'For want of any better word I suppose you could say vengeance. She wants to hurt me. Peter is dead. I am alive. She'll never forgive me for that. She still holds me responsible. I think above all she wanted me to meet young Peter. If what she believes had been true, that would have hurt, badly. Even though it isn't, it still hurt. And she knows it.'

'Is he so very much like his father?'

'The living image. Peter was only a couple of years older when I first met him. I told you—we'd been friends for years.'

'You haven't told Isobel any of this?'

'No.' He lifted his head to look into her face. It was almost full dark. The shadowed sockets of his eyes were lightless. 'And I'm going to ask you not to, either. Poppy, your sister isn't well. She's terribly highly strung, as you know. I'd almost go so far as to say she's unstable. Pregnancy doesn't suit her. Her health, both mental and physical, is very fragile. She mustn't be upset, especially now.

215

She's—' he hesitated '—very possessive. Almost obsessively so. If she believed—' again he paused, then shrugged. 'All right, let's be honest, if she discovered that I married her on the rebound from another woman—and from Eloise, for Christ's sake!—she'd be devastated.'

'But—it was all so long ago.'

'That won't stop Isobel from being hurt and I won't have that. Especially not at the moment. Eloise is playing a game; a sick game, but a game nevertheless. She'll tire of it. I think she already is tiring of it. Hopefully at the end of the summer she'll leave, and Isobel need never know any of this.'

'How do you know she won't tell Isobel herself? She must have realised that would cause trouble for you, if that's what she's after?'

He answered promptly; obviously he had pondered this himself. 'Two reasons, I think. First, it would be too easy; she prefers to play cat to my mouse. Second, and perhaps more important than that, she's come to know Isobel very well. To be truthful, I do believe she has become sincerely fond of her in her own fashion, and she knows that if Isobel gets herself into a state she could easily lose the baby. I don't think even Eloise would go that far.'

Poppy pulled a faint, doubtful face, but said nothing.

Kit reached a hand to her. 'Please, Poppy, don't say anything? To anyone?' He paused, then added, 'Even Michel? The more people know, the more likely it is that there'll be some kind of row. I really don't want that.'

She hesitated for a moment, regarding him levelly. 'All right. I won't say anything. It's your business, after all, not mine. I just wanted to know why you'd lied, that's all.'

He sighed. 'It's one of those stupid things. If I'd told Isobel about Eloise right from the start, all this silliness could have been avoided. But I didn't, and now it's too late to talk about it without hurting her. And, yes, I played into Eloise's hands by lying.'

'The most disturbing thing about lies, even those told with the best of intentions,' Poppy said, 'is that one tends to lead to another.'

In the sudden silence that followed the remark, Isobel's voice called from outside. 'Kit? Poppy? Are you there? Supper's on the table.'

Kit stood up abruptly, picked up the picture and stowed it in the back of a cupboard.

'Kit?' Isobel's voice was closer.

'Coming.' Kit laid a hand on Poppy's shoulder. 'You won't say anything?'

'I won't say anything.'

He dropped a swift, light kiss on the top of her head. 'Thank you.' He held open the door for her.

'Oh, there you are, you two! I thought I'd

217

lost you!' Isobel came across the courtyard, holding Robbie by the hand.

Kit went to her, scooped the little boy up on to his shoulder, put an affectionate arm about his wife. 'You won't lose me as easily as that!'

Poppy heard their laughter as they walked towards the house, heard Robbie's squeals as his father bounced him on his shoulder.

Why, she asked herself, did she have a small, almost indefinable, feeling that somehow, somewhere, the whole truth had still not been told? That Kit's simple, straightforward tale of love and betrayal—surely by no means unique—did not quite explain the situation here? She shook her head firmly. She was being unfair; looking for shadows where there were none.

Yet still her steps were slow and her brow pensive as she followed the family into the house.

*   *   *

In the days that followed, Poppy found herself thinking often of the story Kit had told. It intrigued and affected her that, at the time of which he had spoken, he had been almost exactly the age she was now, though admittedly a lifetime older in experience. Like so many of his generation he had lived cheek by jowl with death and with horror—she had heard and read enough about the War to understand that. He had found love, and lost it. He had been betrayed by a friend, and then seen that friend die—worse, had been himself bitterly blamed for that death. She found herself thinking back on the young man she had met by the river in Kent, and saw, in retrospect, the shadows that had haunted him. And, too, more than once, she pondered on what both Kit and Michel had said of Eloise. In hardly any aspect of the enigmatic, coolly imperturbable woman that she knew—and, she had to face it, Michel's sister or no, thoroughly disliked—could she recognise the warm, impassioned and obviously captivating girl she had once been. A sad little story made all the sadder by the fact that Eloise still held such a savage grudge against Kit that, Poppy suspected, it stood between her and the rest of the world, between her and the possibility of happiness.

But as the warm, calm days followed one upon the other it was not so much that ten-year-old love story that engaged her as the gentle burgeoning of her own relationship with Michel. Since their day together in Siena they had fallen into an easy and affectionate friendship that nevertheless had about it that small spark of suspense, perhaps even of danger, that is engendered by physical attraction. It had become accepted that they saw each other every day, sometimes simply sharing a glass of wine in the kitchen courtyard with the Enevers, Robbie and Peter charging about them, sometimes strolling the woods and fields about the house. Both were aware of the amiably interested eyes upon them; Poppy, occasionally and exasperatedly could not help feeling that she was conducting the affair, if that were how it could be described, in a glorious, sunlit goldfish bowl. Of Eloise she saw little. It was noticeable that Michel always came to the Tenuta. Only when Eloise visited Isobel did her path cross Poppy's, and at those times the most emotion that Poppy could discern with regard to her brother's growing attachment to Kit's young sister-in-law was a mildly amused indifference. Which suited Poppy very well. Things were delicately balanced enough; she had the feeling that an Eloise who chose to set herself against her would be a formidable opponent indeed.

'Peter's terribly good with little Robbie, isn't he?' Poppy shaded her eyes with her hand. She and Michel were standing on a low ridge above the house, watching the two children in the field below as, shouting and laughing, they chased and rolled in the flower-dappled grass. 'It's quite unusual for a boy of his age, isn't it?'

'He's an unusual lad.' Poppy was acutely aware that Michel was looking down not at the playing children, but at her, the sunlight reflecting, lucent, in the pale, attentive eyes.

'Does Eloise mind? That Peter spends so much time up here?'

'No, I don't think so.' The infinitesimal pause before the words was barely noticeable. 'She's quite happy for him to spend time with the little one.'

But not perhaps so happy about the time he spends with the little one's father? Poppy could not ask the question. The rapport between Kit and Eloise's son had been obvious from the start. Looking at it from the new perspective that Kit's story had given her, she could understand—even sympathise—if Eloise were not quite so sanguine about that as she appeared. If Kit had been right, Eloise had had in mind punishment rather than pleasure when she had introduced the two.

They turned to stroll into the woodland, and within minutes were enfolded in an entrancing sun-dappled stillness that was disturbed only by birdsong, the distant cries of the playing children and the sound of their own feet quiet on the soft rich leafmould of the forest floor. Golden dust-motes danced in the shafts of sunlight that struck through the branches about them. The quiet was spell-binding; it was a long time before Michel broke it, and then he spoke quietly.

'You're coming with Kit to the *tratta*?'

'Yes. I'm looking forward to it, though I must confess I haven't quite worked out what it's all about.'

'From what I can gather, it's a sort of lottery, where the *Contrade* who are taking

221

part in this Palio draw their horses, though I'm sure—' he added with soft laughter '—that Umberto would be outraged to hear me describe it so. It's another of these ceremonies so steeped in the culture and traditions of the city that it's hard for an outsider to comprehend the depth of its significance to the Sienese. Umberto is quite beside himself with anticipation. His *Contrada* rides in this Palio. He prays each night for the best horse.'

Poppy glanced at him, interested. 'So they don't all ride in both the races?'

Michel shook his head. 'There are seventeen *Contrade*. It's tradition that only ten ride in each of the Palios.'

'So how are they chosen?'

'Seven run by right; simply enough, the seven who didn't run in the last race. The other three are drawn by lot, in May for the July race and in July for the August one. Umberto's *Contrada*—it's called *Torre*—the Tower—drew lucky in May. He's ready to cut the throat of anyone who suggests they might not win.'

'Umberto? Surely not!' They had reached a clearing, their way barred by a fallen tree. Poppy slanted an incredulous, laughing look at her companion. 'Umberto!' she repeated. 'He wouldn't hurt a fly!'

'Just wait and see. He's boiling over with excitement about it all.'

'I'm pretty excited myself as a matter of

222

fact.' Poppy turned, leaning back against the tree. 'I gather that for this horse-choosing ceremony we're going to the city and staying the night in the house in the Campo that we're going to watch the race from?'

'So I understand. The draw is made at dawn. We couldn't make it from here in time. Anyway, there would be no Umberto to drive us, I think. He has already informed me he will take us to the city by noon. He has duties, it seems, with his cousins. Duties only death would keep him from. There will be a lot to see, a lot to experience. It is a privilege to be in Siena for the *tratta*, so Umberto assures me.' Michel, as he spoke, bent and reached for something. When he straightened, he was holding a small golden flower. 'Tell me something.' The large lids, arched and shadowed, were lowered, masking any expression; he spun the buttercup back and forth pensively in his fingers.

'Mm?' Poppy had tilted her head to the sky, half closing her own eyes against the sunlight. She turned her head to glance at him. Rainbow light dazzled her.

'Do you like butter?' His voice had dropped a tone, and there was laughter in it, warm and affectionate. The lids lifted a little and his eyes gleamed. He pushed himself away from the tree, turned his body to her, was standing very close, smiling, the buttercup held beneath her chin, tickling her skin. His shadow fell across

223

her face, darkening the sun.

Suddenly she could feel her heartbeat, strong and slow.

'Yes,' she said, a little faintly.

'Wait. Isn't the flower supposed to tell me that?'

'Yes,' she said again, valiantly exercising the common sense for which she knew she was, within her own small circle, renowned. 'But you're a little too close, I'm afraid. You're supposed to let the sun shine on it.'

'Oh, no.' He relaxed his fingers. The flower fluttered, glinting, to earth. 'I think I'll take your word for it.' His big hands were on her waist, gently pulling her to him. He lifted a hand to her face, tilting her chin.

She watched him, wide-eyed and still. It could not be denied that she had wondered how it would feel to have him kiss her. She had never much enjoyed being kissed before.

The surprise was of the most pleasant kind possible. The hand that cupped her face was gentle; to her astonishment it trembled a little. His kiss was tender, undemanding.

After a moment, to her even greater surprise, too undemanding.

She lifted her arms about his neck, drew his mouth hard against hers. His arms tightened painfully about her. This time, his kiss was very demanding indeed.

It was some time before they drew away from each other. Michel put her from him, holding her lightly by the shoulders, studying the serene oval of her face, the wide, grave eyes, velvet soft, that searched his, unsmiling. 'Should I apologise?'

She shook her head. 'No.' The word was quiet as a breath. She cleared her throat. 'No,' she said again clearly. 'Not, that is, unless you didn't mean it.'

His smile was slow, and lit his face as the sun lit the forest about them. 'In that case, Ma'mselle, I owe you no apology.'

'I didn't for a moment think you did.' She lifted her mouth to his again.

An hour or so later Kit, working in the vegetable garden, heard their voices and their laughter and lifting his head watched them as they strolled together out of the woods, hand in hand and quite openly with no eyes but for each other. The die then was cast. For reasons that were not entirely selfish, he was glad. He straightened, absently rubbing a dirty hand across his damp forehead. The two young people stopped for a moment, turned to each other. Michel dropped a light kiss on Poppy's nose. Kit heard the happy peal of her laughter; and to his own surprise experienced a small, unexpected and wholly unworthy twinge of envy. Or—in fairness perhaps—not exactly envy. He leaned his crossed arms on his hoe, his blue eyes pensive as he watched their dawdling approach. Only the most unrepentant of sinners would not covet the

225

bright, untainted, innocence that shone from these two. Only the greatest cynic would be tempted to question how long it could last, in this world inured to wickedness.

Poppy had seen him. They quickened their pace to join him. Still leaning on his hoe, he returned their greetings, then, eyes openly quizzical, studied first one face and then the other and was rewarded by a broad grin from Michel and a flustered little smile from a suddenly bright-faced Poppy.

Kit laid his hoe aside. 'I find,' he said, 'that I have a sudden and absolutely irresistible desire for a large glass of wine. Can I persuade you two to join me?'

CHAPTER ELEVEN

The city was seething with excitement. In the end only Kit, Peter, Poppy and Michel had travelled with Umberto; Isobel, who had hoped to come, had in the event not felt well enough and Eloise, in her cool, wayward way, had unexpectedly offered to remain at the house with her and Robbie.

By the time the party from the Tenuta di Gordini arrived at noon on the day before the *tratta*, Siena was already at fever pitch. The 'rat-ta-tat-tat' of the marching drums echoed in the streets, everywhere great silken banners, their symbols emblazoned in jewel colours, billowed in the soft breeze. Women hurried through the narrow streets with trays and with pitchers, and men called and sang as they finished the cleaning, stocking and loving beautification of the well-guarded stables that would receive their prized and pampered occupants the following day, after the draw. Here and there small groups of young men, their everyday clothes brightened by scarves and favours in their *Contrada's* colours practised the intricacies of the flags; swinging, swirling, tossing, catching, deft as jugglers and proud as lords, of their skill and of the honour of serving their *Contrada*.

When they reached the Piazza del Campo, Peter stopped and stared about him, hazel eyes wide in astonishment, at the great draped stands that had risen about the outer perimeter of the square, at the wide, sanded track and the heavy fencing that enclosed and defined it. From the handsome façade of the Palazzo Pubblico ten colourful banners—the banners of those *Contrade* who were to race in four days' time and who at sunrise tomorrow would learn upon which sleek and shining back their hopes would be carried—blazed in the sunshine, bright, brazen and challenging. The place was a hive of activity. Hammers rang as last-minute constructions were put together. People hurried in and out of the Palazzo, the Town Hall of the city. There were many who stood in groups in the spacious area created in the centre of the square and talked, their hands as eloquent as their voices. The atmosphere was electric with a euphoric anticipation that even an outsider could not help but feel a part of.

'Golly! Look at that!' Peter craned his neck. 'There's Umberto's flag—look—the red one with the sun on it. He's told me all about the banners. The black and white one is the Wolf. And the blue and yellow stripy one is the Tortoise. Funny, isn't it, having a *Contrada* called Tortoise? Where's the house we're going to stay in, Kit?'

Kit pointed. 'That one over there. The one with the row of tall windows, see? On the corner, by the steps.'

'Gosh—it looks rather grand!'

Kit laughed. 'It is very nice. The Martellis bought it a couple of years ago. It wasn't in any great shape at the time, but they're making a splendid job of renovating it.'

Poppy and Michel, hand in hand, fell into step with him as they crossed the Piazza, with Peter skipping excitedly ahead. 'How did you meet them?' Poppy asked.

'Through the renovation. Giovanni came to me for some advice when he first acquired the place and we've been friends ever since. His wife Lucia is a delightful woman, and a wonderful hostess. I'm sure you'll love her. And the house really is super. There's a

228

painted ceiling in one of the upstairs rooms that's truly splendid.'

'It's awfully kind of them to have us. I hope we won't put them out too much.'

Kit laughed. 'If I know the Martellis,' he said, 'being "put out" won't enter into it. They're the most charming and hospitable people I've ever come across. They love to entertain, and they love to entertain in style. I think you'll find that we're in for a treat.'

*   *   *

The Martellis were, indeed, exactly as Kit had described them. They were a handsome couple, he tall and heavily built, a picturesque trace of silver in his thick black hair and neatly clipped moustache, she a pretty, plump little woman with fine black eyes and a becoming dimple when she smiled, which was often. Both spoke excellent if heavily accented English. Their delight in seeing Kit was unfeigned and obvious, and was matched by their pleasure in greeting and welcoming the rest of the party. An especial fuss was made of Peter; as in most Italian homes, a child would always be petted and indulged here. Wine was produced and small, sweet cakes, and cool lemonade for Peter. Their bags were whisked away from them by a smiling servant girl. Solicitous enquiries were made about Isobel. Much was made of the fact that Poppy had journeyed alone from England, Lucia happily confessing, amidst laughter, that she would not even dream of going shopping on her own, let alone attempt to cross a continent. The house, five storeys high, the first three of which had now been completely and tastefully renovated, was as handsome as its owners. On the second floor a huge and beautifully appointed drawing-room ran the width of the house; it was this room that possessed the tall, elegant windows that Kit had pointed out, which opened on to a wide balcony overlooking the Piazza del Campo and the Palazzo Pubblico.

'As you see,' Giovanni Martelli said, resting powerful hands on the stone balustrade, 'we will have a splendid view of proceedings, both tomorrow morning and for the Palio itself; you will, of course, be our guests for the race.'

'It's wonderful!' Poppy's eyes were shining with excitement. 'It's so very kind of you, Signor Martelli.'

'Giovanni, my dear, Giovanni! We have no ceremony here. Kit, it is a long time since you were last here. I'd like to show you the ceiling upstairs. The restoration is coming on very well. Then Maria will show you to your rooms—I'm sure you'd like to rest a little after your journey. We will eat early today, of course, for we must be up before dawn tomorrow.' He turned and led the way across the polished floor to the door. 'We have other guests coming to breakfast and to watch the draw. We will be a jolly party, I think.'

They all trooped after him up the wide staircase to the top of the house. The stairs led directly on to a spacious landing, empty and uncarpeted, from which opened a single great door, the impressiveness of which was a little marred by peeling paint and rusted hinges. Giovanni pushed it open.

'Golly!' said Peter, and 'Gracious!' Poppy said in the same breath.

The room into which they stepped was of ballroom proportions—it must, Poppy guessed, take up almost the whole of the top storey of the house. The walls were panelled and painted, as was the ceiling. The room was empty but for scaffolding and planks, the vast wooden floor big as a skating rink. The same tall windows that graced the drawing-room downstairs had been used to even better effect here, since they were set into two walls instead of one, the one side overlooking the square and the other, due to the towering height of the house, looking out over a charming jumble of terracotta roofs and chimneys to a glimpse of the great black and white edifice of the Cathedral. Outside the windows were narrow ornamental balconies of wood and intricately wrought iron. The paintings around the wall were of the city, an enchanting panorama of medieval Siena and its citizens at work and at play. Even stained and dirty as they were, for as yet no attempt had been made to clean them, their quality and charm were immediately obvious. The ceiling was the sky above them, and even only partially restored it was a delight. Beginning in the angle of the corner between the two rows of windows was morning, pale, cool and lovely, the gentle flush of a summer's sunrise glowing beyond the hills that ringed the city. The centre of the ceiling, where the space was widest, was broad, sunny day, which then faded into the corner where they were standing to evening and the dark of night, with a pale, sickle moon. And from those skies peered cherubs and satyrs, winged angels with open record-books and quills in their long, pale fingers and devils who watched with knowing eyes and gleefully brandished their fiery tridents, whilst beneath them, untroubled, the people of Siena went about their business and the business of the city in tranquil ignorance of the watchers above.

'It's wonderful,' Michel said, his voice very quiet, yet still echoing in the empty stillness of the great room.

Kit walked forward, head tilted to look at the ceiling. 'They're making a great job of it.'

'But slow.' Giovanni joined him.

Kit laughed a little. 'And expensive.'

'Very.' There was feeling in the word.

'It's as big as the aeroplane hangars at Biggin Hill!' Peter said, exaggerating only a little; and from one moment to the next, as Poppy had observed was his habit, he turned from a grave little adult to the harum-scarum that she suspected a ten-year-old boy should be, spreading his arms like wings as he ducked and dived about the room making aeroplane noises.

Kit turned, opened his mouth. Giovanni stopped him with a raised hand and an indulgent smile. 'Leave him. He's doing no harm.'

Poppy had wandered to one of the windows, looking out across the roofs. She sensed Michel's presence behind her and smiled as he stepped close, his breath warm on her ear. 'What do you think the angels are writing about us?'

She leaned to him a little. 'What makes you think we're the angels' business?' she asked, and laughed a little. 'Personally, I rather fancy the little devils.'

The aeroplane had come to rest beside them. 'I say! Shame we can't watch the race from up here. It'd be much more exciting.' Peter reached to the handle and turned it. The tall window swung open.

'No!' Giovanni Martelli's voice was sharp, almost a shout. Peter jumped and looked round. The big man hurried across the room, hands spread before him in apology. 'I'm sorry. I did not mean to startle you, little one. But this balcony, it is—' in his agitation he slipped into his own language '—*molto pericoloso*—very dangerous. The wood is

233

rotten. A finger would go through it. Much work must be done before it is safe. These doors are supposed to be locked at all times. The workmen must have opened them yesterday in the heat of the day, and forgotten to close them properly. There.' He had closed the window and turned a small wrought-iron key in the lock. 'Now, my little *aeroplano*, would you care for another glass of Lucia's splendid lemonade before you rest?'

*　　　*　　　*

Later in the day they ate, with the sounds of the square and the city drifting through the open windows of the dining-room. The meal was delicious; Lucia prided herself upon her kitchen and oversaw every dish. The courgettes for the soup must be freshly picked, the chicken chosen live from the market, plump and young, the meringues frothy and crisp and light as air. Much as she loved the peace and quiet, the informality, of the Tenuta, Poppy found herself thoroughly enjoying the urbanity of her surroundings and of her hosts.

Neither Lucia nor Giovanni were native Sienese—both hailed from Rome and had settled here from simple love of the place. Childless, and blessed with inherited wealth, they had reserved their affection for each other and their energy for this house in the city they both adored. They were in a sense more Sienese than the Sienese, and had learned everything there was to learn about the place's intricate history and tradition. The talk, of course, was all of the Palio: of the *Contrade*, of the savage rivalries, the equally fierce friendships, and of the horses—the *barberi* Giovanni called them—all locally bred, all coached and cossetted the year round, trained for the honour of running in the races that were the climax of the city's year. The track around the Piazza was discussed and dissected; the danger of the San Martino and the Casato bends, the perils of loose horses running wild in such a confined area, the even greater danger presented to the riders by the fact that once the race had started no holds were barred. The whips that the jockeys carried could—and would—be used on rival horses and riders as well as on their own mounts, and far more viciously. Indeed, just the year before, a fight had broken out on the starting line before the signal to start the race had even been given.

'It all sounds a bit dangerous to me,' Poppy said. They had moved out on to the balcony and were looking down into the great square, that was becoming more and more packed with people.

'It's no place for faint hearts, that's for sure.' Giovanni smiled down at her. 'That's why the jockeys are so admired. You have to be a very brave young man to ride in the Palio. Tomorrow you will have at least a taste of the racing, for before the *tratta* there are trials to choose the final ten horses, the ones that will take part in the Palio. Then, between now and the real race, more trials will be held, to get horses and jockeys used to the track. But these are much less dangerous affairs. If a horse or a jockey is injured in the trials they cannot be replaced, and the *Contrada* cannot run in the Palio, so you may be sure that they are careful. And the *nerbo*—the whip—is not presented to the rider until just before the start of the actual race. Now—' he turned back into the room '—may I offer you coffee?'

Poppy cast a quick, wistful glance at the excitement below before following him. 'That would be nice. Thank you.'

Michel, seeing the look, reached for her hand. 'Do you really want coffee? Or would you like to come for a stroll with me?'

Her face lit. 'Could we?'

Michel turned to Giovanni Martelli. 'I'm sorry—would you mind?'

Their host was beaming. 'Of course not. Of course not! Off you go at once. You'll find there is much to see.'

'Can I come?' Peter bounced off his chair like a rubber ball.

Michel and Poppy exchanged rueful glances. But before either could speak, Kit laid a playful but determined hand on the shining russet head. 'No,' he said, winking at Poppy. 'Not this time, my lad. There's going to be plenty of excitement for you tomorrow, and we'll be up well before dawn. If you wear yourself out today you'll be fit for nothing in the morning.'

'O-oh.' Peter's brows drew together.

'No,' Kit said again, very firmly, and the boy subsided, though his face was still rebellious. 'Tell you what, though,' he added, 'you and I could pop out later and walk the course, so you see what it's like when you watch the race. How would that be?'

'That'd be good.' The boy's slow, sunny smile broke out as if from behind clouds, and Poppy, unabashedly grateful for the reprieve, thought again how very close these two had become. Indeed, anyone seeing them together could well be forgiven for taking them as father and son. Not for the first time she found herself wondering just a little uneasily if Eloise had noticed, and if so, how she felt about it.

*　　　*　　　*

They spent the afternoon and early evening wandering the festive city hand in hand, engrossed as much in each other as in the sights and sounds, the fever of preparation around them. They found themselves a table beside a marble fountain in a tiny square not far from the Cathedral, ordered wine and cakes, clasped hands across the table and talked, as those balanced on the threshold of love always have, of themselves; of where and how and with whom they had lived, of what they liked and what they did not, of what made them laugh, of what made them cry. Even the young waiter who served them, a bright favour on his shoulder, his mind on the drawing of the horses at dawn and impatient for his day of glory as an Ensign in the great procession of the Palio, had to smile at the young foreigners' self-absorption. Ah, love! Perhaps he too one day would be more interested in a pair of soft brown eyes than in the fierce camaraderie and the dedicated loyalties of the *Contrada* of the Wave. Perhaps. But he doubted it.

As Poppy and Michel made their way back to the house, darkness was falling, windows were beginning to glow with light, and the sound of men's voices lifted in the songs of the *Contrade*—strange, almost medieval chants— could be heard throughout the city. And still excited voices called, from house to house, from street to street, still every square and every corner had its excited little group discussing, exclaiming, voicing hope or opinion amidst laughter or the occasional sound of argument. As they strolled across the Piazza del Campo Poppy glanced at her companion, caught his eye and smiled shyly. He stopped, turned to her and took both her hands, then gently but very firmly he kissed her, to the noisy and enthusiastic approval of a band of young men who, more than a little unsteady on their feet, were crossing the square. One tousled-haired youth slapped Michel good-naturedly on the shoulder as they passed, and the others yelped and called like an unruly pack of puppies, their voices fading as they reached a narrow alley and ran up the steps and out of the Piazza. Neither Poppy nor Michel even glanced after them. They stood quite still, their hands linked, studying each other in a kind of wonder; and it came to Poppy that whatever might come of this, good or ill, here was a moment that would stay with her for ever. 'Would you do that again, please?' she asked, and was surprised to find that this time when his lips touched hers they trembled.

That night, with the house still and quiet around her, she lay beneath a single sheet in the warm darkness and gathered to herself every look, every touch, every word of that afternoon. In her mind's eye she recreated Michel's face with its broad forehead, its large pale eyes and its well-formed mouth that had kissed her, and trembled. She remembered his laughter and his gentle warmth, the feel of his lean body against hers.

Somewhere, sleepily, the old Poppy stirred; take care! she warned herself, and almost laughed aloud at the silliness of it. If she knew one thing, it was that it was far too late for

239

such caution, good sense though caution might be. Poppy Brookes, what has got into you? she asked herself, settling herself more comfortably, punching the pillow. You'll be falling down rabbit holes next, you'll see—

In that strange half-world between sleeping and waking she found her thoughts had drifted to Kit and to the story he had told her about Peter's father; found herself not for the first time wondering if perhaps she should tell Michel, despite her promise. It was odd and uncomfortable to have such a secret from him. She'd talk to Kit about it.

She slept like a child, her hand curled close to her cheek and a small, tranquil smile upon her face.

In a room a little down the landing Michel stood at his window watching the great globe of the moon as it crept into the sky, hanging like a lantern, its light gilding the roofs, the domes, the spires of a city that was settling in excited whispers to rest. Tomorrow, he thought, would be an experience to remember, as would the race in a few days' time. But today—today had been different. Today had been theirs—his and Poppy's. He closed his eyes for a moment; and his smile, had he known it, was as contented as Poppy's own.

*   *   *

Breakfast was an informal and cheerful affair,

240

eaten at first light and attended not just by the English party but by two other families from the city, friends of Lucia and Giovanni. Home-baked bread and the honey-sweet rolls from Calabria called *taralli* were washed down with hot coffee, whilst out in the Piazza the horses were being led into the courtyard of the Palazzo Pubblico to have their draw number painted upon their flanks before showing their mettle to the watching crowds and the *Contrade* Captains who would have the final choice of the ten to go into the draw. The Piazza seethed with people, the very air buzzed with excitement. By the time the first trials were taking place, the whole party was on the balcony, Peter still clutching a large piece of Lucia's delicious almond tart.

There were five races, or trials, with six horses in each, all closely watched by those who had the task of selecting the ten they considered to be the most worthy to run in the final glorious race four days later. Poppy found herself shrieking encouragement as loudly as the most partisan of onlookers as the gallant animals ran flat out around the constricted track, manes and tails streaming, sand spraying from their flying hooves. Right from the start the dangerous San Martino corner took its toll; the slightest miscalculation could unseat a jockey, or, worse, bowl horse and rider over together, a perilous projectile of solid horseflesh and flailing hooves. By the time the

241

rope dropped to start the last race, the crowds were delirious with excitement. This time two jockeys were thrown at the San Martino and their loose mounts careered on, uncontrolled, bringing down another horse and rider. When the horses completed their third circuit and crossed the finishing line, the crowds immediately surged across the track to stand amidst a buzz of excitement outside the Palazzo, where stood a low platform draped in bunting.

'What happens now?' Poppy asked Kit.

Kit pointed towards the platform. 'See the two boxes? In one will go the numbers of the horses the Captains have chosen, and in the other the names of the *Contrade* that are to take part in the Palio itself. Then they're drawn and matched. Then each *Contrada* takes its own horse back to the stable prepared for it. For the next four days the horse becomes the property of the *Contrada* that has drawn it. It'll be cossetted and coached and pampered like a baby. Ah—' A line of colourfully dressed trumpeters had lifted their instruments and a fanfare had rung through the square, causing instant silence to fall '—here we go.'

The trumpets sounded again.

Poppy glanced around. 'Where's Peter?'

'Gone to get some more almond tart, I should think.' The words were interrupted by a roar from a section of the crowd directly beneath them. Backs were slapped, grown men

242

hugged and kissed each other like girls, one youngster threw back his head and crowed like a rooster. A good horse had been drawn. Poppy watched as the animal was claimed by its temporary owners and led proudly through the crowds that parted to make way for it. The sun was high now, and the air warm. One by one the lots were drawn, to be greeted with joy or, occasionally, dejection when a *Contrada* drew a horse it was less than satisfied with. Then at last it was over and the crowds began to drift away, talking animatedly. At last the real business of the Palio was begun, the horses had been seen and judged, and every Sienese would fiercely support one of them, either because it was of his own *Contrada*, or if his was not amongst those to race this time, that of a *Contrada* traditionally allied to his own. Over the next four days more trials would be run, alliances made, vendettas revived. The horses would be jealously guarded, and every attempt would be made to bribe the rival jockeys. The plans and dreams of a long year were coming to joyous fruition.

Much later that afternoon, as Kit, Peter, Poppy and Michel passed through the streets of the city making their way to the meeting place by the Porta Romana that they had agreed with Umberto, the place still had the feeling of carnival. The weather had become sultry and clouds were building to the south, but nothing could dim the bright spirits of the

243

gangs of youngsters who chanted and sang and spun their gallant flags into the air with the insouciance of long and dedicated practice. In one quarter of the city two such groups, old rivals, met—by contrivance or by accident, no one knew or cared—in one of the narrowest streets and a few heads were broken in consequence, but on the whole, at least on the surface, the atmosphere was one of ebullient and happy anticipation.

Umberto and the *calesse* were at the gate before them. Umberto, settled comfortably in to the scuffed leather seat of the little vehicle, was sound asleep and snoring, and showed no sign whatsoever of being anything else for some good time.

Kit surveyed him with cheerfully resigned eyes. 'I think perhaps I'd better take the reins, don't you? It looks as if the *Torre* drew a good mount.'

Michel grinned. 'I wouldn't want to be in his shoes when he gets home. It won't just be the wine that gives him a headache.'

Poppy suppressed a yawn. 'Just looking at him makes me feel tired.'

'It's been a long day.' Michel held out a hand to help her into the trap, then picked Peter up bodily to set him next to the slumbering Umberto before climbing in himself and settling himself comfortably beside Poppy, his arm about her, her head on his shoulder.

'Home, sir?' Kit enquired, gently caustic, one eyebrow cocked.

'Home,' Michel agreed placidly, and leaned his own head back on the worn leather upholstery.

Thunder muttered, far distant, as Kit expertly swung the pony around and on to the road. For perhaps ten minutes he heard the sound of desultory conversation behind him, then silence. When he turned his head to survey his passengers, not one was awake.

The storm, if it were coming, was still a long way off, though the air was still and sultry. Kit clucked to the pony and, nothing loth, she picked up pace and trotted on down the well-known road that led to stable and oats. They'd be home in good time. Kit gave himself up to the smoothly sprung motion of the *calesse*, to the feel of the worn reins in his hands, the welcome brush of air upon his face, and tried to empty his mind. Thought, especially solitary thought, was not always comfortable.

He glanced once more behind him to where Poppy lay asleep with her head on Michel's shoulder. Not for the first time the irony of that tender, growing relationship struck him like physical pain.

Dear God—suddenly sombre, he addressed, as so many do, a being in whom he did not believe but with whom he communed with idiotic frequency—whatever happens, don't let Poppy be hurt. Don't let that be my fault, too.

CHAPTER TWELVE

Poppy Brookes—in common, she presumed, with the great majority of those who knew her—had always considered herself by nature to be a level-headed and sensible soul little given to extremes of emotion or extravagant flights of fancy; the suddenness—and the intensity—therefore of her feelings for Michel took her entirely by surprise, as did the effect of those feelings upon the world about her. Was the sunshine really brighter? The sky bluer? Was the countryside truly more beautiful than it had been? She knew of course, rationally, that it could not be so, yet could in no way rid herself of the impression that they were. It was all quite extraordinary, totally uncharacteristic and undeniably the most enchanting thing that had ever happened to her. She sang about the house like a lark, mentioned Michel's name in at least every other sentence she uttered and serenely ignored the fond and amused smiles that her behaviour elicited from Isobel and Kit. For the first time in her adult life she found herself acting in a manner that could at the very best be called irrational and at the worst foolish; and to her own astonishment did not care a jot. She and Michel saw each other at least once a day, sometimes twice, and even the most casual observer would have seen that he was as beguiled by her as was she by him.

'I do believe my little brother's in love,' Eloise commented to Kit, watching the two come laughing, hand in hand across the meadow towards them. She slanted a pale, oblique look along her shoulder at him. She was not smiling. 'What a strange and ironic affair life can be.'

Kit took a long, slow breath. 'Eloise—'

'Oh, don't worry.' She lifted an elegant chin to look directly at him. 'My quarrel is not with Poppy. And Michel is very special to me; it would be a bad day when I hurt him. Who knows what will come of this? It's far too early to say. Perhaps it is simply a summer love, a romance of sunshine that will die with the season. Perhaps not. We'll see. But rest assured that I shall neither say nor do anything to spoil Michel's pleasure. Not unless I see reason to.' She slipped a hand into the pocket of her jacket, fingering something, and for the first time smiled a little. 'I shall go to find Isobel. I hope she's resting? I know she'll be very disappointed if she is not well enough to come with us to the race.'

She turned and walked away towards the house, spare, erect and supple. He watched after her, face expressionless. Then very briefly he rubbed at his forehead with his fingertips before turning to greet the two young people.

247

Since Isobel, Robbie and Eloise were joining the party going to Siena this time, they were taking two traps, the one from the Tenuta and another that Umberto had borrowed from a friend in the village. Kit was to drive one, Umberto the other.

'Can I ride with you, Kit?' Peter was sitting cross-legged on the kitchen floor with Robbie astride his shoulders. The little boy, drumming his heels and crowing with glee and with absolutely no regard for the ungiving nature of a stone floor, threw himself backwards. Isobel gasped. Poppy yelped. Peter caught the child neatly and expertly and swung him around on to the floor in front of him. 'Can I?'

'More!' Robbie said.

Poppy leaned to scoop him on to her lap. 'Leave Peter alone for a minute, for goodness' sake!' she scolded, her voice indulgent.

'I don't mind,' Peter said, and looked back at Kit with a gaze as clear and brilliant as water in sunshine. 'Please, can I?'

Kit's hesitation spoke for itself. 'I think perhaps—'

Peter cocked his head and waited, eyes steady and confident.

'I think perhaps you should speak to your mother about it,' Kit said cautiously. 'She'd probably prefer for you to go with her. And then there's the problem of space. Isobel

248

needs enough for two—' he flashed a swift smile at his wife who, head back on the chair, eyes closed, did not see it '—and Robbie probably needs enough room for three, and then there's Poppy, because Isobel shouldn't have to look after Robbie on her own.'

'I could look after Robbie,' Peter said reasonably. 'Then Poppy could ride with Michel and Mother.' His quick grin was cheeky as he glanced at Poppy. 'You'd like that, wouldn't you, Poppy?'

To be perfectly honest Poppy was not at all sure that she would; it was unfortunate but true that, Michel's sister or no, too close a proximity to Eloise for any length of time she always found profoundly uncomfortable. She smiled noncommittally and bounced Robbie on her knee.

'I think Kit's right,' Michel said from the armchair where he had been leafing through an ancient newspaper. 'You should speak to your mother. Ah!' He held up a quick, checking finger as the boy opened his mouth to argue. 'Enough. If your mother says you may, then I'm sure Kit will work something out. Let's wait and see.'

Peter pulled a face. 'It's as bad as being at school,' he grumbled.

Michel was amused. 'I'll remind you of that during class in September,' he said drily. He stood up. 'Poppy, will you walk down to the house with me? I found that book you wanted,

249

but forgot to bring it with me.'

Poppy hesitated, glancing down at the child.

'It's all right, Poppy. Give him to me.' Isobel had opened dreamy eyes. 'Come to Mummy, darling.'

'Are you sure?'

'Don't worry, you run along.' Kit took the child from her and very gently deposited him on his mother's lap, where he immediately began wriggling like a demented eel. 'I'll stay with them. Off you go.' He watched as the three of them trooped out into the sunlight. 'I dare say she'll walk home with him, then he'll see her back here,' he said, laughing. 'It could go on all day. I seem to remember there's an old music hall song about it. Come on, young fellow-me-lad. If you can't sit still, then down you come, leave Mummy to rest.' He picked up the wriggling child, set him on his feet, bent to touch Isobel's hand. 'Are you feeling better?'

Her smile was slow, her lids heavy over the harebell gleam of her eyes. Her fingers curled about his for a moment and she nodded.

'Will you be well enough to come with us tomorrow?'

The eyes opened. 'Oh, yes. I promise I will. I shan't miss it. I'm so looking forward to it. Apart from anything else it's ages since I saw Giovanni and Lucia. I wouldn't miss it for anything.'

'We'll make you comfy, you'll see. And

there's no need to worry about this little tinker.' He laid a hand upon Robbie's tangled curls. 'There are enough of us around to manage him. All you need to do is relax and enjoy yourself.'

She closed her eyes again. 'Dear Kit,' she murmured sleepily. 'You're very good to me.'

He looked down at her, unsmiling, before turning away. 'I'll take Robbie outside for a while. You rest for a bit.'

*　　　*　　　*

'Do you think,' Poppy asked, a little carefully, as they strolled slowly down the hillside towards the village, Peter doing his aeroplane impressions a little way ahead, 'that Eloise realises just how fond Peter is growing of Kit?'

Michel shrugged, half smiling. 'I don't know. Why?'

She shook her head. 'I—just wondered, that's all. I'm sorry—' she squeezed his fingers in her own. 'I know she's your sister, but she doesn't strike me as the kind of person to share her only son with anyone.' Not, above all, with Kit Enever; once again she found herself regretting the promise she had given so easily to Kit.

'You're right, of course. But you can understand the boy. He is fatherless.'

'He has you,' she said, swiftly defensive.

'Yes, yes, of course. But I am also his

251

schoolmaster, remember. There is no glamour in me.'

'I think there is.' The words were spoken entirely artlessly; the face she turned to him held nothing of guile nor of coquettishness.

Impulsive and laughing, he swung her towards him, catching her other hand in his, looking down into her face. 'I love you, Poppy Brookes!' he said, and stopped, his own eyes as startled as hers. When she said nothing, he put a gentle finger to her cheek. 'Poppy—I'm sorry—'

'No!' she said. 'There's no need. It's just—' she sucked her lower lip, nibbling it with small, sharp teeth. 'It's just—I don't suppose you feel like saying that again? Just to be sure I heard it right?'

There was a moment's silence. Then, 'I said "I love you, Poppy Brookes."' All laughter had gone from his voice. He waited for a moment before asking gently, 'Shall I say it again?'

'No,' she said faintly, shaking her head. 'I heard it this time.'

'Do me a favour?' The teasing laughter was back now.

'Mm?'

'Don't say "I love you too." Think of something original?'

'I love you three,' she said promptly. 'Four? Five? Do I hear any advance on five?' Her eyes were still locked to his, wide and wondering.

252

'Hey—what are you two doing?' The aeroplane zoomed in to land beside them. Peter's grin was as pleased as it was brightly derisive. 'Do hurry. I'm hungry.'

'We're coming,' Michel said and, hands linked, they followed the scampering child down the hillside in a warm and companionably pensive silence.

*   *   *

On the day of the Palio it was obvious from the moment that Kit drew the pony to a halt outside the house in which Eloise and Peter lodged that Poppy's misgivings had been realised. The occupants of the other *calesse* were ready and waiting for them, Eloise collected as ever in a faultlessly elegant, softly cut beige suit, a pale scarf floating at her neck, Peter sitting ramrod-straight beside her in immaculate shirt and shorts, his floppy sun-hat jammed on his head and every line of his young face set in mutiny. Michel, relaxed in open-necked shirt and slacks, jumped from the trap and crossed to them. His eyes signalled to Poppy; first, love, then a little roll of exasperation that brought an answering grin to her face.

'Eloise wishes Peter to travel with us. She feels it is more suitable.'

Kit steadied the skittish pony. 'I think she's right. To be honest, Robbie's at such a fever

253

pitch of excitement I think he needs a sterner hand than Peter's. Tell Umberto I'll follow him. *Dolce, dolce!*' he soothed the restless pony.

Michel took Poppy's hand, turned it and dropped a light kiss on to the palm. 'I'll see you in Siena.' With his quick, warm smile he turned and ran back to the other vehicle, vaulted into it and spoke to Umberto before settling back into his seat. The diminutive Umberto signalled to Kit with his whip raised to the wide brim of his hat and swung his big-wheeled trap out on the stony track. Kit, the pony's head tossing, followed suit.

Poppy found her hand taken and held softly in her sister's. 'He's such a very nice young man,' Isobel said.

And, 'Yes, he is,' Poppy said, deciding upon the moment that this was not the time to take her sister to task for her lack of imagination in her use of the English language. 'Very nice indeed.'

The journey was a happy one; Robbie, Dog tucked firmly under his arm, having with devilish instinct behaved impeccably for the first couple of miles was rewarded by being installed upon his father's knee with his small dimpled hands upon the reins, and was entranced. Poppy, thus having the responsibility of his safety removed from her, sat beside her sister exchanging desultory comment and laughter and watching the

254

calesse that moved steadily on in front of them, listening for Michel's mellow voice, his instantly recognisable laughter, seeing him turn, as he frequently did, lifting an answering hand to his. She was looking forward to the day as much as she had ever looked forward to anything. In fact as they moved down into the valley and joined the steady stream of festive traffic heading for the city, it came to her that she had never in her life before been as happy as she was at this precise moment.

Obscurely, and only for a moment, the thought bothered her; even her practical soul was aware of the legends about the dangers of tempting the gods. She shook her head, smiling a little.

Isobel cocked her head. 'What is it?'

'Nothing,' Poppy said. 'Nothing at all.'

*   *   *

By the time they had left Umberto to his own concerns and fought their way on foot through the packed, colourful and feverishly excited city to the Martelli house, most of Giovanni's and Lucia's other guests had already arrived and the house was filled with animated and voluble people all dressed in their Sunday best and all, it seemed to Poppy, talking at once. Above the hubbub boomed the sound of the great bell of the Mangia Tower, called *Sunto*, which had been proclaiming the day of the

255

Palio across the Piazza del Campo since eight that morning, and through the tall, open windows came in waves the ever-increasing noise of the already gathering crowds. Although the main ceremonies, the spectacular *Corteo Storico*, and the race itself would take place here in the Piazza later that afternoon and evening, for most of the city the festivities had begun the night before when thousands of *Contrada* members and their guests had attended dinners in the streets to the accompaniment of rousing speeches and passionately partisan songs; for many there had been no sleep at all last night. Many more had been in the square for the Jockeys' Mass at eight in the morning. It was doubtful if there were a single Sienese citizen not caught up in the events of the day.

The Martellis, as might have been expected, had outdone themselves. The food was splendid, varied and plentiful and both the quality and the quantity of the wines more than matched it. The balcony overlooking the Piazza had been decked with bunting, and there were chairs for the ladies of the party. After lunch Poppy and Michel slipped out of the house to savour the atmosphere of the city as *Sunto* once more boomed its summons, this time to the young men of the *Contrade* to don their finery and make ready for the great procession, the *Corteo Storico*. As the two of them made their way back to the Martelli house, the various components of the procession were already parading through the streets to where all would meet in the Cathedral Piazza to assemble into the final magnificent whole.

By the time they arrived, almost the whole party was gathered on the balcony, awaiting the start of the spectacle. A chair was brought for Poppy and she found herself settled between Eloise and Isobel, with Michel behind her, a hand resting lightly on her shoulder. She glanced around. 'Where's Peter?'

'Embarking on his third helping of Lucia's almond tart and lemonade, I believe,' Eloise said drily, 'and encouraging Robbie to do the same. It's all right, Lucia has asked one of the maids to keep an eye on them.' The atmosphere of the occasion seemed to have affected even the normally cool Eloise; there was faint colour in her cheeks and her extraordinary eyes were bright. She looked very beautiful, yet appeared totally unaware of the attention she was attracting from various—male—sections of the crowd below. Even when it was forced upon her in the shape of a young man who was lifted amidst good-natured laughter on to the shoulders of his companions to toss her a flower, her response was no more than a small smile and a nod of the head. Whatever Eloise's faults, vanity was not one of them.

'Listen!' Isobel, unusually animated, cocked

257

her head and took Poppy's hand. 'Here they come!'

The crowds too had caught the sound of the fanfare and, as one man, with a roar had turned in the direction of the entrance to the Piazza through which the procession was to come. And through it they came; the mace-bearers, the standard-bearers, the drummers and the trumpeters, the mounted knights and the sober clerics, the Captains and the Lieutenants, the pages and the ensigns in a kaleidoscope of colour and pageantry, a spectacle straight out of the Middle Ages. Some on horseback, some afoot, the pace was slow and stately. It would take two hours for this splendid pageant to pass. In the crowd, favours and scarves were waved wildly, patches of bright, primary colour as the members and supporters of each *Contrada* stood and acted together, and each section of the procession was greeted by a renewed and rapturous roar. Giovanni, standing between Poppy and Eloise, bent and lifted his voice so that they could hear him. 'See how high the Ensigns toss their banners.' Poppy nodded; the huge, colourful banners so skilfully handled soared through the air like great, flamboyant birds, 'Each *Contrada* wishes to be the best. They compete for the *Masgalano*—the prize awarded to the *Contrada* who is judged to be the most excellent of the year. Rivalry is very strong.'

'Look!' Peter, who was hanging perilously

258

over the balcony, pointed. 'There's Umberto! He's waving!' He waved back so vigorously that he seemed to be in imminent danger of toppling into the crowds below. Michel extended a long arm and towed him back. Robbie, sitting on his father's shoulders, shrieked with delight, bouncing Dog on Kit's head. 'Look, Dog, look! Pretty flags!'

'Where are the horses that are to race?' Poppy asked Giovanni.

He pointed. 'They wait in the inner courtyard of the Palazzo. When the procession is finished, the gun will tell them it is time to come out, they will be given their whips and called to the start. Until that moment no one knows their position on the line. It is a greatly guarded secret, for the places are drawn by lot and some are more advantageous than others. Poppy, your glass is empty. I will fetch more wine.'

Amongst the onlookers the crescendo of excitement was building. When at last in a final display of deftness and skill one Ensign from each *Contrada* stood before the Palazzo and, to the accompaniment of a single drum, enjoyed his personal moment of glory by tossing the huge flag high in the air, the jubilant roars that greeted each throw were literally deafening.

And then, amazingly, silence fell; or at the very least a kind of buzzing quiet. Heady expectation held the crowds. Poppy felt

259

Michel's fingers grip her shoulder; she lifted a hand to cover his. Such was the tension that the thump of the mortar that summoned horses and riders out into the square almost made her jump from her skin. And once more, as the jockeys received their whips and began to line up for the start, the noise began to rise again. The horses danced and jostled, excited and eager, unsettled by the tumult around them. The riders were already using their whips; not upon their own mounts but on their rivals', in an attempt to gain advantage. Then the mortar sounded again, the rope dropped and they were off, hurtling round the square like things possessed, urged on by the screams and shouts of the onlookers who surged at the barriers. And now battle was truly engaged; whips lashed, horses were barged off course, jockeys tumbled and rolled as they were unseated. Poppy jumped to her feet, her hand to her mouth, as two horses collided and fell at the San Martino curve, rolling in a brutal tangle of lashing hooves, bringing another mount down with a crash, its rider tossed into the air like a boneless doll. For perhaps eighty or ninety seconds a dusty and tumultuous pandemonium reigned. Loose horses raced perilously on, still urged on by their vociferous supporters, for this was a race that was won by the horse, not the rider, and a horse could win with or without its jockey in the saddle.

And then it was over. Members of the

winning *Contrada*—Poppy recognised the colours as being that of the Panther—swarmed across the barricades, risking life and limb beneath the hooves of the still-running horses, embracing, back-slapping, dancing in the sand. Grown men were crying. A band had struck up the Palio Hymn. Then in a swirling wave of movement the members of the winning *Contrada*, waving, shouting and singing, ran out of the Piazza, not even waiting to see their victorious flag unfurled from the Palazzo.

'Where are they going?' Poppy asked Giovanni, surprised.

'To the church of Santa Maria di Provenzano, to give thanks. It is the tradition. And then—' he laughed '—ah, then the real celebrations will begin. There will be some very sore heads in the city tomorrow, I can assure you!'

Poppy turned back to the square. An odd, anticlimactic quiet had descended. The horses were being led away, sweating and snorting, one of them limping badly. Faces were downcast, voices low. Only one *Contrada* could win; for the rest there was nothing but ignominious defeat.

'Horsy fell down.' Robbie informed Dog, solemnly. 'Hurt his leg.'

Kit swung the child down on to the floor. 'Umberto won't be too happy,' he said.

Giovanni shrugged. 'They'll all get over it. There is the next race to look forward to now.

In six weeks they do it all over again.' His handsome smile gleamed. 'It is the madness of the Siena summer.'

*   *   *

That phrase recurred to Poppy as the tired party travelled through the warm gathering darkness back to the Tenuta di Gordini. Robbie, curled on Poppy's lap, thumb in mouth, Dog clutched as always in his arms, slept the whole way, and within a couple of miles Isobel too was asleep. The madness of the Siena summer. She supposed with a little stab of amusement that some might say she was suffering a dose of that herself; indeed, if it came to it, she was more than ready to admit that it might be true. The Poppy of old would certainly have said so.

But then the Poppy of old had never been in love.

CHAPTER THIRTEEN

A week or so after the July Palio Eloise unexpectedly announced that she intended to take Peter to Rome for a few days.

'We'll leave you in peace for a while,' she said to her brother, mildly malicious, 'perhaps at last to seduce your little English Poppy?'

He ignored the not-unfriendly jibe. 'You're sure you'll be all right alone? I'll come with you if you wish.' They spoke in French, as they always did when they were alone together.

Eloise shook her head. 'No, there's no need. We'll be perfectly all right.' Her smile flickered. 'Peter will take care of me. And, anyway, I have some small business to attend to. You'd be bored. No, I am resolved; put the time to good use. Seduce your little virgin. I insist! I shall expect a report when I get back.'

'Don't be mischievous, Eloise.' Michel's voice was amiable, 'What Poppy and I do or don't do is none of your business.'

His sister lit a cigarette, blew smoke to the ceiling and regarded him with pale, contemplative eyes. 'But you do want to? Seduce her, I mean?'

'Eloise—!' A faint, amused exasperation tinged the word.

She held up her hand. 'All right, all right! I'm sorry.' She put her sleek head on one side, still watching him, real curiosity in her eyes. 'Do you love her?' she asked, suddenly and directly.

Michel nodded calmly, submitting with patience to an inquisition he had been expecting for some time. 'Indeed I do.'

Eloise swung an idle foot, her face thoughtful. 'In what way do you love her?'

Michel frowned a little. 'What do you mean?'

'Exactly what I say: in what way do you love her? As a friend who may become a lover? As an attractive, sensible girl who may become a wife? As a grand passion? An obsession? Would you die without her?'

Her brother shook his head helplessly. 'Eloise, I'm not like you! It hasn't occurred to me to pigeon-hole it in any of those ways. I love her. I love to be with her. She makes me laugh, she makes me happy. She's pretty and she's fun and I don't believe she has a malicious bone in her body. What more can I say? I love her.'

'Yet you don't want to seduce her?' Eloise raised mockingly amused eyebrows, 'What a paragon you are, little brother!'

He had to laugh. 'I didn't say that—'

Her own laugh was quick and husky as she leaned forward to stab a long and slender finger at him. 'Ah! So you do! Then my suggestion is not such a silly one after all, eh?'

'I told you, it's none of your business.' His words were gentle, tolerant, but very firm. 'Now—would you tell me something?'

'What's that?'

'Do you like Poppy?'

She thought for a moment, then shrugged a little. 'Yes, I suppose I do. She's a nice enough little thing, if a touch lacking in fire. Unless—' she cast a sly glance at him '—unless there are hidden depths that are not immediately obvious?'

'Is anyone truly what they seem?' Michel asked mildly.

There was a pensive silence. Then, briskly, Eloise rose, dropped a sisterly kiss on his cheek and went to the door. 'What a startlingly serious question. I'd better be getting back. I'll see you later.' As she turned, she threw back over her shoulder a bright, impenitent glance, and her laughter was soft. 'I still think you should seduce her. It would be good for both of you.'

*   *   *

A little uncomfortably, Michel found himself remembering those words more than once in the days that followed, and they came to him again a week or so later when, having seen Eloise and Peter off to the station with Umberto on the first stage of their journey to Rome, he walked up the hill to the Tenuta and came upon Poppy, bareheaded and in grubby shorts and shirt, pulling weeds out in the vegetable garden. She looked up at his footsteps, jumped to her feet with a glowing smile, pushing her hair back from her damp forehead with a dirty hand. 'Michel!' She raised her face happily for his kiss.

He kissed her gently, put her from him, holding her shoulders. 'Eloise thinks I should seduce you whilst she is away,' he said solemnly.

For a moment the brown eyes were startled, then, 'What, now? Oh dear,' Poppy said with composure. 'If I'd known, I'd have done the weeding in sequins. You wouldn't guess it, but I look very fetching in sequins. Have I blown my chance?'

He gave a small shout of laughter. 'My darling Poppy, you look very fetching, as you put it, as you are. Any man would find himself hard put not to seduce you.'

'Well, you're the only one around at the moment,' she said, encouragingly, 'unless you count Robbie, and he's asleep and just a little inexperienced for my taste.' She kissed him again. 'Would you care for a glass of wine while you consider it?' She took his hand to lead him into the little back courtyard. In fact Michel had spoken nothing but the truth; in the few weeks she had been here she had blossomed. The sun had gilded her smooth skin and brightened her shining hair, her eyes were soft and clear and almost always close to laughter. Poppy was no Eloise, to veil her feelings with a subtle skill and a schooled face; every time she looked at him, her love and happiness shone clearly through, unguarded.

He followed her into the kitchen, where she fetched glasses and poured dark wine from a cask into a jug. 'Where are Kit and Isobel?'

'Gone for a walk. Isobel doesn't get enough exercise. I'm sure it's part of her trouble. Since it's a little cooler today, Kit persuaded her to

266

take a stroll with him. Did Eloise and Peter get off in good time?'

He nodded. 'They're on their way. They'll be back on Friday.'

She had turned, jug in hand, studying his face. 'Isn't it strange—just a few weeks ago I didn't even know you existed. Now, I'm so pleased you didn't go off to Rome with them. I'd have missed you so.'

'I did offer—oh, not because I wanted to go, simply because—well, Eloise is my sister and I thought I ought at least to make the effort.'

Poppy led the way out to the table, set the jug and glasses on it. 'I dare say she's pleased to have Peter to herself for a while.'

'Yes, I think that's true. She also said she had some business to attend to, and I'd be bored.' He took her hand as she passed and raised it to his lips, kissing the grubby palm. 'I didn't argue.'

'Business? In Rome?'

'Money, I should think. Siena isn't exactly the centre of the financial world and although Peter's father's family help to support him, she keeps a very firm eye on the money and interests her grandmother left her.'

Poppy sat down, poured the wine, pushed a glass towards him and rested her chin on her knuckles, looking at him. A warm and easy silence fell. A cicada chirruped close by. Two colourful butterflies danced in the still air.

'I have a bone to pick with you,' he said,

267

smiling.

She did not look over-alarmed. 'Oh?'

'Isobel told Eloise, and Eloise told me that it is your birthday soon.'

'Oh—that. Yes. In three weeks or so.'

'And that it is no ordinary birthday.'

She grinned. 'My twenty-first. Grown up at last.'

'You didn't tell me.'

She sipped her wine. 'It didn't occur to me.' Their eyes were still locked in a perfect, private communion that had little to do with the desultory conversation.

'Dog's hungry,' said a small, firm voice from the doorway of the kitchen. 'So's Robbie.'

The spell was broken. Laughing, Poppy rose and picked the little boy up, planting a kiss on his smooth, sleep-flushed cheek. 'We'll have to do something about that, won't we? Egg and soldiers for Robbie and a biscuit for Dog. Do you think he'll be able to manage that?'

The child nodded gravely. 'Robbie help him,' he said kindly.

$$* \qquad * \qquad *$$

It was inevitable, of course, that sooner or later they would have their first quarrel, and equally inevitable that the spark that started the blaze should be struck in innocent and light-hearted conversation. They were strolling along the woodland path towards the tower.

268

The sunlight glittered through the trees in slender shafts of gold, the air was very still, and rang with birdsong. High above the treetops swifts and swallows swooped, the soaring curve of their flight the very essence of grace and freedom. Poppy tilted her head to look at them. 'I love swallows. They're my favourite birds. They nest under the eaves every year at home. I always think that they bring the summer with them.'

He smiled at that. 'I spent the summer vacation in Paris a few years ago, staying in an attic apartment on the Left Bank. Swallows were nesting right outside the window. They woke us each morning with their chatter.'

'I've never been to Paris. Is it as romantic as they say?'

'Yes, it is. At least, I think so.' He squeezed her fingers in his. 'Perhaps we'll go there together one day? Would you like that?'

'I'd love it. Would your friend let us stay in the romantic attic on the Left Bank?'

He shook his head. 'She doesn't live there any more. She went to America a couple of years ago. But there are lots of apartments in Paris. And lots of swallows.'

They walked on in silence. The tower loomed ahead, the swallows circling and diving about it. Poppy had lost interest in them. She was watching her sandalled feet as they scuffed through the soft leafmould of the woodland floor. 'Michel?' she asked at last, in a voice

269

that did not quite succeed in its effort to appear casual. 'Did you say "she"?'

He looked at her, but she kept her head determinedly down. 'Yes,' he said gently, 'I did.'

'But you said—' She lifted her head suddenly to look him in the face. A faint flush stained her cheeks. 'You said you stayed with her. You said "woke us up". Did you mean—that is—' She stopped, biting her lip and the colour in her face deepened.

They had both stopped walking. Michel was watching her, his face faintly, almost amusedly, puzzled. 'Darling, I told you. It was a long time ago.'

'That wasn't what I asked,' she said stubbornly.

He laughed a little, teasingly. 'You didn't actually ask anything!'

'Well, I'm glad you think it funny.' Poppy herself was astounded at the emotions that had so suddenly and surprisingly engulfed her at Michel's casual reference to his past.

'Poppy—' Michel laid a hand on her arm. She shook it off, turned and began walking again towards the ruined building. Michel looked after her for a moment then hurried to catch her up. 'Poppy!' he said again, more sharply.

'Might I ask the name of this "she" who went to America?' she asked, her voice chill.

'What does it matter? I haven't seen her for

years.'

'It matters to me.' She knew she was being quite unjustifiably childish, yet not for the life of her could she stop it.

'Her name was Chantal.' Michel, now, was equally brusque. 'But, Poppy, what on earth does she have to do with us?'

'You've never mentioned her before.'

'Because she doesn't *matter*.' His voice was lifted in exasperation. 'I haven't mentioned her because I haven't thought about her. It's as simple as that.'

She turned to face him, her head high. 'But you did—' she struggled for a moment '—sleep with her?'

He sighed, his irritation dying. 'Yes,' he said quietly. 'I did. But—'

'And how many others have shared your bed?' Poppy was scarlet with anger, mortification and a furious, and she knew totally irrational, jealousy. 'Do you always dismiss your women so lightly?'

His anger was rising again. 'As a matter of fact it was she who dismissed—as you put it—me. But I still don't see it has anything to do with us. Good God, I'm nearly thirty years old! Do you expect me to have lived like a saint?'

'Of course not! But I expected—' She stopped, suddenly aware that if she spoke another word she was going to burst into tears. She flung away from him, clamping her lips against their trembling.

'Poppy, you're simply not being reasonable! It's not the past that counts—it's the future. Our future.'

'Our future? How do I know we have a future? How do I know you won't be standing with some other woman in a couple of years' time talking about the girl you met in Italy, and what a fool she made of herself over you?' She let out a small, miserable sound and bowed her face to her hands, shoulders shaking.

He came to her in bewilderment, putting an arm about her shoulders. She stood, rigid and shaking, in the circle of his arms. He tried to pull her into his shoulder, but she resisted, her face still hidden. 'Poppy, Poppy!' He shook his head. 'The only foolish thing you're doing is making a quarrel out of nothing. Yes, I did live with Chantal for a few weeks. Yes, I suppose we did believe we were in love. But we weren't. We were too young.'

She lifted her tear-streaked face fiercely. 'As young as I am, I suppose?'

'Yes, as young as you are. But, my darling, you're different—'

'How, different?' She had stopped crying, but her breath was still coming in hiccoughing sobs.

He smiled a little at her woebegone face. 'Just different. I love you. You know I do.'

'Then make love to me.' The words were flung like a challenge.

272

He looked at her in silence for a long time. Then he shook his head. 'No, Poppy. Not now. Not like this.' His voice was quietly tender.

'You see?' Poppy's own voice rose in a wail. 'You *don't* love me!' But this time she made no move to prevent him drawing her into his arms, and once there, she stood still and quiet as he held her to him, stroking her hair. It was a very long time indeed before she said something, the import of which was muffled in his damp shoulder.

He bent his head to her. 'What did you say?'

'I said I'm sorry!' She would not look at him. 'I'm sorry,' she said again, less forcefully. 'I don't know what's the matter with me. I know it's none of my business—'

'It is your business. Anything to do with me is your business. As anything to do with you is mine. It's just that what's past is past—there's nothing either of us can do about that. It's silly to be jealous.'

That brought her head up. 'I'm not jealous!' she flashed indignantly, and then, as he surveyed her with affectionately quizzical eyes, added with wayward honesty, 'Well, only a little.'

He laughed. 'There's no need. And there's no need to doubt that I love you either.' He drew her close again.

She tilted her head to look up into his face. 'Then why don't you want to make love to me?'

'I told you. Not now. Not like this. It wouldn't be right. You surely know that?'

She nibbled her lip, her eyes on his. 'To be truthful—' she hesitated and then went on in a rush '—I don't know anything. About—that sort of thing, I mean. I've never—' She shrugged and did not finish the sentence.

'All the more reason to take care. Poppy, can't you see that it's *because* I love you that I won't do anything that might hurt you?'

She was playing with his shirt button, clicking it with her fingernail, eyes veiled by the dark sweep of her lashes.

'I saw someone once. Making love,' she said very quietly. 'Accidentally, when I was a child.' Her lashes lifted and dropped again as she glanced at him and away. 'It frightened me.'

'Oh, Poppy, Poppy!' Eyes and voice were soft as he hugged her to him. 'Don't be frightened. There's nothing to be frightened of, I promise.'

She flashed another quick look up at him, and this time he was relieved to see a glint of the old subversive amusement in her eyes. 'From what you've just told me,' she said, a little tartly, 'you should know. Though, come to think of it—' with a sudden change of mood as swift and complete as the one that had precipitated the silly quarrel she laughed and took his hand, turning to walk on '—it's a good job that one of us knows what they're doing, I suppose!'

274

In the event, Eloise and Peter stayed away for almost a week. The first Poppy knew of their return was when she glimpsed Eloise in the distance, walking from the Tenuta back towards the village. There was no mistaking the tall, decisive figure. Poppy had been out in the woods, hunting early blackberries for a pie. Hot, sticky, her forearms scratched and welted and her fingers smeared with juice, she was not sorry that their paths had not crossed; Eloise always managed to make her feel like a graceless and slightly tiresome child as it was. In this state she would have been at a greater disadvantage than ever.

Isobel was sitting in the shade of the courtyard, her feet up, an almost empty glass in front of her. On the table beside it lay a large and decorative box tied with a silken red bow. She looked round with a start as Poppy came around the corner of the house.

Poppy dropped a quick kiss on her sister's cheek. 'Was that Eloise I just saw?'

'Yes. They got back last night. Had a lovely time, apparently.' Isobel saw Poppy's eyes on the box and added brightly, 'She brought me a box of chocolates from Rome. Wasn't that kind?'

'It certainly was. Is that lemonade? I'm so dry I'm spitting sawdust.' Poppy picked up the

275

glass and finished its contents in a swallow. 'I'll get you some more. Would you like me to take these inside out of the heat?' She leaned across the table to pick up the box and, as she did so, exclaimed in surprise. 'Good Lord— how many chocs are there in here?'

In the same breath and with almost the same movement, Isobel had leaned forward to take the box from her. 'No,' she said sharply. 'It's all right. They'll take no harm here. But, yes, I should like some more lemonade, please.'

Poppy grinned. 'Lemonade and chocolates. Yum.'

Her sister shook her head. 'You'll just have to wait. I don't want to open them yet. The box is so pretty, don't you think?'

'Please yourself.' Cheerfully Poppy swung into the kitchen to get the lemonade. 'They're your chocolates.'

*   *   *

Poppy could not but guess that there was some conspiracy afoot regarding her birthday, which fell on the fourteenth of August, just two days before the August Palio. It so happened that Isobel had an appointment with a doctor in the city for a check-up on the tenth, just a month before the baby was due. It came as no huge surprise to Poppy when Michel announced his intention of going into Siena on that day with the Enevers, on business entirely of his own. To be truthful, much as she tried to deny it to herself and to everyone else, Poppy was beginning to look forward to the event. It was, after all, a milestone. She had marked it in her mind as Independence Day. This very year had seen the introduction of equality in the British voting system; women now were enfranchised at twenty-one, as had always been the case with their brothers. 'Grown up at last,' she had said to Michel, and yes, it was true. After August the tenth she would have to ask permission for nothing. Including marriage. Whenever the thought occurred—which it did rather too frequently to be comfortable—she very sensibly dismissed it. Who in the world had suggested marriage?

'We'll take Robbie with us,' Kit said. 'He needs some new shoes. So you'll have the entire day to yourself. Do what you like. Do nothing. You certainly deserve a day off.'

Poppy shook her head. 'I'm going to have to do some washing. We're all running out of things to wear! But apart from that, perhaps I will put my feet up.'

As it happened, on the day of the trip the hot, still weather had broken. A blustery wind blew, and there were a few clouds scudding across a sky that for the past couple of weeks had been resolutely clear and blue. Poppy, far from being disappointed, found the change refreshing; lovely as the settled southern weather was, she occasionally found the constant heat wearing. For a day or so a fresh wind and cooler temperatures would be welcome.

Having seen the others off, she hummed about the house collecting and sorting clothes to be washed, putting a great pan of water on to boil, setting the washboard up in the sink. The wind that rattled the doors and windows would make short shrift of drying the washing. She picked up the basket and went upstairs to Robbie's room, stopped as she passed his parents' bedroom door. As always, it was untidy. The clothes that Isobel had promised to sort to give to Poppy were tossed on a chair; some had slipped to the floor. With a small, exasperated smile she pushed the door open further and went into the room. As she straightened from putting the clothes into the basket, her eyes fell upon a bright splash of colour protruding from underneath the unmade bed. Curious, she slid it into the open with her foot. It was the box of chocolates that Eloise had brought from Rome. The ribbon had been taken off, and it had obviously been opened. Poppy, a little piqued, bent to pick it up. It seemed hardly necessary for Isobel actually to hide the things—she stopped. This time, with the box fully in her hands, it was perfectly obvious that it must contain something other than chocolates. It was far too heavy, and as she had moved it, something had

278

clearly chinked. She stood for a moment, looking down at it; then, on impulse, opened the lid.

There were no chocolates. Several small phials lay snugly on a silken bed. Two were empty, a third had been opened. A sickly sweet odour drifted from the box.

And this time, on the instant, Poppy recognised it. For a moment her head swam with it. She smelled again those headily scented flowers that she had hated and that her mother had so loved, and then the smell of her sick-room as she had lain victim of the brutal illness that had wasted her to death. The two smells—that of the hothouse flowers and that of the medicine that her mother had had to take in ever-increasing doses to give her relief from the savage pain—had become inextricably entwined in the memory of the child who had watched her mother die.

Had this, then, been Eloise Martin's 'business in Rome'?

Very slowly Poppy took one of the phials from the box, put the lid back on and dropped the box on the bed. It took a moment for her to realise that of all the emotions her discovery had stirred the predominant was anger; sheer, scorching anger. An anger that could not wait. Still holding the phial, she slipped from the room, ran down the stairs, paused only to take the pan from the stove and then went out into the wind, banging the door behind her.

CHAPTER FOURTEEN

'From the expression on your face, my dear,' Eloise said coolly, 'it seems to me that you know exactly what it is. It's laudanum.' Dressed in silken soft-cut pyjamas of a pale green that almost exactly matched her eyes, she was seated at a small table upon which stood a mirror, a hair-brush in her hand, her shining cloak of hair spread about her shoulders. The room into which Poppy had unceremoniously burst a couple of minutes before was almost clinically tidy. A photograph of young Peter stood beside the bed, a small collection of creams and lotions and a glass jewel-box were neatly aligned before the mirror.

'Laudanum that you brought from Rome.' It was a flat statement rather than a question.

'Yes.'

'For my sister.'

'Yes.'

'How dare you!' Poppy was raging; it was only with extreme effort that she kept her precarious grip on her temper and did not raise her hand to slap the lovely, supercilious face.

Eloise laid down the brush and, still seated, turned to face her fully. 'But, my dear, she asked me to.'

'If she asked you to pick up a gun and shoot her, would you do it?'

'Let's not be melodramatic, darling. And do try to keep your voice down.'

Poppy's control snapped. 'To hell with keeping my voice down! Not content with tormenting poor Kit because he survived the war and your precious Peter didn't, you're now turning his wife into a junkie! Well, that wife is also my sister! And I'm going to stop it, you hear?'

There was a small, thoughtful silence. Then, 'Well, well,' Eloise said, 'so that's what he's told you, is it?'

Poppy stood watching her, breathing heavily, saying nothing. In her temper she had broken her promise to Kit not to mention to anyone what he had told her. Who knew what mischief this woman might try to wreak now? Too late, she realised where her fury had led her.

'Poppy, I think we need to get some things straight. First, your sister is a sick woman. She needs medication—'

'Not like this! Not in these quantitics!' Poppy flashed back. 'And not when she's a month off bearing a child!'

Eloise ignored her. 'Second, your darling Kit is a liar. A liar and a murderer.' Her voice was perfectly controlled. Outside, the wind whistled and buffeted about the house, the trees beyond the window bowing and tossing turbulently.

Poppy was staring at her. 'I don't believe you,' she said, flatly. 'I don't know what you're talking about.'

Eloise had picked up the phial and was turning it thoughtfully in her long, pale fingers. 'Have you never noticed,' she asked after a moment, 'that when an honest person—let's say an honest man—lies, he does it extremely well? Simply because we don't expect a lie, we believe what we hear. Oh, how he has fooled you, Poppy.'

'I don't want to hear any of this. I just want—'

'Oh, but you're going to, whether you like it or not.' The pale eyes glinted with a sudden deadly rancour. 'You think *him* the injured party? You think *me* the villain of the piece?' Her soft laughter was wholly unpleasant. 'Just tell me—what did he tell you?'

'He told me about the war. About you and him. And about how Peter came and took you from him.'

She nodded, her eyes fixed unblinkingly on Poppy. 'And did he tell you how Peter died?'

'Yes. He was killed behind enemy lines, trying to reach a truck to get away in. Kit said it was pure bad luck; it could just as easily have been him.'

'He lied,' Eloise said.

'He told me that you believed he had deliberately abandoned Peter.'

'Oh, no, he didn't abandon him. At least, not until after he was dead.' Eloise leaned forward and suddenly her face was blazing. 'He killed him. *Kit killed Peter.*' She spaced the three words deliberately apart, speaking very clearly and calmly, only the faintest tremor in her voice betraying her.

Poppy stared at her. 'I don't believe you.'

'Believe me. It's true.'

Poppy lifted a challenging chin. 'How do you know? How can you possibly know? You weren't there.'

'No. But someone else was. Someone Kit didn't know was there. A wounded German, hiding in the loft of one of the barns. He saw it all. Peter wasn't killed as he ran towards the truck. He couldn't run. His knee had been shattered by a bullet. He was waiting for Kit to bring the truck to him. Kit did. He drove it straight at him. Ran him down, and left him there in the mud. Peter hated the mud,' she added sombrely, her eyes distant. 'He always hated it.'

'I don't believe you!' Poppy whispered. 'I *won't* believe you!'

Eloise, coming out of her reverie, shrugged.

'How did you—how did you get to hear this story?'

'Peter was dead by the time the German reached him. The man went through his pockets—looking for cigarettes, he said, though I think he probably took more than

283

that. Anyway, he found my photograph and a letter with my address on it. A year or so after the war he was still in hospital. I don't know, perhaps in an attempt to make amends to the man he had robbed, he wrote to me and told me the story. He had no idea, of course, of who the man driving the truck was. But I had. Oh, yes, I had. I went to visit the German, but by the time I got there he, too, was dead. I decided there and then that I would find Kit. That I would make him suffer, as he had made me suffer.' She paused for a moment. 'Do you blame me?' she asked, hideously reasonably.

Poppy had taken a step away from her, shaking her head. 'I still don't believe you.'

'I have the letter.'

'That's no proof. You could have forged it.'

'True. But I didn't.' Eloise turned her head sharply as a sudden gust of wind caught a door in the house and slammed it. She sat listening for a moment, but there was no sound but the wind. 'I didn't,' she repeated quietly.

'What do you want?' Poppy asked into the quiet.

Eloise answered promptly. 'Revenge. Peter haunts me. I haunt Kit, in his name. It took me a long time to find him. I won't give up so easily now. I told you—I want to see him suffer for what he did.'

'So you started by making my sister dependent upon laudanum,' Poppy broke in bitterly.

284

'It was part of the game to begin with, I admit, but—'

'*Game!*' Poppy repeated, aghast. 'Eloise, it isn't Isobel who's sick, it's you!'

'I was about to say that I have truly grown to like poor Isobel. She's not stable. You must know that. And the laudanum does help her.'

Poppy pursed her lips fiercely, but said nothing.

Eloise put her head on one side, and the shining raven hair slithered about her shoulders. 'Will you tell her? About me and Kit?'

'No. It would upset her too much. There's no need.' Poppy remembered all too well her own perhaps unreasonable but nonetheless painful reaction to Michel's revelation about the girl called Chantal. How much more adversely might Isobel's reaction be in her present fragile state?

'I agree. So—what will you do?' Eloise asked interestedly.

'I don't know. But I'll at least do my best to get her off that filthy stuff!' She pointed to the phial that Eloise still held.

Eloise shook her head. 'Kit's tried that. I doubt you will succeed where he has failed.'

There was a moment's bleak silence. 'Kit knows?' Poppy's voice was raw with pain.

'Poor Poppy. It gets worse, doesn't it? Yes, Kit knows.'

Very slowly Poppy turned and walked to the

285

open door, where she turned, to find Eloise watching her with something outrageously close to sympathy in her face. 'I still don't believe you. Kit wouldn't do something like that. He couldn't. He doesn't have it in him.'

The brief flash of warmth was gone. 'Believe what you like, Poppy,' Michel's sister said, the words truly indifferent, and she turned back to the mirror, lifting her arms and beginning with deft hands to put up her hair.

'Does Michel know? What you claimed happened? What you're doing?'

Eloise reached for a hair-grip. 'You must surely know him well enough to know that my principled young brother would not approve. Will you tell him?'

Poppy nibbled her lip. 'I don't know.' She stood for a moment, watching the smooth, competent movements. 'Eloise?'

'Yes?' Her hands stilled, the other woman met her eyes in the mirror.

'Please—go away and leave them alone. Nobody's getting anything out of this! Think of young Peter.'

'I do.' Eloise's voice was suddenly fierce. 'I do think of him! I think of him fatherless! His father didn't even know I was with child when he was killed. Oh, yes, Poppy—I think about that often. And no, I won't go away. You English have a saying, I believe—"*Revenge is a dish best eaten cold.*" I have waited a long time.' She smiled a small, chill smile. 'I will not give up my supper now.'

*   *   *

The Enevers arrived back from the city in the early evening, Robbie all but asleep on his father's shoulder. Isobel walked into the kitchen first, talking as she came. 'Hello, Poppy. Goodness, what a wind! But at least it seems to be dropping a little now. I wouldn't be surprised if we got some rain. They'll be disappointed in the city if this weather keeps up for long and spoils the August race—' She stopped so suddenly that Kit, walking behind her, almost cannoned into her.

'Hello, Isobel,' Poppy said into the silence.

Kit, who still had not seen what rested upon the table by Poppy's hand, hefted Robbie a little higher on his shoulder. 'I think the best thing is to get this young man to bed right away.' His eyes fell upon the bright box, and he too fell silent. 'I'll take him up,' he said at last.

Neither sister spoke as he left the room. It was, at last, Isobel who broke the silence. 'That's mine.' Her voice was cold with anger. 'Where did you get it?'

'I went into your room to collect the dirty clothes. You'd left it sticking out from under the bed.'

'How dare you? *How dare you!*' Unwittingly, Isobel echoed Poppy's own cry to Eloise. She reached a shaking hand to snatch the box.

287

Poppy did nothing to prevent her. Isobel clutched the thing to her as if it were a precious child. 'You had no right!'

'I know. And I'm sorry. But it's done. And now I have to talk to you.'

'I don't want to talk about it.'

'But, Isobel, you *must*—'

Her sister shook a curly, stubborn head, her face set. 'No. It's none of your business.'

Poppy stared at her in disbelief.

Isobel's eyes were huge, ablaze with fear and anger. 'I mean it. This has absolutely nothing to do with you. You have no right to interfere. I've promised Kit I'll try to give it up. After the baby. But not now. I can't. Poppy, you don't understand!' Sudden tears welled, spilled, and ran unheeded down the thin face that had once been so smooth and bonny. 'You could never understand, no matter how hard you tried! You're not like me. You're strong. I don't think you're afraid of anything. I'm afraid of everything. Everything! I'm afraid of life and I'm afraid of death. I'm afraid of losing Kit. I'm afraid—terrified!—of having this child.' She paused for a moment, dashing a hand across her wet cheeks, fighting unsuccessfully against her tears. 'I get so depressed. I get so that I feel that life simply isn't worth living. I don't know why. It's just something in me. I'm sometimes afraid I'm going to lose my mind entirely,' she added in a miserable whisper, and bowed her head, sobbing.

Poppy leaned forward, urgent and fierce. 'But, Isobel, can't you see? This isn't making it better!' She gestured towards the box. 'If anything, it's making it worse!'

'*No!*' There was desperation in her sister's eyes and voice. 'You don't understand,' she repeated in stubborn despair. 'You don't know what happened before. You don't know how awful it's been.'

'You've both told me—'

'No.' Isobel's voice was quieter now, though the tears still ran. 'Neither of us has told you the whole truth. Neither of us has told you that I once attacked Kit with a kitchen knife because I convinced myself that he was going to leave me. Nor that, in Paris, I twice tried to kill myself.'

'Isobel!' Appalled, Poppy reached a hand across the table to her.

Isobel, her head bent, took it, her own hand cold and lax. 'I don't know if I really meant to do it, or whether I just wanted to make Kit feel guilty.' She lifted drowned eyes to her sister's face. 'You don't know what it's like to be me.'

Poppy could find absolutely no reply to that. When Kit came back into the room they were still sitting at the table, hands clasped, in silence.

'Isobel,' Kit's voice was gentle, 'do you think perhaps you should get some rest? It's been a very long day for you.'

Isobel nodded unhappily. Poppy watched as with infinite tenderness Kit put an arm about his wife and helped her to her feet. She turned her wet face into his shoulder for a moment, and stood trembling a little within the comfort of his encircling arm, before, still supporting her, he led her from the room.

He came back perhaps ten minutes later. Poppy had not moved. She neither spoke nor turned her head when he entered the room. Her face was sombre.

Kit walked to where the bottle of whisky stood on the dresser. 'Drink?' he asked quietly.

Poppy shook her head.

He poured a glass for himself and crossed the room to sit in the chair that Isobel had vacated. 'I'm sorry. We should have told you. You were bound to have found out sooner or later.'

'Is it true that Isobel tried to kill herself in Paris?' Poppy asked abruptly.

There was a short silence. 'To be honest, I'm not sure. She certainly tried to harm herself. Whether she actually intended to die, I don't know. I suspect probably not. She was in a very disturbed state at the time. That was when she was first prescribed laudanum. She became dependent. She went through a very bad time breaking the habit.'

'And when Eloise turned up here, she discovered that and started supplying her again?'

He glanced at her. 'You've made that connection, then?'

Very deliberately, holding his eyes, Poppy said, 'I've spoken to Eloise.'

The silence this time was much longer.

'You've spoken to Eloise,' Kit repeated carefully.

'Yes.'

He waited.

'She told me that you killed Peter,' Poppy said.

He drew a great, sighing, resigned breath and dropped his face into his hands for a moment.

All of that unhappy day the niggling seeds of doubt had been growing. She waited until he lifted his head to meet her eyes before she asked bluntly, 'Did you?'

'No.' The word was quiet, the more convincing for being entirely unemphatic.

'She says she has a letter, from a witness.'

'Who then conveniently died,' said Kit, wryly. 'Yes, she's told me that, too.'

'Have you ever seen the letter?'

He shook his head. 'It's no kind of evidence, anyway. Anyone could have written it. She could have written it herself.'

'That's what I said.'

He put his elbows on the table, turning the glass in his hands, his eyes pensive upon it. 'I didn't kill Peter, but I can't prove it. Any more

291

than Eloise can prove that I did.'

'The circumstances were such that you could have done.'

'Yes.' The word was simple. He lifted his eyes, clear and steady, to hers. 'I can't help you, Poppy. You have to make up your own mind.'

To take the word of a stranger whom she disliked—however she felt about her brother—against that of someone she had known and loved for most of her life. The choice was made for her. 'I believe you.'

'Then there's no point in speaking of it again, is there? The past is past, and its dead are buried, whatever Eloise likes to think. Isobel is our priority; we must concentrate on protecting her. From herself, and from others.'

The words reminded Poppy of the reason for their trip. 'What did the doctor say?'

He shook the sombre mood from him. 'He seemed to think she's doing well. She must rest, of course, and not become agitated. Her blood pressure is up. But, apart from that, physically she's fine. Which reminds me—' he smiled a little over the rim of his glass '—Lucia came with us—my Italian isn't quite up to something like this—and heard us talking about your birthday. She wants to throw a party for you. On the day of the Palio.'

'That's kind.' Even preoccupied as she was, Poppy herself could hear the ungracious lack of enthusiasm in the words and added hastily,

292

'It really is. There's no need. They hardly know me.'

'They want to. And since we're all going to be there anyway, we can hardly refuse, can we?'

She shook her head. 'Kit—'

He sipped his drink, eyebrows raised enquiringly, waiting for her to go on.

She was frowning, nibbling her lip.

'What is it?'

'Michel,' she said. 'I hate having secrets from him. It's a sort of lying, isn't it?'

He considered for a long moment, absently running a finger around the top of his glass until the sound of it rang in the silence. 'I have no right to ask it,' he said at last, 'but I'd really much rather you didn't speak to him about all this. I can't see how it could help and it might very well do greater harm. Michel's a splendid chap—I've never known nicer—I don't think he'd like or approve of Eloise's purpose here. She's causing enough mischief already. If we rouse her further by implicating Michel—and possibly turning him against her—God knows what she might decide to do. We mustn't let Isobel be any further upset. Can you imagine her reaction if Eloise chose to tell her about the past? If she finds I've been lying to her? No, I truly think the fewer people who know, the better. I'm sorry to ask, but would you please say nothing? For Isobel's sake? At least for a while?'

Reluctantly she could see the logic of that, and was acutely aware too that the secrets of which they spoke were not hers to share, even with Michel—perhaps even especially with Michel. She nodded.

He tossed back his drink and set the glass on the table. 'Thank you.' He stood up. 'I'd best go and check that Isobel's all right.' He came around the table to stand behind her, a light hand on her shoulder. 'Don't worry. And don't let this spoil your special birthday. Everything will be all right, I promise. Eventually Eloise will get tired of her games and leave us alone. I'm sure of it. I think she may even be getting a little bored already. With any luck, she'll leave with Peter when he goes back to school.'

'I will not give up my supper now.'

Poppy smiled, a little wanly. 'Perhaps.'

*   *   *

'Eloise, how is our small invalid?' Michel, passing from Bernado's house on his way to the Tenuta, had come across his sister, leaning at her gate, obviously waiting for him, a small package in her hand. 'Is he well enough to come with me today?'

Eloise shook her head. 'He still complains of feeling unwell. A touch of the sun, I'm sure. The silly child will not keep his sun-hat on. But I'm sure it's nothing serious.'

294

'He'll be well enough to come to the race on Friday?'

'Oh, yes. I think so.' She held out the parcel. 'Will you take this up to the house with you? A small present, for Poppy's birthday. Wish her many happy returns from me.'

Michel took it, tucked it into his pocket, feeling as he did so the hard edges of the little box that already rested there. Then he leaned to kiss his sister's cheek. 'Give Peter my love. Tell him to get well quickly. I'll see you later.' He turned and left her. In a moment she heard him whistling cheerfully; the very set of his shoulders, the jaunty lift of his head speaking of happy high spirits. She watched him, half-smiling, until he disappeared around the corner.

*   *   *

In the event, Poppy's birthday did not turn out to be the disaster she had foreseen. In the couple of days that had followed her discovery, they had all behaved with careful courtesy to each other, and the subject had not been mentioned again. On the day of her birthday Kit brought her breakfast in bed, and when she came down to the kitchen it was to find it and the courtyard decorated with paper chains, ribbons and coloured bunting. A birthday cake with her name on it rested in pride of place upon the dresser shelf and a small pile of gifts graced the big old table. Robbie could scarcely contain his excitement and pride as he stood before her clutching a card upon which were stuck brightly coloured paper shapes. 'I maked it for you,' he said, glowing with self-importance, 'for your birfday.'

Poppy bent to hug him, took the sticky, dog-eared thing that was smudged with small fingerprints. 'Darling, it's beautiful! Thank you.'

'Maked chains, too,' he said, eager that she should not miss the importance of his contribution to the festivities, 'with Mummy.' He picked up Dog, tucked him comfortably under his arm, beaming immodestly.

'*Buon compleanno, Signorina!*'

'Umberto! How lovely!' The little man was standing in the doorway, his smile at least as wide as Robbie's and his arms full of cut flowers. 'For me? *Grazie!*' In her delight she kissed him, and his brown skin darkened further in a blush of pleasure. Touched, she took the flowers, burying her face in them; then as she lifted her head she caught sight of a small brown package on the table, a package with English stamps upon it and addressed in a hand so familiar that even in these unexpected circumstances she recognised it immediately. 'How on earth did that get here?' She picked up her father's gift, turning it in her hands in unfeigned astonishment.

Isobel was smiling at the expression on her

296

sister's face. 'It was waiting at the post office when we went into town the other day. You didn't think he'd forget, did you?'

'Well, yes,' Poppy said, surprised into honesty. 'I suppose I did.'

'Aren't you going to open it?'

The package held a short, stilted note of congratulation—signed, equally stiltedly by both her father and Dora—and a gold ring set with sapphires that both young women recognised immediately as having belonged to their mother. It was an unexpectedly thoughtful gesture that brought quick tears welling to Isobel's eyes and even set Poppy blinking.

'Open Robbie's!' Robbie demanded impatiently, and the moment was gone. Smiling, Poppy sat down at the table. Robbie had chosen for her—all by himself, his straight-faced parents assured her—a little china statue of a dog with quite the ugliest face Poppy had ever seen. 'Look, Dog,' the child said, holding up his precious toy. 'Dog,' and beamed again at the adults' laughter. Isobel and Kit had bought her a beautifully made leather handbag; but Kit, in addition, had painted her a little picture of the Tenuta nestling on its hillside, the tower rising behind it.

'A small keepsake,' Kit said, as she kissed him in thanks. 'I'd have made it bigger, but I had to bear in mind you'll have to take it home

297

with you!'

'It's lovely, really lovely! I'll treasure it—' Poppy turned as a shadow fell across the doorway. 'Michel!'

The party complete, Kit insisted on opening one of the two extravagant bottles of champagne he and Isobel had brought back from the city for the occasion. Everyone exclaimed delightedly over the pretty pendant Michel had found for her, and a touch more surprisedly over the silk scarf that Eloise had sent. The moment Poppy opened the package, she smelled the drift of perfume that clung to it; the perfume that Eloise always wore. Very carefully she folded the pretty thing and put it back in the paper. 'It's very nice,' she said politely. 'Please thank her for me.'

'I shall.' Michel bent to kiss her, took the pendant from her and straightened to fasten it about her neck. 'There.' He stepped back, holding her hands in his, pulling her to her feet. *'C'est belle, non?'* There could be no mistaking the warmth in his eyes as he looked at her; nor, Kit thought a little ruefully, watching them, could any onlooker misinterpret the happy glow on Poppy's face as she thanked him. He did not for a moment begrudge them their love, but not for the first time he found himself wishing that Poppy had found someone else to fall for. Someone not quite so closely connected to Eloise Martin.

It was a long and happy day. In her

bedroom that night, Poppy lit the lamp and stretched tiredly. The ring her father had sent glinted upon her hand, and she looked at it pensively. Then she turned to the mirror to inspect the pretty golden pendant Michel had given her. She touched it gently with her fingertip, smiling before setting the ugly little dog carefully in place on the chest of drawers. 'Dog likes dog,' Robbie had informed her gravely. She smiled again. Then she shook the scarf Eloise had sent out of its wrapping and stood looking down at it. Again the wave of perfume drifted from it, heavy on the warm night air. Wrinkling her nose, she picked the thing up, opened a drawer, stuffed it as far to the back as it would go and slammed the drawer shut with a satisfying bang. And though it could not be said that her thoughts exactly matched those Kit had harboured that morning, the faintest of echoes was certainly there.

*   *   *

The day of the August Palio was a day of still air and blazing sunshine. The vast arena of the Piazza del Campo was once more a carnival of noise and colour beneath a burning sky. If any of the party who had driven in from the Tenuta had expected that this second event might, by reason of being so close, not have lived up to the tensions and excitements of the first, any such thought was confounded from the moment they entered the city. The place was vibrant with energy and expectation, glittering with colour, ringing with music. Once again *Sunto*'s iron tongue rang out its summons to the devotees of the *Contrade*, once again the proud and cossetted mounts were led through the streets, coats gleaming in the sun, to their moment of glory, once again the great theatrical procession came together and the picturesque confusion of the city was tamed to pageant.

In the Martelli house the happy coincidence of the race with Poppy's birthday had been taken advantage of to the full. There were presents, flowers and a candle-decked cake. The place was, if anything, more packed than before; there were people she had met and people she had not, yet all seemed as eager to congratulate and celebrate, and the food—that must, she estimated bemusedly have taken a week to prepare—and the generously flowing wine did much to contribute to the festive atmosphere.

Robbie, with his tangle of blond curls and wide, flower-blue eyes was made much of; petted and fondled and kissed upon the cheek until, in disgust, he crawled under the table, pulling Dog with him, and refused, to much charmed hilarity, to come out. Peter, still pale and a little withdrawn after his unexpected bout of illness, answered politely when spoken to but did not, Poppy noticed, apart from that make much effort to socialise with the other children. Even given the language barrier, this was unusual.

'Peter? Are you all right?' She laid a hand on the thick, shining hair. 'I must say you still do look a little poorly.'

'I'm fine, thank you.' There were dark rings beneath his eyes, and his voice was listless. 'I just keep getting bad headaches, that's all.'

She was concerned. 'Is it too noisy for you? Do you want to lie down?'

He shook his head. 'No, honestly. I'm all right, I promise.'

'Poppy—come. You must blow out the candles on your cake. And a wish—you must make a special wish.'

The crowd parted to allow her to the table, where Giovanni stood beaming his handsome smile beside the cake. He held up his hands for silence. *'Uno!'* he called as Poppy drew breath, and the crowd picked up the count enthusiastically. *'Due! Tre!'* The audience broke into loud applause as, on the count of three Poppy extinguished the candles in one go. 'You have made your wish?' Giovanni demanded exuberantly.

She nodded, smiling.

He wagged a finger, playfully serious. 'Then tell no one! Or it will not be fulfilled.'

For one second Poppy's eyes encountered Michel's and, mortifyingly and very prettily,

301

she found herself blushing. Obviously at least one person in the room had come close to guessing what she had wished for; she could not for the moment decide if that were a good thing or a bad, and her shy colour deepened.

Outside in the square a trumpet sounded. All heads turned. There was a rush to the balcony. Poppy, as guest of honour, was settled with some ceremony in the best seat by Giovanni, with Michel behind her as before, his long fingers moving very gently, stroking the slender bones of her shoulder. Poppy, her face hidden by the wide brim of her flower-decked sun-hat, closed her eyes for a moment, aware in that all but perfect moment of nothing but the closeness of his body to hers, the perilous, almost hypnotic pleasure engendered by those stroking fingers. The bustle on the balcony subsided and, in common with the rest of the onlookers, all eyes were turned to the opening through which the *Corteo Storico* would enter the Piazza. It was very hot; and Poppy had drunk far more wine than was usual for her. She leaned back a little, pressing her body into Michel's, and was rewarded by a quick, acknowledging squeeze of his hand. His fingers, warm and dry, slipped beneath the collar of her shirt, stroking the skin of her neck.

The procession, a gaudy feast to eye and ear, burst upon the Piazza to an ecstatic roar of applause.

*　　　*　　　*

Perhaps because of the wine, or perhaps because of what came later, Poppy never could remember clearly the events of that afternoon—neither the procession nor the formalities, nor the race that followed except as a kaleidoscopic and dizzying muddle of colour and movement, of heat and excitement, of deafening noise and surging, chanting crowds.

Only a few clear memories stayed with her, indelible images to haunt her.

The feel of Michel's fingers stroking the skin of her throat.

The heat of the sun on her bare forearms.

The roar of triumph that greeted the winner of the race.

The uncomprehending moment of horror and shock when, at the moment that the victorious *Contrada* rioted out of the square to the Cathedral to celebrate their victory, the splintering of timber and the crash of falling masonry mingled with shrieks and cries as the upstairs balcony collapsed into the steep and narrow alley beside the house.

The hideous sight of a small, broken body lying amongst the wreckage, Dog still clutched in a bloodied hand.

And, in the pandemonium that followed, her sister's distorted, horror-stricken face as she screamed and screamed and screamed, harrowingly and monotonously, as if she would never—could never—stop.

CHAPTER FIFTEEN

It was a long and difficult labour and one that, in such cruel circumstances, did not at first bode well for mother or for child. For twenty-four hours the shocked household attended the exhausted and grieving Isobel. Kit, with a fortitude and strength that could only draw admiration, stirred from his suffering wife's side only when absolutely necessary, to help the city officials who were investigating the accident, and to start the arrangements for the funeral. In sober truth, for all the horror of the thing, there was little to investigate; the facts spoke for themselves. The child, energetic and inquisitive, had had the run of the house. Far from there being too few guardians, there had been too many, and no one had thought to question his whereabouts for those few fatal minutes. One of the workmen, horrified and grieved at the result of his carelessness, came forward to admit that it was more than likely that he had once more forgotten to lock the window that led out on to the balcony; might indeed, he acknowledged, even have actually left the thing open. It was sheer luck that no one else had been hurt—the crowds had still been in the square, and the alley had been empty at the time of the tragedy.

'Poor little boy.' Poppy's head ached from weeping, and the tears still would not stop. 'Poor, poor little boy—and poor Isobel—' She laid her forehead upon Michel's shoulder, her own shoulders shaking.

Gently he stroked her hair, his face sombre. 'My darling, I hate to have to leave you like this—'

She stepped back from him, blowing her nose furiously. 'Don't be silly. You have to go. We must think about Peter. This is no place for a child at the moment. He needs you, and we can't keep him here any longer. He'll make himself ill if we don't get him away. No, you must take them home.'

'You'll get word to us? About Isobel?'

'Of course I will. Umberto is staying with us. He'll come to you when there's news.'

'How is she?'

Poppy shook her head, tears brimming again, said nothing.

'Michel?' The voice from the doorway was quiet. Eloise, collected and exquisite in black, stood there holding Peter's hand. The child, pale and stricken, stood silent, his eyes huge and desolate in his drawn face. 'We're ready to go.'

Michel hugged Poppy very tightly, and kissed her wet face. Poppy bent to Peter. The child's cheek was cold as marble as she kissed it. She said nothing; there was no comfort to be given.

'Goodbye, Poppy.' Poppy was grateful that Eloise neither kissed nor attempted to touch her. 'Look after Isobel.'

'We will. We'll send news when there is any.'

Poppy watched them leave, then turned to go back upstairs to where her sister, agonised, terrified and all but demented with grief, struggled to rid herself of her burden.

At three o'clock on the morning of the following day Isobel bore a daughter; tiny, fragile, but miraculously whole and alive. Isobel herself, torn and at the limit of her endurance, lay like one dead as doctor and midwife worked over her. Poppy held the tiny, sleepy scrap in her arms as Kit, on his knees beside his wife, chafed her hand between both of his, murmuring to her; words of love, words of grief, words of encouragement. At last the bruised blue eyes opened, fixed upon Kit's. 'The baby?' she asked, her voice hoarse with exhaustion.

'A little girl, my darling. A beautiful little girl.' Kit stood, took the baby from Poppy and laid her in her mother's arms. Isobel turned a haggard, haunted face to look at the child and, through the silent tears that trickled into the sweat-darkened curly tangle of her hair, very faintly she smiled.

Kit, defeated at last, dropped back to his

knees, buried his face in the bedclothes and cried as if his heart were broken.

*   *   *

There was no question that mother or child could be moved, and even if there had been, the Martellis would not have heard of it. The third floor of the house was given over to the Enevers and Poppy and to the nurse who had been brought in to tend to Isobel and her tiny daughter—who, despite her size and a tendency to sleep for overlong periods, showed no sign of anything but a stubborn determination to live and thrive. Lucia it was who, concerned about the state of Isobel's health, found a plump and motherly wet-nurse who had just herself given birth to a daughter. Isobel, still worn out, could not pretend to anything but relief.

'Have you decided on a name?' Poppy asked, the day after the birth, after having seen Umberto on his way to the village to take news to Eloise, Peter and Michel.

Isobel, head tiredly propped on pillows, nodded. 'Elizabeth,' she said. 'After Mama.'

Poppy leaned to kiss her, and gently to touch the baby's soft warm head. 'What a lovely idea.'

'I wanted a little girl so much.' The words were a whisper. Isobel's eyes were on her daughter. 'But now—' She trailed off, the tears

307

of weakness coursing again.

'Darling, don't.' Poppy took her hand. 'Please don't.' She bit her lip, knowing that at the moment words, no matter how well intentioned, no matter how much meant to comfort, could only make things worse. Little Robbie had not yet been buried. And the grief at his loss could not be buried with him.

With Giovanni's help Kit had made the final arrangements for the funeral, to be held at a small English cemetery to the north of the city on the following Monday. A couple of days before, Poppy drew Kit to one side. 'If you'll hire a *calesse* for me,' she said, 'I'll go back to the Tenuta for a couple of days. The others need to be told about the funeral, Isobel needs some of her things, you and I need clothes for the funeral.' She hesitated. 'And—someone has to—' the hesitation was infinitesimal '—straighten up the house,' she added.

'Poppy—no—'

She shook her head stubbornly. 'I insist. I'm not needed here, you've plenty of help, and Isobel needs you, not me. You can't leave her. I'll do it. It'll make me feel at least a bit useful. Michel's there. Umberto's there. It was pretty silly, actually; if I'd been thinking straight I would have gone back with him. I shan't be alone. And there are things that need to be done. You know it.'

Tiredly he sighed, pushing a hand through his hair. 'If you're sure—?'

'I'm sure. Ask Giovanni to find me some transport. I'll get my things together.'

*   *   *

It was the most melancholy journey of her life, and the loneliest. As she travelled the now-familiar road every turn brought its memory; of the flower-blue, limpid eyes, of the baby chuckles, the droop of a fair, sleepy head on his father's shoulder. A few short days before they had driven down this valley in laughter and happy anticipation. Now Robbie was gone, and all was changed. It was an oppressively hot day, with thunder grumbling in the distance and no breath of air stirring. Even the spanking pace of the *calesse* did not generate any cooling breeze, but rather a stifling warmth, like the breath of an animal, in her face. The driver hunched upon his seat, keeping the pony at a trot, intent upon executing his errand as quickly as possible. Not a word passed between them for the whole of the journey.

They reached the village as it lay in its midday stupor. Shutters were closed, doors curtained. Smoke from cooking fires hung heavily in the air. The driver slowed his pace. A child cried. A woman called. Chickens scratched in the dusty road. The temptation to stop as they passed Umberto's house, to search out Michel, was almost overwhelming, but she

309

resisted it. She had set herself a task, and it was a task she had to do alone. Her own concerns would come later. She had time this afternoon to do what needed to be done; her reward then would be time with Michel. Time alone. Time, perhaps, to escape, for just a little while, the desperate weight of grief and regret. But not yet. First she must face the house, and the memories that it held.

The taciturn driver set her down outside the gate, accepted the money she proffered with grunted thanks—the first words he had spoken—swung the pony round and trotted back down the hill.

Poppy picked up her bag, crossed the still, hot courtyard with its uneven paving stones and dilapidated buildings and walked round to the back of the house. The huge old key to the door was in her bag. She fitted it into the lock, turned it with both hands, and the door swung open upon the familiar kitchen. Despite the fact that the range had long gone out it was suffocatingly warm, and there was a stale smell to the place. She propped the door wide, threw open the windows. The dull, stormy light was eerie, the silence complete. It was, she thought in morbid fancy, as if the house itself had died.

She shook her head. 'Come on, Poppy Brookes,' she said aloud, brisk and sharp. 'Soonest started, soonest finished. Or something like that. Stop moping and get on with it.'

She relit the stove before going to her room to change into a loose shirt and an old pair of slacks. Then, on the principle that if one starts with the worst then things can only get better, she went straight to Robbie's room.

She threw nothing away. Several trips to the attic saw the room cleared and tidy, with only the furniture left as a reminder that the place had ever been occupied. It was not done without tears. Just once, as she surveyed the pathetic little box of toys and clothes that she had packed so neatly and carefully, she almost broke down entirely. For a moment she dropped to sit on the top stair of the attic flight, knuckling her eyes like a child. She sat so for a long, still moment. In the stuffy atmosphere perspiration plastered her hair to her skull, trickled uncomfortably from her hairline, ran down her cheeks. At last she stood, went slowly down the stairs, paused for one last look into the room she had just cleared before firmly shutting the door and going on down into the kitchen, where, with no compunction whatsoever, she poured herself the last of Kit's whisky before setting about what needed to be done there.

As she worked, the storm grumbled nearer, the sky darkening, thunder beginning to echo along the hillsides. A few heavy drops of rain splattered through the leaves of the vine outside the window, forerunners, she assumed, of a downpour. Oddly, neither the weather nor her own isolation, alone in the vast house, bothered her. On the contrary there was something about the storm that seemed entirely appropriate to the day. She stacked away the last plate, looked at the small pile of crockery and cutlery she had left on the table—a baby plate and dish, a cup and a mug, a tiny spoon and fork. One more trip to the attic, and she would be done. Kit and Isobel could look at and cherish these things at some later time, when hopefully the pain would have eased. But at least they would not have to face them until they were ready to. She reached for the cardboard box and old newspaper she had set beside them and packed them carefully away. As she picked the box up and turned to the door the rain, as if a floodgate had been opened, began in earnest, and with it came a quick, gusting wind. Thunder rumbled in the valley and lightning crackled. She set the box back on the table and went to the outside door to close it against the sudden onslaught. And caught her breath, startled, as a tall figure, head down against the rain, hurried around the corner of the house and into the yard.

'Michel! *Michel!*' Idiotically, instead of waiting for him to reach the door, she ran to him, out into the rain and wind, into the vice-hug of his arms, and stood there, safe at last, at least for the moment, from the need to be strong, from the need to be alone. His kiss was fierce and tender, and left no room for doubt that he was as happy to see her as was she to see him. The rain was warm and wonderfully refreshing after the sweaty heat of the day. They took their time; it was a long, lovely moment before, without words, they turned and walked indoors.

He held her hands, looking at her with that gentle, quizzical smile that she so loved. Like her he was drenched, his dark hair plastered to the neat, high-domed skull, rainwater gleaming on the sharp bones of his face, glittering upon his lashes. 'Hello,' he said.

'Hello.'

'Why didn't you tell me you were here?'

'I was going to. I'd have come down in an hour or so. There were some things I needed to do here.'

His hands tightened very slightly on hers, encouraging and sympathetic. 'I came up yesterday. I was going to do it for you. But the house was locked.'

'It was a kind thought. Thank you.' Not for a moment had either gaze wavered. They stood as if each were attempting to see through to the very heart of the other. 'How did you know I was here?'

'Eloise saw you go past. She assumed I knew. I called in just now, and she told me. I came at once.'

The rain was lessening a little into a steady, drumming downpour, and the clouds still lowered, bringing the darkness of night to the day, shadowing the corners of the vast kitchen. Their linked, wet hands were warm. Water dripped from Poppy's hair and ran down her back. 'We're making puddles,' she said.

'Does it matter?'

'No.'

Their kiss this time was impulsive, long and fervent; a kiss to rouse them both, and to prompt them, too, when at last they drew apart to sudden, delicate caution. Poppy stepped back, aware all at once that the all-enveloping shirt, wet, was plastered to her body like a second skin. Self-consciously she crossed her arms over her breasts.

He shook his head. 'Please.' His light voice was very quiet. 'Don't do that.'

Her eyes on his, she let her hands drop to her sides. He stepped to her, lifted her chin in his hand and kissed her again, quickly and lightly. 'A glass of wine,' he suggested, 'would go down very well. Don't you think?'

They sat at the table, lamp unlit, as the storm growled and grumbled around them, holding hands, a jug of wine between them, their prosaic tongues speaking of the events of the past few days, their less rational eyes and clasped fingers sending other messages entirely.

'How's Peter?' Poppy asked at last, her own news having been delivered and discussed.

Michel shook his head, his pale eyes clouding a little. 'Still very shocked. He's very quiet. He won't talk about what happened.'

'It's natural, I suppose. He was so fond of Robbie. And he's very young himself to witness such a thing. I'm sure he'll get over it.'

'Yes.'

A log in the stove shifted and crackled. Beyond the open door the rain still flittered through the vine leaves. Full dark had fallen; every now and again there was a murmur of thunder, the faintest flicker of lightning over the hilltops. Gently Poppy disengaged her hand, fetched the lamp to the table and lit it. Before she could step back, Michel had caught her wrist and drawn her to him, his head upon her breast. 'I love you.'

'And I you.' She was trembling.

'Don't be afraid.' His hand, too, was at her breast, softly stroking.

'I'm not.' But, suddenly, and intemperately, she was. Afraid, exalted, enchanted.

He was undoing the buttons of her shirt, baring her breasts to the light. She stood utterly motionless, hardly breathing. His face, lifted to hers, gilded and shadowed by the dim rays of the lamp, was intent, watching, with hard-held and fragile self-control, her every reaction, studying for any withdrawal, any protest.

She made none. His long hands brushed her breasts. She it was who caught his head in her hands and brought his mouth to her nipple.

After a moment, with a sound half gasp,

half groan, he stood up abruptly, his hand once more about her wrist, not painfully, but with strength, holding her a little from him. Still she stood in silence, breathing shallowly and fast; still she trembled. But her face was serene. 'I hope you're not thinking of leaving?'

He began to speak, cleared his throat. 'Perhaps I should.'

'Perhaps you should,' she agreed, equably, 'but you'd better not. I might have to come after you with a knife. A bit operatic, don't you think? Even given the backdrop.' She lifted her free hand, drew his mouth down upon hers. The rain fell steadily, a warm curtain between them and the world beyond. The shadowed house was still, silent, impassively compassionate about them. It had seen it all before: love and anger, birth and death, all came to the same in the end. Now was the only moment.

Poppy it was who took his hand and led him from the kitchen, lifting the lamp high to light the way, not faltering as they passed the closed door next to Kit's and Isobel's bedroom. Beyond the long window of her own bedroom the pyrotechnics of the storm, though distant now, continued to light the sky in the direction of the city, a firefly light through the curtain of rain.

*   *   *

'When will you be going back?' Michel asked quietly, into the darkness. They were lying naked and relaxed together, Poppy's head on his shoulder, in a tranquil quiet no longer broken by the rain. Outside the window something rustled, and an owl hooted, flittering on soft wings.

Poppy stirred a little, ran a light finger over his chest. 'Sunday. Umberto will take me. You'll be coming to the funeral?'

'Of course. So—we have all day tomorrow, you and I?'

'Yes.' The word was a breath in the darkness. And all night. She did not say it, but the lover's thought was there between them. A day and a night. A lifetime.

He turned his head to look at her. 'Perhaps tomorrow the sun will shine for us again?'

'I don't care if it doesn't. I find, suddenly, that I am very fond of rain.'

They lay in silence for a long while, Michel's fingers softly and rhythmically stroking her shoulder, his breath in her hair. 'Perhaps,' he ventured at last, 'I should go?' He did not move, nor did the caressing finger stop.

Sleepily she snuggled closer to him. 'Oh dear! Am I boring you already?'

She felt his laughter through his body. 'Don't be silly!'

She came up on one elbow, looking down at him as if she would memorise every line of his face in the lamplight. 'Then no,' she said, 'you

317

shouldn't go. Stay. Please me. And show me how to please you.' She grinned her gamin, anarchic grin, and whatever was left of his heart was lost. 'You are a teacher, after all.'

*　　*　　*

He left at first light, promising to return later with fruit and cheese for breakfast, and leaving Poppy curled sleepily amongst the bedclothes. Despite her best intentions, within minutes she had dozed off again, and woke with a start after a sound and refreshing sleep to find the sun well up in a cool, clear sky and the birds singing their hearts out in the woodland behind the house. She stirred and stretched, then suddenly stilled as the full memory of the night before came back to her. She lay for a very long time, her eyes wide and unseeing upon the stained ceiling, a small smile curving her lips. She drew a long, sighing breath, ran her hands lightly down her body, remembering. She was a little sore; but she had expected that. She was, for this moment, utterly, blissfully happy; after the events of the past week she would not, this time yesterday, have believed that possible. With a surge of energy she swung her feet to the floor and ran to the mirror, peering into it, studying her own face, a little put out that nothing appeared to have changed. There should surely be *something* to mark this rite of passage?

Something to show the world that Poppy Brookes had grown up at last? That Poppy Brookes—she almost danced away from the mirror and stood by the window for a moment, stretching her arms above her head—that Poppy Brookes was in love?

She glanced at her watch. Ten o'clock! Michel would be back any minute. For a mischievous moment she was tempted to jump back into bed and pretend to be asleep when he came, just to see what might happen, but then with a quick grin she decided against it. When he came back they would have the rest of the day—to say nothing of the night— together. She would set the little outside table—put some flowers on it—borrow Isobel's prettiest china—even as she was thinking it she was flying about the room, washing, dressing, brushing her hair until it shone. Only when she hurried from the room and turned the corner into the passage where the other bedrooms were did her surge of happiness falter. She stopped for a moment outside Robbie's closed door, touched it gently with her fingertips, then briefly rested her forehead against it, closing her eyes. Nothing, not even the discovery of love, not even the finding, for the first time in her life, a fount of true personal joy could overcome or ease that pain. Only time, she supposed, would do that.

In more sober mood she went down to the kitchen.

*   *   *

An hour or more later, she was still waiting, table prettily laid, for Michel. She had made one pot of coffee only to pour it down the sink when it cooled too much to be drinkable, had made herself tea and sat drinking it alone in the sunshine, with just the smallest shadow of unease beginning to shade her happy confidence. He would come. Of course he would. He had meant everything he had said last night. Of course he had. The worms of doubt began to wriggle in her mind; how many dire warnings had she seen and heard about the girls men slept with and the girls they married? For the first time she found herself thinking of the details of her behaviour the night before with a slight stain of colour in her cheeks. The first stirrings of fear, almost of panic, churned in her stomach. She reached a hand for her cup, and seeing its nervous trembling drew it back again. He would come. He would!

Five minutes later he did, full of apologies, crushing her to him, kissing her with all the ardour she could wish. 'I'm sorry, my darling, I'm sorry.' He put a bag of fruit on the table, and now she saw what she had not in her relief and pleasure in his arrival at first noticed. A faint thread of worry fretted between his brows, and his smile, though warm, was brief.

He looked around, glancing into the kitchen. 'I don't suppose you've seen Peter this morning?'

She looked at him blankly. 'Peter? No. I haven't seen him since I arrived. Why?'

He chewed his lip a moment. 'That's a pity. I had hoped he would be here.'

Poppy, too, was frowning now. 'But Michel, why? What's happened?'

'Nothing.' He was quick to reassure her, but his face belied the words. 'Eloise says he wanted to talk to me last night. Apparently he went to my room and waited for quite a long time.' His eyes flickered to Poppy's face and seeing there the faint rise of colour, reached for her hand, shaking his head gently. 'Don't worry. Anyway, apparently the boy came back late not having found me, of course. Eloise said he was very quiet; she thought he was getting one of his headaches again, so this morning she let him lie in bed. But when she finally went in to wake him he wasn't there.'

'What do you mean he wasn't there?' Even as she spoke, Poppy heard the idiocy of her own question and added hurriedly, 'I mean— where was he?'

'That's the problem. We don't know. That's why I hoped he had come here. Presumably he's looking for me, but so far as I know he didn't come to the house this morning.'

Poppy was thinking. 'I did sleep late,' she said. 'He could have come, and thought there was no one here?'

Michel shook his head, unable now to disguise his concern. 'Darling, I'm sorry. I'd better go back to let Eloise know he isn't here. We've already been through the village, and to the places she knows he likes to play. No one seems to have seen him.'

'I'll come with you.' Briskly Poppy had begun to gather the cups and saucers ready to take them back indoors.

'No.' Michel's hand restrained her. 'It's best you stay here, my love, in case he comes. I'm sure we're worrying about nothing. He's probably safely back home already. But—just in case—I have to go back to tell Eloise. I'm sorry. I'll be back as soon as I can.' He bent to kiss her upturned face. 'I love you,' he said, and was gone, his long legs taking him around the corner and out of sight in moments.

Poppy, nonplussed, stood for a moment watching the spot where he had disappeared, then, picking up the cups and saucers, went back indoors. Once in the kitchen she set them upon the table and went to the stairs. It was an unlikely chance, but worth a try. 'Peter?' she called, her voice echoing into the gloom. 'Peter? Are you there?'

Silence.

She called once more, advancing up the stairs a little, but still there was no response. Would he have gone into the closed part of the house? He might have done, she supposed. He was after all a ten-year-old boy with a ten-year-old boy's nose for adventure. But a swift search revealed nothing. If he had been there, she was sure he would have answered her calls. She went back downstairs and on the way slipped into her bedroom to fetch her sun-hat, which she had left on the chair by the window; and as she bent to pick it up a tiny glint of colour and movement caught her eye in the morning sunlight, deep in the woodland beyond the window. She stared, screwing up her eyes. Had she really seen it? The smallest flash of blue in the shadows amongst the dappled greens and golds?

She dropped the hat and ran down the stairs and out into the courtyard. 'Peter? Pe-eter?' She strained her ears to listen, but any sound was masked by the song of birds and the stirring of leaves in the breeze. She ran a little way up the path. 'Peter!' Again she stood still, listening. Again there was no reply. She walked further into the woods, towards the tower, and was about to call again when a sudden, startled flock of pigeons fluttered from the building and wheeled about the sky, wings beating in the air. Something, or someone, had alarmed them from their roost. Poppy quickened her footsteps, half-running towards the tower. The air was still and dusty, and smelled of decay and of the bird-droppings that were everywhere. It was utterly quiet. A pigeon swooped from the roof and she glanced up. And 'God Almighty!' she whispered, almost beneath her breath.

The child, sitting, shoulders hunched, high above her in the window embrasure neither moved nor spoke. He had his back to her and quite obviously his legs were dangling over the crumbling edge; it brought the sickness of vertigo to Poppy just to think of it. 'Peter?' It was such an effort to keep her voice low and calm that she sweated with it. 'What on earth are you doing? Sweetheart, please come down. You shouldn't be up there. It's too dangerous.'

She saw by the slight movement of his head that he had heard her, but he neither acknowledged her presence nor spoke. She moved to the bottom of the crumbling, unguarded steps. 'Peter, please come down. You're being very silly.' She caught her breath. Very slowly the small figure had begun to rock, back and forth, back and forth, rhythmically. A shower of small stones and ancient mortar cascaded from the ledge at the movement. Panic gripped her, dried her throat, thundered in her chest like a drum. *'Peter!'* She fought for a moment to control herself, drew a deep breath. 'Peter, you're being very naughty. Come down at once.' Desperately she tried to combine authority with gentleness and was aware she was succeeding with neither. 'What's the matter?' Her voice was almost pleading. 'Peter, please tell me. What's the matter?'

'Robbie's dead.' The child's voice echoed

within the decaying walls. He did not stop the rocking movement. Another small avalanche of stones fell around Poppy, and she winced. 'Robbie's dead,' Peter said again, dully.

Poppy's skin in the stuffy heat was stone cold and slick with sweat. She stood helpless, her head tilted back, watching him. 'I know. I know!' She tried to keep her own distress from the words. 'But it isn't your fault. Hurting yourself won't bring him back. Please come down, there's a good boy?'

This time he did turn a little, to look down at her, and she flinched from the look on his face. 'It is,' he said. 'It is my fault.'

'No!' She shook her head vehemently. 'It isn't! Just because you weren't with him—'

'I was.' The quiet words cut across hers and stunned her to silence. 'I was with him.'

There was a long and difficult silence.

'What do you mean?' Poppy asked at last, very carefully.

The boy had turned away again, shifting a little on his precarious perch. His voice floated down to her, light and disembodied. 'I was with him. In the room with the ceiling—' His voice faded to silence.

Poppy's mind was racing. 'You mean you went up there, to watch the race? And— Robbie followed you?'

He shook his head. 'I took him.'

'That still doesn't make it your fault! The window had been left open.'

'No, it hadn't.' The words were unnaturally calm and flat. Once again the russet head turned and the burning eyes looked down at her. 'I opened it.'

The silence this time was truly terrible.

'I don't believe you,' Poppy said at last. 'Peter, why are you saying such things?'

'It's the truth.'

'But why? *Why?* Why would you do such a thing?'

He leaned forward a little and instinctively she held up her hands in a sharp gesture, as if to prevent him from falling. 'Because his father killed my father,' he said, and his voice was suddenly savage. 'Mother said so.'

Poppy was aghast. '*She* told you that?'

He shook his head. 'No. She told you. I was there. I heard you. You were shouting. I came up to see what was going on. You'd left the door open.'

The words were like a physical blow. *To hell with keeping my voice down!*

Poppy bowed her head, closing her eyes against the memory.

'I thought Robbie was really lucky to have a father like Kit.' There were tears now too in the tight little voice above her. 'I thought he was smashing. *I wanted him to be my Dad!*' Suddenly he was sobbing hysterically, his hands over his face. A small piece of loose masonry bounced off the wooden rungs of the ladder and hit the floor. *'I hate him now. I hate him. That's why I opened the door. He killed my father. He killed him! That's why I pushed Robbie out!'* The words were disjointed, a howl of anguish and rage.

Poppy was fighting physical sickness; there was bile in her throat. When she spoke, her voice shook so badly she could hardly get the words out. 'Peter, we'll talk about this later. I'm coming up to get you. To help you down.'

She went up the first few crumbling steps on all fours, frantic fingers clutching at any handhold she could find. Above her the child was sobbing wildly, completely beyond control.

'Poppy!' Michel's voice behind her almost made her lose her footing. She froze. He came to her, held out a hand to support her. 'Come down. I'll get him.' He neither hesitatcd nor questioned. She had no idea how much he had heard. Her legs were trembling so badly that they almost failed her as she stepped thankfully on to firm ground, backed away as Michel started carefully up the steps. 'Peter!' His voice was authoritative. 'Calm yourself. And turn around. Put your feet on the platform. Wait for me.' His foot slipped. Poppy watched, heart pounding, as he righted himself. The boy had lifted his head at the sound of his uncle's voice, his sobs quietening a little. 'Turn around,' Michel said again firmly, inching his way up. 'Come away from the edge. I'm coming up to get you.'

'I went to find you last night.' The child's

choking voice whispered in the enclosed space. 'I was going to tell you then. I wanted to tell you. But I couldn't find you. I couldn't find you!'

Last night.

Poppy bowed her head in despair.

It took fifteen perilous minutes to bring the child down, fifteen minutes that to the watching Poppy seemed half a lifetime. When at last, dusty, sweat-streaked and dishevelled, Michel at last helped Peter down the final few steps she could do nothing but close her eyes for a moment, weak with relief. She felt Michel's arm about her shoulder, and opened her eyes to find him beside her, his other hand upon Peter's shoulder. Peter had stopped crying, though his thin, dirty face was still tear-streaked. He was standing quite still, watching Poppy with opaque, almost expressionless, eyes.

'I did do what I said I did,' he said, a frightened, stubborn defiance in every line of his small face.

Poppy looked at Michel, and saw from the bleak, impassive set of his mouth that he had indeed heard enough to know what the words meant, but 'We'd best take him back to his mother', was all he said as he turned to lead the way out into the noon sunlight.

CHAPTER SIXTEEN

The late afternoon sun, sinking towards the mountainous skyline of the west, cast a flood of golden light through the windows of Eloise Martin's fastidiously ordered room. In the yard below, children were playing, their voices and laughter ringing in acute contrast to the constrained silence within. Poppy sat sombre and quiet, watching the other woman. She had had her say, she had offered her bargain; now it was up to Peter's mother if she accepted it or not. Eloise stood with her back to the room, looking out of the window. Poppy could see the flawless, clear-cut profile, still and expressionless as a carved effigy. She had stood so for a very long time. Poppy folded her hands and her lips and waited.

'So,' Eloise said at last, her low voice calm, 'it is agreed.' She turned, her sleek head high, her pale eyes direct and dauntless. There had been tears, but now they were gone. There had been flat disbelief, but her son's stubborn corroboration of what Michel and Poppy had had to tell had dispelled that. There had been, for a moment, horror, and perhaps an awareness of culpability, but that, at least apparently, had not lasted long. Eloise was herself again, elegantly and obdurately composed, coolly self-contained.

Poppy stood up. 'You do understand that I mean what I say? If I ever hear that you've been anywhere near Kit, Isobel or the child again then I shall tell what I know, whatever might happen in the future between me and Michel. This is between you and me. Don't think I won't do it.'

The other woman shook her head slowly; even, austerely, smiled a little. 'Oh, I don't. I have underestimated you once, Poppy Brookes. I shan't make the same mistake again.'

'By the same token,' Poppy added, 'providing you do stay away I see no profit to anyone by saying anything. There's been grief enough. It would only hurt them more. A tragic accident is one thing—something that perhaps eventually they will come to terms with. This would crucify them.'

Eloise said nothing. She stood unmoving, her face impassive once more.

Poppy turned to leave.

'Are you not going to wait for Michel?' Eloise asked, softly.

Poppy turned, and shook her head. Michel was in Peter's room with the exhausted and unhappy child, watching over him as, at last, he slept. Much as she wanted to see him, much as she longed for the reassurance of his love, for the moment he belonged here and she did not. In her revulsion at what she had discovered, her every instinct was urging her to get away from this place; to escape from the nightmare. Even her feelings for Michel could not overcome her need for a breathing space, for time to come to terms with the anguish of what she now knew. 'No,' she said. 'Best not, I think. Peter needs him. And so do you. We'll have time together later. I'm going to find Umberto. It isn't too late for me to ask him to take me back to the city this evening. Perhaps you'd explain to Michel?'

Eloise nodded. 'I'm sure he'll understand.'

Again Poppy made to leave, and again the other woman's voice stopped her. 'Poppy?'

Poppy waited.

Eloise looked at her steadily for a long moment. 'You do realise that you'll never know?' she asked at last.

'Know what?'

'Whom to believe. Me or Kit. About what really happened to Peter's father.'

Poppy fought hard but not entirely successfully to keep her composure. 'I believe you lied,' she said, hating the tremor in her voice in face of the other woman's calm.

Eloise shook her head.

Poppy stared at her. 'I said the last time I was in this room that you were the sick one,' she said very quietly, 'and now I say it again. And now I tell you—' she took a breath to control the sudden, choking anger, lifted a steadily pointing finger towards the other woman '—that you've passed your sickness on to your son.'

This time she left the room silent behind her. And as she ran precipitously down the stairs and out into the yard where the children played, noisily and happily as children should, it came to her, with no remorse whatsoever, that she had just said to Eloise the cruellest thing she had ever said to anyone.

Face pale and still as marble, Eloise watched from the window as the slim, leggy figure ran up the street towards Umberto's house. She did not move as she heard the click of the door opening behind her, but stood like a statue, arms folded across her breasts, her hands holding her upper arms as if, in the full flood of sunlight, she were cold.

'Has Poppy gone?' Michel asked, wearily and a little surprised.

'Yes. To find Umberto. She's going back to the city. To her family.' She turned, looked at her brother with direct and steady eyes. 'I fear it has all proved too much for her. She has taken flight from us. You can't blame the poor child, Michel. She's very young.'

There was a very long silence. Then, 'Yes, of course. I suppose it was bound to happen,' and Michel left the room, closing the door quietly behind him.

*　　　*　　　*

On the morning of the funeral a note arrived,

exquisitely written, gracefully worded. Eloise expressed once more her sympathy for the unhappy accident, her confidence that Isobel's little daughter, whilst never taking the place of the child that had been lost, would nevertheless prove a comfort and consolation to her bereaved parents, and gently excusing herself, her brother and her son from attending the funeral. Peter, she explained, had been so badly affected by the tragedy that she feared for his health; she and Michel were to take him home to England and under the circumstances it seemed prudent to leave as soon as possible. They were to catch the Florence train on Tuesday afternoon.

'Tuesday afternoon?' Poppy said blankly. 'That's tomorrow.'

Kit looked up from the note, the flare of hope and relief in his tired eyes quickly veiled. 'You didn't know?'

She shook her head.

He touched her arm with a sympathetic hand. 'He'll call before they leave.'

'Perhaps,' she said, then, looking down at the workaday clothes in which she had been helping Lucia in the kitchen, she added, 'I'd better go and get changed, I suppose. I want to look in on Isobel before we leave.'

Alone in her room she stood looking bleakly out across the sunlit square. Tomorrow. Michel was leaving tomorrow, apparently without so much as a word. Why had he not included a message for her? At least some word of love, of reassurance? Why would he leave her to face this day of all days alone? Through a wretched and wakeful night she had bitterly regretted the impulse that had carried her away from him. But, surely, he had understood? Surely the bond between them was not so fragile? Surely he wouldn't leave without coming to her? The night of their loving seemed a lifetime ago; but, surely, he could not have forgotten? Unless—

Unless he had come to regret their entanglement. Unless he saw and wanted to grasp in this a convenient way out.

Sick at heart, she turned away to face the melancholy day.

Little Robbie was laid to rest with simple ceremony in a graveyard sheltered by an ancient, evergreen holm oak whose great branches spread like a canopy, shading and protecting the spot where he lay. There are always tears at a funeral; but those shed for a lost child must surely be the saddest. It was a subdued group that made its way back to the city, to the house where a new flame of life had been kindled, and was being nurtured with love and with hope. Whilst Kit sat with Isobel and the baby, Poppy joined Lucia in playing hostess to the mourners, handing round food and trays of drinks, trying not to remember that the last gathering in this room had been her own ill-fated birthday party.

There had been no word from, nor sign of, Michel.

*   *   *

Once again, though weary to the bone, she slept badly that night. Once again she went over and over the harrowing events of the past days in a mind that refused to rest. And once again she wept; for Robbie, for poor, weak Isobel, for Kit, whose fragile and heroic self-control that day had all but broken her heart; and for herself. Was Michel really going to be so cruel as to leave without attempting to see or speak to her? Did he really care so little? Or—worse—was his pride so high, so tender, that he could not bear what she knew of Peter? As the pastel wash of dawn lightened the sky and the spires and domes of the city stood stark against it, a miserable anger grew. Let him go, then. He wasn't the only man in the world, not by a long chalk. Let him get on his beastly train. Let him leave. Good riddance. She wished him joy of his elegant, manipulative sister and her flawed and damaged son.

She lay, grieving and sleepless, until she judged it the time when she could decently get up. Even so, the whole household was astir by the time she went downstairs; no one it seemed had rested too well. She paid her morning visit to Isobel—on doctor's orders all visits but Kit's were restricted—and found her pale but strengthened and remarkably calm. With her fair curls and shadowed blue eyes, and the tiny, sleepy baby in her arms she was the very picture of motherhood. The peaceful room, with its baby clutter and baby smells, its blinds drawn against the sun, was a world apart; a world, hopefully, of care and of healing. On this particular morning, however, it was too much for Poppy. Restless and aware of a precarious temper she went back downstairs.

Kit it was who cornered her a couple of hours later, joining her as she stood on the balcony. She was leaning, her shoulders resting against the wall between the long windows, long legs crossed, hands jammed in the pockets of her slacks, scowling across the square. She neither moved nor spoke as he walked out from the drawing-room. He went to the parapet, leaned his elbows upon it and turned his head to eye her quizzically. There was a long and, on Poppy's side at least, uninviting silence.

'You know where the station is,' Kit said, at last, mildly.

'And he knows where this house is!' Poppy snapped back, not without logic. 'It's his choice, not mine.'

Kit shook his head slowly. 'Oh, Poppy, Poppy—this isn't like you! Where's my smart, practical Poppy? Go and find him. Speak to him! If only to give him a piece of your mind. The train leaves at two.' He pushed up his cuff to look at his watch. 'You've plenty of time.'

'No.' The word was obdurate.

'You're sure there hasn't been some misunderstanding?'

'On the contrary. I'm sure there has.' She was herself surprised at the bitterness of that. She snapped her mouth shut.

He pushed himself upright, shrugging resignedly. 'Mohammed and the mountain come to mind,' he said ruefully. 'And blowed if I'd want to get in the path of either of them. But think about it. As I say—even if only to give him a piece of your undoubtedly sharp mind.'

'I doubt if screaming at him in public could possibly be in the least bit therapeutic!' Poppy said drily.

He looked at her in a creditable attempt at amazement. 'You? Scream?'

Tears were pricking her eyes again. 'I could,' she said tartly, 'very easily. Here and now if you don't stop nagging me.'

'I'm not nagging you.' His voice was so gentle her composure almost broke. She bit her lip fiercely. 'I just want to see you happy, that's all.'

'He knows where I am.'

Sighing, he turned to leave her, hesitated. 'It's not in character,' he said before he went in. 'It doesn't fit at all with what I know of the man. But—there's someone else involved in this. Think about it.'

She did, and almost for too long. She had left herself perilously short of time when she slipped out into the square and set off, half running, through the steep and narrow streets that led down towards the Porta Ovile, the gate in the ancient walls that was closest to the station.

*   *   *

She arrived with perhaps five minutes to spare. The train was standing at the platform, shrieking steam, the place was an ant-heap of activity. Half Siena, it seemed, had chosen to travel to Florence this afternoon. Townsmen smart in suit and tie, peasants with baskets, piglets and chickens. A crocodile of schoolchildren, escorted by two formidable, black-robed nuns. She stopped in dismay. Oddly and foolishly, it had not occurred to her to realise that, once here, Michel might not be waiting alone on an empty platform. Feverishly she began to push through the crowd. He must be here somewhere. He must!

'Scusi—Scusi—' She elbowed her way through frantically, looking about her, standing on tiptoe. So far as she could see, neither he nor Eloise were anywhere in the crowd. Which meant they must already be on the train. 'Scusi—'

338

In the event Michel saw her before she saw him. 'Poppy! *Poppy!*' No one in the vicinity could fail to hear the bellow, and many eyes turned in amusement to the tall young man who, leaving the door swinging behind him, jumped from the train and ploughed through the now thinning crowds to where the girl stood, struck to stillness at the sight of him. There were more smiles when her tongue loosened. Even though most of the interested listeners could not understand a word of what she said, the tone spoke, eloquently, for itself.

'How could you? *How could you?* How could you leave without saying goodbye at least? What the hell kind of game have you been playing?'

He caught her by the shoulders and kissed her, briefly and hard.

She struggled free. 'Let me be! Tell me! Why didn't you come?'

'I thought you didn't want me to.'

Doors were slamming. The train whistle shrieked again.

'Michel!' Eloise's imperious voice.

'What do you mean? Why wouldn't I want you to?'

'Eloise said—' He stopped, a sudden tautness in his good-natured face.

'Eloise? Bloody Eloise! Why believe *her*?' She was openly crying.

'*Michel!*'

He raised a hand without taking his eyes

339

from Poppy's face. 'I'm coming.' Then, 'Poppy, I love you so much. Please don't cry. I thought I was doing the best for you.'

'By leaving me?'

'I thought it was what you wanted.'

'Was that what she said?'

He made a small, disarmingly helpless, gesture.

The guard was marching officiously down the platform, flag tucked under his arm, slamming the open doors as he went.

Eloise leaned through the window to throw the door open again. *'Michel! Viens!'*

Michel began to hurry back towards the train, drawing Poppy with him by the hand. His voice was urgent. 'I was wrong?'

'You've never been so bloody wrong!' Tears were still streaming down Poppy's face. 'You never will again! I hate you! No, I don't. No, I don't!' They had stopped by the open carriage door.

'Tell me you love me.'

'I love you.'

He leapt the step into the carriage. Poppy caught the briefest glimpse of Eloise's face, coldly furious, her last mischief undone.

Michel leaned from the window, and caught her hand painfully hard. A whistle shrilled. 'Marry me.' He raised his voice against the noise. 'Please, Poppy!—Marry me!'

The train was moving. Still holding Michel's hand, Poppy walked beside it.

'Poppy, please! Marry me—'

Steam billowed, engulfing them for a moment.

'Poppy!'

The train had picked up speed. She was almost running. 'Yes.' She shouted the word just as she had to let go of his hand. 'Yes,' she said again, quietly, to herself, as she saw the gleam of delight in his face, his open hand still stretched towards her, and stopped, watching as the train snaked slowly from the platform, gleaming in sunshine, trailing its ribbon of smoke.

Michel, leaning perilously far from the window, waved once more.

She lifted her hand; stood in utter stillness as the train chugged busily into the sunlit distance.

'Signorina? Scusi?' She turned. A plump little man in a gold-braided peaked cap that would have done justice to any admiral was standing behind her, a broom in his hand.

She stepped aside with an apologetic lift of her hand. He put his head on one side, his eyes sympathetic, looked from her to where the train was disappearing into the rolling hills. *'Ah—l'amore!'* he said with an exaggerated shrug and an even more exaggerated roll of the eyes.

Even Poppy's Italian was up to that. She nodded, considering the thought. 'I'm very much afraid you may be right,' she agreed with a bright and friendly, if somewhat absent-minded, smile, and turned to start the climb up the steep hill back to the city.

We hope you have enjoyed this Large Print book. Other Chivers Press or Thorndike Press Large Print books are available at your library or directly from the publishers.

For more information about current and forthcoming titles, please call or write, without obligation, to:

Chivers Press Limited
Windsor Bridge Road
Bath BA2 3AX
England
Tel. (01225) 335336

OR

Thorndike Press
P.O. Box 159
Thorndike, Maine 04986
USA
Tel. (800) 223-2336

All our Large Print titles are designed for easy reading, and all our books are made to last.